OH, FUDGE!

D0365880

Nancy Coco

KENSINGTON PUBLISHING CORP.

http://www.kensingtonbooks.com

KENSINGTON BOOKS are published by

Kensington Publishing Corp.
119 West 40th Street
New York, NY 10018

All Kensington Titles, Imprints, and Distributed Lines are
available at special quantity discounts for bulk purchases for
sales promotions, premiums, fund-raising, and educational
or institutional use. Special book excerpts or customized
printings can also be created to fit specific needs. For details,
write or phone the office of the Kensington special sales
manager: Kensington Publishing Corp., 119 West 40th Street,
New York, NY 10018, attn: Special Sales Department, Phone:
1-800-221-2647.

Kensington and the K logo Reg. U.S. Pat & TM Off.

ISBN-13: 978-1-4967-0164-0
ISBN-10: 1-4967-0164-X
First Kensington Mass Market Edition: September 2017

eISBN-13: 978-1-4967-0165-7
eISBN-10: 1-4967-0165-8
First Kensington Electronic Edition: September 2017

10 9 8 7 6 5 4 3 2 1

Printed in the United States of America

"A five-star delicious mystery that has great characters, a good plot and a surprise ending. If you like a good mystery with more than one suspect and a surprise ending, then rush out to get this book and read it, but be sure you have the time since once you start you won't want to put it down. I give this 5 Stars and a Wow Factor of 5+. The fudge recipes included in the book all sound wonderful. I am thinking that a gift basket filled with the fudge from the recipes in this book, along with a copy of the book, some hot chocolate mix and/or coffee, and a nice mug would be a great Christmas gift."

    —**Mystery Reading Nook**

"A charming and funny culinary mystery that parodies reality show competitions and is led by a sweet heroine, eccentric but likable characters, and a skillfully crafted plot that speeds towards an unpredictable conclusion. Allie stands out as a likable and engaging character. Delectable fudge recipes are interspersed throughout the novel."

    —**Kings River Life**

All Fudged Up

"A sweet treat with memorable characters, a charming locale, and satisfying mystery."

    —**Barbara Allan**, author of the Trash 'n'
    Treasures mysteries

"A fun book with a lively plot, and it's set in one of America's most interesting resorts. All this plus fudge!"

    —**JoAnna Carl**, author of the Chocoholic mysteries
    (NAL)

"A sweet confection of a book. Charming setting, clever protagonist, and creamy fudge—a yummy recipe for a great read."

    —**Joanna Campbell Slan**, author of The Scrap-N-Craft
    Mysteries and The Jane Eyre Chronicles

"Nancy Coco's *All Fudged Up* is a delightful mystery delivering suspense and surprise in equal measure. Her heroine, Alice McMurphy, owner of the Historic McMurphy Hotel and Fudge Shop (as much of a mouthful as her delicious fudge), has a wry narrative voice that never falters. Add that to the charm of the setting, Michigan's famed Mackinac Island, and you have a recipe for enjoyment. As an added bonus, mouth-watering fudge recipes are included. A must-read for all lovers of amateur sleuth classic mysteries."

 —**Carole Bugge**, author of *Who Killed Blanche Dubois?* and other Claire Rawlings mysteries

"You won't have to 'fudge' your enthusiasm for Nancy Parra's first Mackinac Island Fudge Shop Mystery. Indulge your sweet tooth as you settle in and meet Allie McMurphy, Mal the bichon/poodle mix, and the rest of the motley crew in this entertaining series debut."

 —**Miranda James**

"The characters are fun and well-developed, the setting is quaint and beautiful, and there are several mouth-watering fudge recipes."

 —*RT Book Reviews* (**3 stars**)

"Enjoyable . . . ALL FUDGED UP is littered with delicious fudge recipes, including alcohol-infused ones. I really enjoyed this cozy mystery and look forward to reading more in this series."

 —**Fresh Fiction**

"Cozy mystery lovers who enjoy quirky characters, a great setting and fantastic recipes will love this debut."

 —*The Lima News*

"The first Candy-Coated mystery is a fun cozy due to the wonderful location filled with eccentric characters."

 —**Midwest Book Review**

**The Candy-Coated Mystery Series
by Nancy Coco***

ALL FUDGED UP

TO FUDGE OR NOT TO FUDGE

OH SAY CAN YOU FUDGE

ALL I WANT FOR CHRISTMAS IS FUDGE

ALL YOU NEED IS FUDGE

OH, FUDGE!

*Available from Kensington Publishing Corp.

This book is for Ashley.
I'm so proud of you and all you do.
You never stop amazing me.

Chapter 1

The Mackinac Island Butterfly House didn't open until ten AM on Monday, but I had a message from Blake Gilmore, the current manager, that she needed to see me about a possible tour group staying at the McMurphy. I walked my puppy, Mal, around the back of the Butterfly House looking for an open door. I saw movement in the greenhouse and figured Blake was watering plants or checking the butterflies.

"Hello? Blake?" I called as I opened the back door and pushed through the plastic flaps that kept the butterflies in the greenhouse. I was hit by the tropical humidity of the glass building. Bright blue butterflies floated about and I was careful where I walked as different sizes and shapes and colors of butterflies alighted on every surface. Mal tugged on her leash, pulling me through the lovely winding, lush trail of the greenhouse that contained the live butterfly collection.

Suddenly I heard a short scream. My heartbeat sped up and Mal and I ran toward the sound. I stopped short at the sight in front of me. "Tori?"

Mal tugged at her leash, but I held her back.

There beside the cascading waterfall fountain was my cousin, Victoria Andrews, kneeling over a woman. Tori held the handle of a gardening trowel in her hands. The rest of the trowel was stuck firmly in the chest of a woman I didn't know. The woman's jeans-clad legs were oddly angled. Her hands spread out, but empty. A pool of blood blossomed from beneath her checkered blouse. Butterflies landed on her and took off as if she were no more than a rock or convenient plant.

"Tori, what's going on?" I couldn't tell if Tori was pushing the trowel in or pulling it out. But when she saw me, she let go of the handle and held up her hands as if I were the police and had just said, "Freeze!" Her blue eyes filled with fear. Her long blond hair was pulled back in a low ponytail, but a streak of blood caressed her cheek. Her bow-shaped mouth trembled and her tanned skin looked ashen. "Tori? What's going on?"

She stood and wiped her bloody hands on the front of her jeans. I could see that she was shaking from head to toe. "It's not what it looks like," Tori said with a wobble in her voice.

Mal dragged me toward the scene. "No," I said and tugged Mal back as I took out my cell phone. "Tori, sit down." I ordered as I pointed to a nearby raised bed made of bricks. "You're in shock." I dialed 9-1-1 and eased my cousin over to the round flower bed to sit on the edge. Mal jumped up beside her to comfort her and ended up with blood on her white fur.

"Nine-one-one, this is Charlene. What is your emergency?"

"Hi, Charlene."

"Allie McMurphy, this can't be good. Where are you? I'll send Rex over there right away."

"Thank you," I said. Rex Manning was the lead policeman on Mackinac Island and a good friend. "I'm at the Butterfly House. Tell him to come around to the back. We're in the greenhouse."

"He's on his way," Charlene said. "You said 'we'?"

"Yes, it's me, my cousin Victoria, and—"

"Another dead person?"

"Well, she certainly looks dead," I said. "I haven't touched her."

"Then how do you know she's dead?"

"There's a hand spade sticking out of her chest and she's not moving." I wasn't going to tell Charlene that my cousin might have been the one to put the spade there. Not until I had all the facts. "Let me check for a pulse."

I skirted around the pool of blood and put my fingers on her neck. She felt warm, but there was no pulse. I shook her shoulder. "Are you okay?" But her eyes simply stared lifeless into the skylights. "She doesn't respond to verbal cues and I didn't feel a pulse."

"Enough said," Charlene said. "I swear we've never had this much trouble until your Papa Liam passed. God rest his soul."

It was then that Tori moaned. "I think I'm going to be sick."

"Charlene, I've got to go," I said and hung up the phone. I had a doggie doo bag in my pocket. I carried them with me whenever I walked with Mal. I handed it to Tori. "Breathe into the bag," I said. "I think you're hyperventilating."

"It's not breathing that's a problem," Tori said before she turned her head and emptied her stomach into the bag.

I put my hand on her back as she heaved. "It's going to be okay," I said.

Mal put her paw on Tori as if to comfort my trembling cousin.

"What happened? Did you stab her?" I asked. "Was she attacking you?" The dead woman appeared to be middle-aged. Her feet were ensconced in gray and pink walking shoes. She had black hair pulled back into a neat ponytail. There was a streak of white hair along the left side of her face. She had high cheekbones, thin lips, and wide-open brown eyes that stared at the glass ceiling.

"No, no, she wasn't attacking me," Tori said and lifted her head from the baggie. "I didn't kill her. It's Barbara Smart. I was supposed to meet her here this morning to talk about a fund-raiser. I found her like that."

"But you were holding the handle of the trowel." I had to point out the obvious.

"I wanted to help her. I thought if I pulled it out I might be able to do CPR, but as I tugged, more blood came out and I was afraid I was only making things worse. Then you came in. Did I hear you correctly? She didn't have a pulse?"

"No, she didn't," I said. "Didn't you check for one?"

"I know it's the first thing they tell you to do when you take a CPR class, but I didn't. I panicked and knelt down and shook her shoulder. I thought I heard a moan so I tried to take the blade out. That's when you got here."

"Did you see anyone?"

"No," Tori said and hung her head. Tiny purple butterflies landed on her shoulders. "You and your dog were the first live people I've seen."

"Wow, okay, so what time was your meeting? Was Blake supposed to be here? After all, Blake manages the Butterfly House."

"Barbara and I met with Blake last night. Blake had another meeting this morning, but she told Barbara and me that we could meet here to finish the details."

"Wait. You were here last night?"

"Yes."

"And you didn't call me? It's before the ferries come so you had to have stayed on the island last night. Why didn't you let me know you were coming? We have room at the McMurphy. You could have stayed with me."

She gave me an angry look. "I didn't think I was welcome at the McMurphy. You own it, not me— even though our great-grandfather started it."

"What?" I straightened away from her. "Papa Liam always said your family didn't want anything to do with the McMurphy even after my father moved us to Detroit. It's the only reason I took it over."

"Listen, can we talk about this later?" Tori said. "Barbara's lying there dead."

"Sure," I said. "But we will finish this conversation. Where are you staying?"

"Dad still owns a cabin on the far north side. I'm staying there."

"What's going on?" Officer Rex Manning walked in through the vinyl flaps from the back door. His black police boots clomped on the brick pavers that were laid down to form the winding trail between the raised beds. "Charlene says you found another body?"

"Hi, Rex," I said, and stood. Mal jumped off the edge of the flower bed and raced over to beg Rex to pet her. He reached down to pat her and noticed the blood on her paws. "Sorry, kid, can't touch you when you have evidence on you." He looked up at me with his flat blue gaze. "What happened?"

Rex wore a perfectly pressed police uniform. He took his hat off the minute he entered a building, showing off his shaved head and square jaw. The man had the build of an action movie hero and the attitude that went with his good looks. An orange and black monarch butterfly landed on his arm.

"I had an early appointment with Blake," I said. "The front door is closed until ten AM so I came around back. I saw movement in the greenhouse and I thought it was Blake so I came in. I heard a scream and rushed toward the sound to find my cousin Victoria, here, kneeling over the woman with the garden trowel in her chest." I pointed at the body.

"I see." Rex walked over and checked the pulse point at the dead woman's throat. He glanced over at Tori who had put the doggie doo bag down by her feet and had her head between her knees. "This woman is dead," Rex announced and picked up her wrist. "She's still warm. I don't think she's been dead long, but we'll have to wait for the coroner's report to know for sure." He stood and went over to Tori. "Tori Andrews?"

Tori looked up at him. "Hi, Rex."

I frowned. How did they know each other?

"It's been a while," Rex said as he squatted down to look Tori in the eye as she hung her head. "I thought you were in California."

"I am," she said and took a deep breath then blew it out slowly. "Up until yesterday."

"You have blood on you. Can you tell me what happened?"

Mal tried to nudge herself between Rex and Tori. Rex gently pushed Mal back and sent me a look that silently told me to take care of my pet. I scooped up my evidence-covered pup and took a step back, knowing that the EMTs were most likely on their way along with the county CSI guy, Shane Carpenter.

"I was supposed to meet Barbara here this morning, but when I arrived she wasn't in the office. So I came out here looking for her," Tori said and put her head between her knees. "I heard a noise and came this way. That's when I saw her lying there by the fountain. I called her name and knelt down to shake her. You know, like you are supposed to do for CPR."

"Is that how you got blood on you?" he asked. Rex was calm and there was kindness in his tone I hadn't heard in a while.

"Yes," Tori said. "I thought I heard her moan and was going to pull out the trowel. I grabbed the handle and then thought, *What if that will make things worse?* So I stopped. Then Ally came in. She got me to sit down."

Rex looked at me. "Why did you come here?"

"I had a meeting with Blake."

"I see." Rex stood. "Did you see anyone else?"

"No," I said and shook my head.

Just then Blake came around the corner. "What's going on? I saw Rex's bicycle parked out front. Wait!" She froze in place and put her hands over her mouth. "Barbara?" It came out as a shocked whisper. Then her knees buckled. Rex and I got to her at the same time and each took one of Blake's elbows and helped her slowly to a bench. "Barbara? Oh, Barbara! What happened?" She glanced from me to Rex to Tori. "Tori?"

"I found her like this," Tori said.

Mal put her front paws on the bench seat and looked from one distressed woman to the other as if unsure how to comfort them both.

"Is that a trowel? Who would do such a thing?"

"We'll find out," I said, and patted Blake on the shoulder. Blake was an older woman in her mid-fifties. She had light brown hair highlighted with blond streaks that shimmered in the daylight. Her face was round and pretty. She was of average build and could pass for younger. Today she wore a pair of jeans, sneakers, and a white polo shirt with the Butterfly House logo monogrammed on the left breast.

George Marron and Walt Henderson came in through the vinyl strips that covered the front entrance to the greenhouse with a stretcher between them and their EMT bags in their hands.

"What do we have?" George asked. George was the lead EMT on Mackinac Island. He had long black hair that was pulled back in a single braid, copper skin, and the high cheekbones of his Iroquois ancestry.

"Dead body," Rex said in a low tone. "She's probably been gone about forty-five minutes to an hour, but we'll have to wait for the coroner to find out for sure."

"Cause of death seems pretty clear," Walt said. Walt was a tall, thin man with gray hair and a hawk-like nose. He had sharp features and dark brown eyes. His skin had the weathered look of a fisherman or at the least someone who knew their way around the water.

"Tori Andrews," George said. "When did you get back on the island?"

"Hi, George," Tori said and tried to sit up

straight. "Sorry, I can't." She grabbed the doggie bag and heaved again.

George let go of the stretcher and went over to her. I watched as he checked her pulse and eyes. "You're in shock." He waved for Walt to bring a blanket over, then slung the blanket around Tori's shoulders. "Are you hurt?"

"No," Tori said, and shook her head.

"There's blood. I should check," he said.

"It's Barbara's." Tori closed her eyes. "I tried to take the spade out of her chest, but I couldn't. It was making things worse. Oh my, there's blood everywhere."

"Okay, well, let's take you back to the clinic and get you checked out just in case. Okay?" George looked at Rex who nodded.

"I'm fine, really," Tori said.

"You should go," I said. "They can give you something to settle your stomach and, besides, the crime scene guy will want your clothes. You're covered in evidence."

"Come on," George said and helped her to her feet. "Allie and I will take you to the clinic."

"What about Barbara?" Tori asked as she glanced at her friend one more time.

"Walt and Rex will take good care of her," George said.

"Come on, Blake," I said and tugged Blake to her feet. "Come with us. You look a little shocky yourself."

"I can't leave Barbara," Blake said with tears in her brown eyes.

"It's okay. Rex is with her," I said and locked my arm with hers. "Tori can really use our comfort right now. Right?"

"It is better if you ladies stick together," George said as he walked Tori out the door.

Shane passed us on the way out. He wore his navy blue CSI jacket and ball cap. His horn-rimmed glasses emphasized his concerned eyes. "I hear you've found another crime scene."

"Not me this time," I said. "My cousin Tori did." I pointed toward George and Tori.

"Tori Andrews?" Shane said, and his face burst into a wide smile. "When did you get back on the island?"

"Yesterday," I muttered. "She just didn't tell anyone."

"I had meetings," Tori said.

I frowned as Shane made his way into the build-ing. "Gee, Tori, everyone seems to know you."

"They should. I went to school with all of them up until senior year when Dad moved us out to California. Unlike you, Allie," Tori said, "I'm not a fudgie."

I bit back a retort. After all, Tori had just found a woman lying dead in a pool of her own blood. That kind of shock did things to people. I looked at George who simply shrugged at me.

"Poor Barbara," Blake said, bringing my attention back to the older woman who clung to me. "Poor Barbara. She didn't deserve to die."

"No," I said and patted Blake's arm. "She didn't."

"Who could have done such a thing?" Blake asked. "Barbara wouldn't hurt a flea."

"I didn't know Barbara," I said, "but no one deserves to die like that."

"I've got to put up a sign," Blake said and pulled away as if to go back into the crime scene. "I've got to let everyone know that the Butterfly House is closed. I've got to let Barbara's family know."

"The police will take care of her family," I said and gently guided Blake back toward the ambulance. "You need to take care of yourself. Trust me, you've had a shock. You should go to the clinic and get checked out."

George helped Tori into the ambulance—one of the few motorized vehicles allowed on the island for safety purposes.

"Let George help you," I said. Mal nudged Blake as if to let her know that she was not alone in her sorrow.

"Thank you, it's so upsetting," Blake said as I helped her up in the ambulance. Mal jumped up with them.

"Is it okay if Mal goes with you?" I asked George.

"She should be quarantined until any evidence she's carrying is collected," he said and slipped bags on her paws. "Are you staying?"

"I should give my statement and see if there is anything that Rex or Shane needs," I said.

George nodded and closed the doors on the ambulance. "We'll take good care of these girls. You can pick Mal up after Shane gets his evidence."

"Thanks." I waved them off as he slowly drove away. I turned and looked at the trail to the Butterfly House entrance. What a terrible thing to happen in such a fun and beautiful place. First thing I should do was to put a note on the door. The next was to go back inside and see what I could do to help figure out who would do such a terrible thing. Last was to figure out why my cousin Tori didn't feel that she could stay with me. Was she hiding something? Was it something that had to do with the dead woman on the floor of the Butterfly House?

California Fudge

Ingredients

1½ cups sugar
¾ cup sour cream
½ cup of butter
12 oz. white chocolate chips
7 oz. marshmallow crème
¾ cup walnuts
¾ cup chopped dried apricots (or any candied fruit)

Directions

In a large heavy saucepan, bring sugar, sour cream, and butter to full rolling boil. Stir constantly for 7-10 minutes until it reaches softball stage or 234 degrees F on a candy thermometer. (Make sure thermometer doesn't touch the bottom or side of the pan.)

Remove from heat. Add white chocolate chips and stir until melted. Add remaining ingredients and stir until blended. Pour into a buttered 8-inch square pan and cool completely. Cut into 1-inch squares. Makes roughly 2½ pounds of fudge. Enjoy!

Chapter 2

"It's so weird watching George bag Mal's paws," I said to Shane. "Is that necessary? She only touched Tori."

"It's all evidence," Shane said. "I'll process Mal first once I finish taking photos. That way you can take her home."

"She's going to chew those bags off," I said. I imagined Mal walking stiffly, doing her best to shake off the bags as if they were snow booties. "I hope George is prepared."

"I'm sure he can handle Mal. They like each other."

"At least this time you don't need my clothes."

"We will need Tori's clothes," Shane said. "Can you go get her a new set?"

"No," I said and frowned. "She isn't staying with me."

"Really?" He looked surprised.

"Not because I didn't want her, if that's what you're thinking," I said and hugged my waist. "I didn't even know she was coming into town."

"She must be staying at her father's old place," Shane said. "You really should take her a change of clothes."

"I suppose," I said. "Can I take Mal?"

"No, she needs to stay. One I've processed her I'll give her to Brent. He'll watch her until you get back with the clothes. Do you remember where your uncle's place is?"

"Of course I remember," I said.

"They keep a spare key under the third rock from the door."

"How do you know that?" I crossed my arms. I didn't know that. In fact, I barely remembered where my uncle's cabin was. I planned on texting my mom for the address.

"Everyone who went to school with Tori knows where the key is," Shane said with a shrug. "It was part of sneaking her back into bed if she partied too much."

"Tori was a partier?"

"Island living," Shane said with a shrug. "Can you get her some clothes?"

"Sure." A quick text to my mom and I got the address to my uncle's cabin. It was near the airport. I biked over and let myself in with the key that was right where Shane said it would be.

The cabin was small: two bedrooms, one bath, with an open living room, and kitchen. Tori hadn't been there long. There were still coverings on most of the furniture. The first bedroom door was open, her suitcase spread out on the bed. She hadn't even unpacked before heading out this morning. I grabbed her a pair of cargo shorts and a T-shirt because it was a warm day. I headed out and then thought again and went back for a pair of flip-flops. They might want her shoes if she had any blood on them.

The thought had me checking my shoes. Today I wore white tennis shoes. Luckily they were still unmarked, except for some dust from my travels. I found an old tote in the kitchen and put her things inside it. Then I went out, locking the door behind me, careful to return the key to the same place.

I shook my head as I got on my bike. How could you feel safe knowing that everyone on the island knew where you kept your key? Why lock the door at all?

As I biked down the hill, I passed Mrs. Howard. "Good morning, Allie," she said and waved. "I heard that you found another dead body this morning."

That was fast. "It was actually my cousin Victoria who found her," I said as I slowed to a stop. "I'm taking Tori a fresh set of clothes now."

"Oh, yes, I saw her come in last night from the boats," Mrs. Howard said. "Tell her I said hello and I'm sorry."

"Sorry?"

"That she found a dead body. I can't imagine that was a nice welcome back to the island. Where is she living now? Is she moving back to the island?"

"I thought she was living in California," I said. "But she's working on a fund-raiser for the Butterfly House. I don't know if that means she's moved back or not."

"I don't understand." Mrs. Howard drew her gray eyebrows together. She wore a denim shirt over a white tee and denim cropped pants. "I thought you two were family. Don't you talk?"

"We talk," I said. "But not since Papa died."

"Oh, yes, I can see why that would happen."

"What would happen?"

"A split in the family since you inherited the hotel and she didn't."

"She lives in California," I said. "I didn't think she wanted to inherit the hotel."

Mrs. Howard shrugged and slipped on her gardening gloves. "You never know what you want until it's taken away from you."

"I suppose that's true," I said. "But all she has to do is talk with me. There is always room at the hotel for family."

"All that's good and true, but you might need to tell her."

"I didn't think I had to," I said and frowned. "Why is everyone on Tori's side with this?"

"We watched her grow up here," Mrs. Howard said with a shrug. "She is one of us."

"But she left the island," I pointed out.

"It doesn't matter," Mrs. Howard said. "What matters is that, unlike you, she's not a fudgie."

"I'm not a fudgie," I said. Fudgie was the name the islanders gave to the many tourists who came to sample the fudge. Mackinac Island was known as the world capital of fudge. It wasn't an insult to be called a fudgie, but I felt as if being labeled that meant I was not quite accepted in the island society. "I spent almost every summer here."

"So do a lot of fudgies," Mrs. Howard said. "We were all surprised when you got the McMurphy and not Victoria."

"Why am I just now finding this out?"

"Maybe because you never asked. Now, tell me more about the dead person. Was the scene gruesome?"

I made a face. "I've got to go take these clothes to Victoria. I'm sure the details of what happened this morning will be in the paper tonight. Have a nice day." I left Mrs. Howard to her gardening and hurried back to the clinic.

"I brought you clothes," I said to Victoria as I entered the curtained area in the clinic where she sat wearing a hospital gown.

"Thanks," Tori said with a frown. "How did you know where to get them?"

"Shane told me," I said. "How do you feel safe knowing that so many people know about your spare key?"

"Only the people from the island know," she said with a shrug and took the tote from me. "No one here would hurt me."

"Well, someone hurt Barbara," I said.

"True." She stopped and shuddered. "I don't think I'll ever get the scene out of my mind."

"I'm sorry," I said. "Have you been processed yet?" I had discovered enough bodies to know that they collected your clothes and then evidence from under your fingernails as well as taking photos of you when they processed you.

"Shane just left," she said. "They told me I could take a shower if I wanted, but I'd rather just go home and take one there." She dug out her clothes. "Thanks for thinking of the shoes."

"You're welcome. I understand they usually take them as well to check for evidence."

Tori tugged the shorts on under her hospital gown. Then pulled off the gown and slipped on the T-shirt.

"You really should stay with me at the McMurphy. There's room, you know."

She grabbed her flip-flops and put them on. "I'm fine at Dad's place. I'm not staying but a couple of weeks."

I searched for something to fill the silence. "At least come for dinner. You can meet the new staff. I understand you and Barbara were working on a fund-raiser for the Butterfly House improvements. You can meet my friend Jenn. She's a professional event planner."

Victoria looked up at me. "I'm perfectly capable of planning a fund-raiser." She stood. "Listen, Allie, you don't have to pretend we're friends. Just go about your day. I'm fine."

"You are not fine," I said and crossed my arms over my chest. "You found Barbara dead."

"Yes, well, I'm sure I'll get over it. Just stay out of it. Okay?" She opened the curtain. "Go back to making fudge. I'm going to see if I can be discharged. Thanks for the clothes." She dismissed me and walked away.

"Fine," I muttered, "but you can't say I didn't try."

Chapter 3

"Barbara Smart," Frances, the hotel manager and longtime friend of my grandparents, said. She sat on the tall stool behind the reception desk of the McMurphy. Frances was a retired teacher in her seventies. She looked ageless with her brown bobbed hair, colorful reading glasses, and minimal makeup. Today she wore a peasant blouse and long flowered skirt. "She was an interesting person."

"In what way?" I asked. I held Mal. I had picked her up from the police station and, once home, Frances had given her a bath.

"She was notorious for flirting with all the men. At one point in her twenties she confided in me that she was going to marry Richard Smart for his money. Richard was thirty years older than Barbara, you see. We all wondered what she was doing with the old guy." Frances shook her head. The new engagement ring on her left hand sparkled under the lights as she made notes for the day's staff meeting.

"It's possible to love someone older than you," I pointed out.

"True," Frances said. "But Barbara was a beauty and ruthless. She married Richard and within ten years he was dead and she was free to live out her days on his fortune. She confided in me that it was her grand plan all along."

I frowned. "What did her husband die of?"

"Cancer, poor fellow. He went fast. At least he was happy."

"What else do you know about Barbara?" I asked and leaned against the reception desk. The Historic McMurphy Hotel and Fudge Shop had been in my family for over one hundred years. I recently remodeled it to take it back to its original Victorian splendor. Except for the addition of glass walls around the fudge shop. When we adopted a stray cat we named Carmella or Mella for short, I had closed off the fudge shop. I wanted to give Mella the chance to roam without getting underfoot and possibly burned by hot fudge or melted sugar.

The lobby of the McMurphy was large, with the fudge shop on the right and a fireplace on the left with a comfy sofa and chairs for seating. I had free Wi-Fi installed to encourage people to come and sit in the lobby and possibly buy more fudge. Toward the rear of the lobby was the bar-height reception desk that was Frances's domain. Behind her were small cubbies with slots for mail or notes for each of the rooms. Across from her was more seating and the back of the room housed the elevator. The elevator was the old-fashioned cage kind.

It only went up two floors but it was convenient when we had guests who couldn't master the twin staircases that led to the guest rooms.

"Why do you want to know about Barbara?" Frances asked and studied me from over the top of her reading glasses.

I shrugged. "She's dead. I witnessed my cousin trying to pull a garden trowel out of her chest. I want to know who put it there and why."

Frances went back to her computer screen. "You want to investigate."

"You make it sound like a bad thing," I said. "My cousin was involved. What if she needs help?"

"You don't even like your cousin," Frances accused.

"It's not that I don't like her," I said and put Mal down. "It's that I don't know her anymore." I sighed. "It's been years since we were kids and played together, but I still want to help her."

"You think she's involved in the murder?"

"She's in town to meet with Barbara and help with a fund-raiser for the Butterfly House. She also was the one with her hands wrapped around the garden trowel handle when I arrived on the scene. What do you think?"

"I think you shouldn't be in such a rush to judge."

The heat of a blush rushed up my cheeks. "I'm not judging. I only want to know more. Did you know about the fund-raiser?"

"Yes," Frances said. "It was suggested at the garden club."

I raised an eyebrow. "Did you mention that Jenn

was a party planner? They didn't have to call in Victoria."

"I mentioned it," Frances said with a shrug. "But some people thought your cousin should get the job, not Jenn."

"Oh, right, because Jenn's a fudgie and Tori's not," I said semi-sarcastically.

"Exactly." Frances stopped what she was doing and turned to me. "Don't be insulted. But Jenn is a fudgie and Victoria grew up on the island. People love and trust her. They wanted a reason to see her."

I tried to keep my expression neutral. "Okay, I guess I could see that." Jenn Christensen was my best friend from Chicago. She had come to Mackinac Island for the summer to help me get through my first tourist season. Since Papa Liam had died before I had a chance to work a season with him, I needed the help. Jenn was a party planner and organizer. She'd already helped me put together some really great events for the people on the island and the families who stayed at the hotel. I guess I was a little jealous. I wanted my friend to get the job.

"It was Barbara who contacted Victoria in the first place," Frances said. "Tori must be devastated."

"She seemed more pissed off than devastated," I said. "But then it could just be because she was talking to me."

"Perhaps."

I let a pause swirl around us for a moment. "You know I had no idea Victoria would be upset over my inheriting the McMurphy. She lives in California."

"You lived in Chicago," Frances pointed out.

"Yes, but I was only there to get my degrees in culinary studies and candy making."

"And before that you lived in Detroit."

"Only because Dad moved us."

Frances shrugged and went back to work. "I'm simply pointing out that your circumstances aren't much different than your cousin's."

"I thought she had a new wine country tour business," I said. "Isn't she into California wines? Or was it a pet grooming business? I can't keep up with her new start-ups."

At the sound of the word *grooming*, Mal froze, then went off to hide in her bed beside Frances's chair. My puppy didn't shed so that meant she needed to be taken to the groomer about every six weeks. Like me, she felt that a day at the spa was more torture than pampering.

"It doesn't mean she doesn't want to come back to her home and help plan a fund-raiser for the Butterfly House," Frances said. "Besides, you two are related. You should be taking care of each other, not at odds over Liam's lack of forethought when writing out his will."

I thought back to Papa Liam's funeral. Victoria had been there of course. I hadn't noticed her. I was so caught up in my grief of losing my papa. Then terrified at the idea of running the McMurphy by myself. I'd completely overlooked my cousin.

The thought made me frown.

"What is up with the scowl?" Jenn asked as she bounded down the stairs. My friend Jenn was tall and lithe and gorgeous. Today she wore crisp, green linen crop pants and a lightweight silk tank in a green leaf pattern.

"Allie is discovering there are more people than herself in this world," Frances said.

"I know there are others," I said and made a face. "I serve them fudge every day. Plus I think of you guys all the time."

Jenn stopped and looked from me to Frances and back. "Wait, what brought this on? Are you two fighting? Because you don't fight."

"We're not fighting," we both said at the same time.

"Then what's going on?"

"My cousin Victoria is in town to plan a fundraiser for the Butterfly House."

"And"—Jenn put her hands on her hips—"why the fuss?"

"I thought you would be a better choice," I said.

"Why? Isn't your cousin from here?"

I wanted to give her the evil eye, but refrained. "Yes," I said with a sigh. "She's from here. But she now lives in California. And she didn't tell me she was coming back to the island. And she won't stay here because she's upset that Papa Liam didn't leave her partial ownership in the McMurphy."

"Wait, I thought you were the only heir—isn't Tori a cousin on your mother's side?"

"No," I said. "Papa Liam's sister is Tori's mother."

"Gee, how old was she when she had Victoria? I mean, isn't Victoria our age?"

"She just turned thirty," I said. "My great-aunt had her when she was forty-nine. In those days they called them oops babies."

"What? Why?"

"Because she thought she was going through menopause and discovered she was pregnant when she went into labor," Frances supplied.

"Crazy," Jenn said.

"Don't mention it to Victoria," I said. "She hates that story."

"I don't know why she hates it. It's all true," Frances said.

"No one wants to be considered an accident their entire life," Jenn said wisely. "Well, we should have Victoria over for dinner. You did invite her to stay here at the hotel, right?"

"I did, but she won't," I said and crossed my arms. "She'd rather stay out at her father's dusty old cabin in the woods."

"Then how did you know she was on the island?" Jenn asked.

"You must have been working all morning," I said.

"Why do you say that?"

"Because Mal and I discovered Tori standing over a dead body."

"Oh no! Who? Where?"

"At the Butterfly House. It was Barbara Smart."

"Oh man, and I didn't get to bring you new clothes," Jenn said with a twinkle in her eye.

She was dating Shane and liked it when I had to call her to a crime scene to bring me fresh clothes.

"Shane said to tell you hi," I said. "He bagged Mal's paws and asked me to go bring Victoria new clothes."

"Why did he bag Mal's paws?" Jenn asked as she picked up my pup. "They look fine to me."

"She jumped on Tori and got blood from the body on her paws. Shane needed to verify that by sampling the streaks on her paws."

Jenn held my pup out in front of her and crumpled her face. "She didn't lick the blood, did she? Because she just kissed me."

"I don't know," I teased. "Dogs do like to lick their paws."

"It's why Shane bagged them first," Frances said with a wise nod.

"Ew, ew, ew," Jenn said and put Mal down. "I need to go wash my hands and face and brush my teeth." She ran back up the stairs.

I looked at Frances and she looked at me. "Are you going to tell her that Mal got a full bath or should I?"

"I say we leave her to her own assumptions," Frances said as she went back to her computer screen. "She could use a little excitement in her life."

The door to the McMurphy flew open, the bells on the back jingling as Liz McElroy, the local newspaper reporter, came rushing inside. "I just heard your cousin is a person of interest in the death of Barbara Smart," Liz said. Her face was flush and her green eyes sparkled. "Do you have any comment for my article?"

"When it comes to family," I said, "you should know by now, Liz, that I have no comment."

Creamy Almond Fudge

Ingredients

4½ cups sugar
13 oz. of evaporated milk
¾ cup of butter
3 (7 oz.) chocolate bars broken up
12 oz. dark chocolate chips
2 cups chopped almonds
7 oz. of marshmallow crème
1 tsp. vanilla

Directions

In large saucepan mix sugar, milk, and butter. Over medium heat bring to rolling boil. Stir constantly for 7-10 minutes until it reaches softball stage. Remove from heat. Stir in chocolate bars and chips until melted. Add remaining ingredients and blend. Pour into buttered 8-inch pan. Cool—do not refrigerate. Cut into 1-inch squares and serve.

Chapter 4

Liz McElroy was close in age to me and Jenn. She was a tall, athletic girl with curly brown hair and a great big heart. Today she wore cargo pants, a pair of athletic shoes, and a dark blue T-shirt. "What do you mean you can't comment?"

"How do you know Tori's a person of interest?" I asked.

"I saw Rex Manning walking her into the police station," Liz said. She pulled out a little notebook and pencil to take notes. "Mrs. Gilmore told me that you found your cousin Victoria looming over Barbara Smart's dead body this morning with the handle of the murder weapon in her hand. Knowing that and seeing Rex escorting her inside, I put two and two together."

"I think he's just investigating," I said. "He knows Tori would never do such a thing."

"Are you sure about that?" Liz asked. "Because I heard that Tori and Barbara got into a big fight last night. Several people saw Tori stick her finger in the center of Barbara's breast bone and say she would kill her if she didn't keep her nose out of things."

"She did not!" Frances said.

"That's what I heard," Liz said. "I've got three witnesses. If I've got them, then you know Rex has them as well. So now, Allie, do you have any comments for my article? Do you think your cousin is capable of murder?"

"Anyone is capable of murder under the right circumstances," I said. "But I don't think Tori did it. What was the motive? Do you even know what they were fighting over?"

"No," Liz said, "but I intend to find out. And you can bet that Rex will find out, too. So I can quote you as saying anyone is capable of murder under the right circumstances?"

"No, don't quote that," I said with a shake of my head. "People will think I'm talking about my cousin. I'm not. She was trying to save Barbara, not kill her."

"Do you know that for sure? Because they were arguing."

"She's my cousin. She wouldn't ever get mad enough to stab someone with a gardening trowel."

"So the murder weapon was a hand spade?" Liz snagged onto my slip. "A weapon of opportunity I would guess." She wrote down a note. "Is there anything else you can tell me?"

"There isn't anything I can tell you," I said. "Really, Liz, I've said too much already. Just know that there is no way Victoria killed anyone. Not even accidentally."

"So you think it was an accident? Perhaps she

picked up the spade in the argument and they fought and Barbara was stabbed."

"I didn't say any of that," I protested. "I thought you were my friend."

"I am your friend," she said. "I'm simply trying to figure out Rex's angle on this."

"Their arguing the night before is circumstantial. No one knows what happened this morning, except Victoria. I believe her when she says she found Barbara that way."

"That means someone else was in the Butterfly House and killed her moments before Victoria got there and moments before you got there. Did you see anyone else?"

"No." I drew my eyebrows together. "I didn't see anyone but Mrs. Gilmore who came in later after I'd called nine-one-one. But then, they could have slipped into Insect World or any one of the front offices."

"Hmm"—Liz tapped her pencil on her notepad— "it sounds to me like your cousin is the best person of interest." She made a note. "Is there anything else you want to tell me?"

"No." I shook my head. "Liz, you can't quote me. I really don't know anything about this. I didn't even know Victoria was in town."

"You didn't?" Liz looked at me. "But she's your cousin."

"She's not talking to me. Apparently because Papa Liam left me the McMurphy and not her."

"Interesting." Liz made yet another note.

"Hey, that's not for public consumption."

"Everything is for public consumption, Allie."

Liz winked at me. "But only if it is a clue to who murdered Barbara."

"Did you know Victoria was going to plan the fund-raiser for the Butterfly House?" I asked.

"It wasn't a secret as far as I know," Liz said. "She was a year behind me in school but everyone keeps up with everyone on the island."

"But she moved to California years ago," I pointed out.

"She's still considered a native." Liz shrugged and her dark curls bobbed. "People keep in touch."

"Apparently not with me," I muttered. Mella, my new cat, jumped up on the reception desk and rubbed her face against my sleeve, begging to be petted. I absently stroked the calico cat from her shoulders to the end of her tail a few times.

Liz glanced at her watch. "Listen, I have to go. I've got a deadline. Promise me you'll keep me posted on the investigation."

"What investigation?"

"The one you're going to do to keep your cousin out of jail. That is if you really believe that she didn't murder Mrs. Smart."

"She didn't murder anyone," I said and raised my chin.

"Let's hope you can prove that," Liz said. She turned on her heel and waggled her fingers at me and Frances. "See you soon."

"Are you going to investigate?" Frances asked.

I stopped stroking Mella and she gave me a sour look and hopped down off the desk. "I'm not really in the business of murder investigations."

"You are really good at it," Frances pointed out. "This could go a long way toward healing the rift you two girls have."

"Darn it, there is no rift," I said. "I've got fudge to make."

"And a murder to investigate," Frances called from behind my back.

I wanted to turn and stick my tongue out at her for being right. But I controlled myself. I had a fudge demonstration to start in fifteen minutes and I needed to prep.

Demonstrating how fudge is made is one of the best marketing methods for selling fudge. People like to watch how it's done, but they don't want to stand in the street or in the lobby for the entire time it takes to make fudge. So I usually posted the times we demonstrated fifteen minutes after I really started. It took a while to boil the sugar and water and base flavors to the right consistency to begin the turning process.

The candy had to reach soft boil stage before we could remove it from the heat and add butter then toss it to the right consistency and add the more delicate pieces. I boiled together sugar and corn syrup, fresh milk and cocoa in a large copper kettle. When the mixture reached full boil, I quit stirring and left it for a few minutes to reach the proper temperature. I had to be careful not to over boil it and burn it, but also if you kept stirring constantly the mixture would take twice as long to reach the right stage of sugar boil.

Today's demonstration was dark chocolate cherry walnut fudge. The cherries were from

Travers City, Michigan. The walnuts were also grown in Michigan. I tried to keep ingredients as local as possible. People from all over the world wanted to taste Michigan when they came to the island. I spent my time chopping ingredients and waving to people who stopped by the big window to watch.

When the fudge was at the right temperature, I clipped on my microphone and grabbed Sandy, my chocolatier and assistant fudge maker, to help me start the demonstration. This was one of the parts I loved best about making fudge. With the large glass front windows and the glass-enclosed fudge area, people could gather and watch from three sides as we picked up the copper pot of boiling candy and poured the contents onto the cooling table with the marble top.

I told the same stories Papa Liam used to tell as I grabbed a long-handled, metal-topped scraper and started to push the fudge base toward the center of the table. As I pushed the scraper, I lifted and tossed the hot syrup into the air to add volume and to cool. People watched in fascination as the mixture slowly started to thicken and hold its shape. When it hit a certain thickness, I swapped out the long handle for a shorter scraper and explained the art and science of fudge.

The short handle allowed me to pick up the thickening fudge and form a long pool of it in the center of the buttered marble. I then reached for the cherries and added them to the top along with the walnuts. Finally, I folded them into the fudge with the scraper working quickly now as the fudge began to set. I created a smaller loaf in the center of the table and expertly cut one-pound pieces, adding them to the long tray that went into the candy counter. I cut off small tasting pieces and plated them. Sandy took the plate around the crowd offering free samples. Meanwhile I took orders at the counter as people purchased fresh fudge. Today we had five types—maple walnut, brown sugar pecan, dark chocolate cherry, milk chocolate, and classic cocoa.

Once the crowd dissipated, I saw Officer Rex Manning come into the McMurphy. "Sandy, can you clean up?" I asked and took off my apron and chef's coat leaving my white polo and black slacks. "I think Rex wants to talk with me about this morning."

"Sure," Sandy said and turned to the sink.

Sandy Everheart was a local girl and expert chocolatier. She had come back from culinary training in New York to take care of her ailing grandmother. Unfortunately for her, but fortunately for me, all the jobs on the island had been filled for the season. I needed an assistant, and Sandy—who was clearly overqualified—took the job. I couldn't pay her what she was worth, but I paid her what I could and offered her space in my kitchen to create chocolate sculptures and build her own business. It had turned out to be a great partnership. Sandy's sculptures brought people into the McMurphy who might have otherwise never stopped by. I was hoping to offer Sandy permanent space at the fudge shop.

"Hello, Rex," I said as I walked out of the kitchen

and closed the glass door behind me so that the cat didn't get into the area. "What brings you by today?"

He took off his police hat. His steel blue gaze was welcoming but concerned. "I thought we could talk about what happened with your cousin this morning. Do you have time?"

"Let's go up to my office," I suggested.

Rex was a good-looking man with that muscled action hero look. He shaved his head, but it looked good on him. Whenever he was close, I felt all feminine. I had to work to remind myself that he was simply a good friend. That I was dating Trent Jessop.

But Trent had been gone to Chicago on business for the last week. I pretended I wasn't lonely when he went away.

"Liz tells me that you brought Tori in for questioning," I said. We entered my office. It was a nice space on the fourth floor beside the owner's apartments. But it was crowded with file cabinets along the walls, and two desks in the center that faced each other. One desk was mine. The other was Jenn's. Jenn was helping me with my first season as owner of the McMurphy, but like Sandy, she also was establishing a side business. Jenn was a party planner by profession and had taken to planning events on the island like a duck takes to water.

I wonder what Papa Liam would think if he knew that we were running three businesses out of the McMurphy. They all went hand in hand as the party planning brought business to the hotel.

Jenn booked weddings and anniversary parties and other family groups that would rent out the entire space.

I was saving my pennies to reinforce the roof and create a rooftop area that looked out to the lake. The idea was that we could hold big events and parties up there. While I saved money for that project, I was also in the process of getting it permitted by the historical society and the neighboring establishments. I didn't want any complaints about the change in the building or the noise that came off the roof.

"Come on in." I waved Rex toward a creaky wooden office chair. He took a seat and I sat across from him. "How's the investigation going?"

"It's going," Rex said and propped his hat on his knee. "Why don't you tell me exactly what happened this morning?"

"Again?"

"Again," he said. "You might remember something now that the shock of it has worn off."

"Okay," I said and blew out a long breath. "Mal and I were going to the Butterfly House to meet with Mrs. Gilmore."

"Why?"

"She wanted to talk to me about scheduling a tour group and putting up posters and possibly flyers in the McMurphy."

"I see. She wanted to meet before the museum opened?"

"Yes. They get quite busy this time of year and she hoped to have a nice chat before things got crazy. I arrived with Mal, but the front doors weren't open yet."

"So what did you do?"

"I went around the building to see if she had left the back doors open. I thought I saw someone in the glass area so I stopped and tried the door. It was open."

"Who did you see?"

"Not anyone I could recognize. Mostly I saw movement and a shadow," I said. "I wish I could be more specific. The vinyl strips distorted everything. I thought it was Mrs. Gilmore, but it had to have been Victoria."

"Or Barbara Smart," Rex said.

I sat up straight. "Do you think she was killed as I arrived?"

"What happened when you found the door open?"

"I entered the greenhouse with Mal and called out for Mrs. Gilmore."

"What did you see?"

"Nothing out of the ordinary," I said and sat back against my seat. "Mal pulled me toward the right and then I heard a noise."

"What was the noise?"

"I'm not sure. It sounded like a small scream and someone moving through the building, bumping things, I guess."

"You called out for Mrs. Gilmore?"

"Yes, when I first entered, but she didn't answer. After I heard the scream, Mal and I hurried around a curve in the path and I stopped short. There was my cousin Victoria kneeling over the body of an older woman. Tori looked at me with desperation and shock on her face. Her hands were covered in blood and she had one hand on the handle of a garden trowel that was stuck in the chest of the body." I shuddered at the memory.

"And then what happened?"

"Tori told me she found her like that and tried to pull out the spade, but it made things worse. Poor Tori. I told her to back away and sit down on the edge of the flower bed because she was pale as a ghost and looked like she was going to be sick. Which she was by the way—I don't think a killer would stay there and be sick."

"I'm not making any judgment on whether she killed Barbara or not," he said. "I'm simply gathering facts. What happened after Tori sat down?"

"Mal jumped up to see her and that's how she got blood on her paws."

"What were you doing?"

"I called nine-one-one. Charlene asked me to check the body for a pulse and there wasn't any. She wasn't that warm—the victim, not Charlene. It wasn't as if she just died. I imagine if I found someone dead within moments of their death there would still be heat in the body. Right?"

"Yes."

"Well, she was cool. You remember. You arrived shortly after I checked for a pulse."

"You think that Barbara was dead when your cousin put her hand on the spade handle?"

"Yes, don't you remember that you told George you thought she had been dead a while?"

He sent me a serious look. "You should have also heard me say I wasn't a coroner."

"I remember," I said. "We're not doctors, but we've both been around enough dead bodies to know when someone has been lying dead for a while."

He sat back. "Did you know Victoria was in town?"

"Why does that matter?" I muttered.

He raised an eyebrow. "So you didn't know."

"Apparently there's a lot of things about my cousin I don't know."

"Like whether she could kill someone when she felt threatened?"

"What? No!" I sat up straight. "You didn't see her face. She was scared and sick."

"It could have been from regret."

"Why would she stay there for me to find her? It doesn't make any sense. She stumbled upon Barbara just as I stumbled upon her."

"That's a lot of stumbling," Rex pointed out.

"Okay, I'm not liking you too much right now." I glowered at him.

He chuckled and stood. "I'm just doing my job, Allie."

I stood. "Good. Then you'll find whoever killed Barbara."

"I have a strong lead," he said.

"Not Tori," I pressed.

"She had her hands on the murder weapon. I've got fingerprints and a witness."

"It doesn't mean she did it," I panicked.

"Thanks for the information, Allie." He stepped out of my office and I followed him.

"My cousin didn't kill her," I pressed. "I'll prove it if I have to."

He stopped short. "Trust me to do my job, Allie."

"I do trust you," I said. "I trust you to know Tori didn't do this."

"Have a good day, Allie." He sent a small wave and took the stairs two at a time.

I crossed my arms. It wasn't that I didn't trust him to do his job. It's that sometimes he got things wrong. I turned back to my office bound and determined to find out who really killed Barbara Smart.

Chapter 5

"You need to stop sleuthing," Trent said through my cell phone. It was close to my bedtime and I had Trent on speaker. He'd been gone more and more on business these days and he had a ritual of calling before I went to sleep each night.

I bristled at his tone of voice. "I really don't appreciate you telling me what to do," I said.

"I'm not telling you what to do," he said. "I'm simply telling you that I worry about you. It's a lot of pressure to run the hotel and fudge shop for your first season—and without any experience to guide you."

"Frances is here," I pointed out, scowling. "Jenn is a big help. I haven't been doing that badly and I sleuthed for you."

"I didn't want you to then and I don't think you should now," he stated. "Running a business is hard work, Allie. I know Liam made it seem like it was all fun and games, but by now you should have gotten the idea of how much work goes into it. Have you even taken a single day off?"

"What do you mean?"

"I mean, have you been off the island for a day? Have you even just gone to the beach and relaxed? No, you haven't," he said, and I thought I heard him running his hand through his hair. "All work and no play will burn you out."

"I'm not burned out," I said and folded my pajama-covered legs under me on my bed. "I like to sleuth and I have you and my friends to keep me from burning out."

"Not if you don't listen to us."

I let silence dance around my room for a couple of heartbeats. I pursed my lips in consternation. "I've spent my whole life preparing for ownership of the McMurphy. I'm not going to burn out three quarters of the way through the first season. I'm made of tougher stuff than that."

"Trust me, honey, I know how tough you are. But you don't need to be that tough," he pointed out. "Didn't you say your cousin wasn't even talking to you?"

"She doesn't know I will let her have partial ownership if she wants."

"You shouldn't do that either," he said. "The McMurphy is yours. If you give her half, she could sell you out."

"Tori wouldn't sell me out."

"How do you know that?" he asked. "You didn't even know she was angry at you in the first place."

"She's my cousin. She wouldn't do anything like that."

"You'd be surprised, honey, what people will do over inheritance. Trust me. I've watched the vultures fight over family fortunes one time too many in my life."

I gathered my hair in my hand and twisted it into a messy bun. "But Victoria is my family and we aren't that way."

"Then why isn't she talking to you?"

He had a point. I scrunched up my face. "Fine, I'll take your advice into consideration." Oh, beware when I became agreeable. It meant I wasn't happy, not happy at all. "Speaking of all work and no play, when are you going to be back on the island?"

"I've got to be at our Chicago office for another week," he said. "Henry reassured me that the stables are doing well and not to worry about the island business. The board of directors wants to acquire another company and that takes a lot of negotiation."

"I miss you," I said. I did. Even if he was a little high-handed with his demand that I stop sleuthing.

"I miss you, too," he said. "Take care of my girl. Try to take a day off now and then."

"I'll think about it."

We said our good nights and I lay back on my bed and looked at the ceiling. I loved the McMurphy. I'd grown up spending most of my summers on Mackinac Island helping Papa Liam and Grammy Alice run the hotel and fudge shop. Grammy was the best at keeping the hotel clean and the patrons happy. Papa was the best at fudge making and storytelling. When Grammy Alice died,

Papa had hired Frances. I was lucky to still have her, but Trent was right about one thing: I was trying to do two jobs at once and that was without sleuthing.

That said, angry with me or not, I wasn't about to let Victoria remain a suspect. My thoughts whirled. Who would kill Barbara Smart? Heck, I didn't know Barbara enough to even begin to imagine. Whoever it was, I highly doubt it was planned. Killing someone with a hand spade had to be very difficult. Most likely, whoever killed Barbara was arguing with her, picked up whatever was nearby, and stabbed her.

The real question in my mind was who was the shadow and movement I saw in the greenhouse? Was it Victoria looking for Barbara? Or was it the killer fleeing the scene?

I rubbed my hand over my face, suddenly exhausted. I may never know who I saw. But that didn't mean I shouldn't try to find out.

The next morning, I made a trip to the senior center. I brought fudge with me because what senior didn't want to be bribed with candy? I'd learned a few weeks back that the senior center was a wealth of local information. The seniors there all knew each other and they knew what happened on the island. My hope was that I could get a few of them to tell me everything they knew about Barbara Smart.

"Allie, what kind of fudge did you bring?" Mrs. O'Malley asked. It was craft day and today the ladies were learning to crochet little animals. The senior center was a bright square building with a kitchen on one end and centers set up in the big open space. There were windows on three walls and the floors were smooth linoleum. This is where Papa Liam spent his last days. Here at the tables where the men sat playing cards.

The ladies sat on a grouping of couches and chairs, patterns set out in large print on the coffee table between them. Mrs. O'Malley was a short, round-faced woman with dark black hair cut into a pixie and bright orange reading glasses perched on the end of her nose.

"I brought two kinds: chocolate cherry and peanut butter," I said. "No nuts this time."

"Good," Mrs. O'Malley said. "You're learning."

"I like nuts," Mrs. Morgan said from her perch on a wingback chair. She was a tiny older woman with snow white hair, mischievous eyes, and a pointy chin. She reminded me of an elf. Today she wore a T-shirt and cropped polyester pants. Her feet barely touched the ground.

"They'll break your teeth," Mrs. O'Malley proclaimed as she selected a piece of the chocolate.

"Maybe they'd break your teeth," Mrs. Morgan said, "but mine are strong. We Morgans are known for our strong teeth. Allie, next time bring some of that wonderful pecan pie fudge you make."

"I can do that," I said with a nod and passed her the platter of fudge. She selected a piece of peanut butter fudge.

After handing out fudge to Mrs. Albert and

Mrs. Helmsworth and Mrs. Tunisian, I sat down on the empty end of the couch.

"We heard you found your cousin Victoria murdering Barbara Smart," Mrs. O'Malley said and studied me over her glasses. "That must have been terrible."

"She wasn't murdering her," I protested. "She was trying to save her."

"I heard she had the handle of the garden trowel in her hand when you first saw her."

"She was trying to pull it out."

"That's what she said," Mrs. Abernathy said. Her fingers worked the yarn and hook. "We know the story, dear. We all know the story. It's in the news. What we want to know is what really happened. You girls aren't exactly on speaking terms. Still you insist that she is innocent. Why?"

"Because Victoria would never do this."

"Really?" Mrs. Morgan said. "We all heard that she was seen arguing with Barbara the night before."

"Why would they argue?" I had to ask. "What could Mrs. Smart possibly do that would motivate Tori to kill her?"

"We heard Barbara told Wanda Sikes that Tori's father was embezzling from the yacht club," Mrs. O'Malley said. "Wanda told Harriet Gross, who told Victoria. Tori confronted Barbara about it the night before the murder."

"If that's true, why would Tori agree to meet with Barbara in the morning? She would have told her to forget about her working with them on the fund-raiser."

"Of course she did," Mrs. Helmsworth said. "But then Wanda Sikes called Victoria and assured her that no one else believed the rumor. Wanda offered to meet Victoria instead of Barbara. But it seems Barbara showed up and Victoria got angry."

"Why would Barbara say such a thing about Tori's father?"

"There was a rumor that when Tori's dad was young, he was a busboy for the yacht club and took some money out of petty cash."

"That's hardly embezzlement," I pointed out. "How old was he? Sixteen? How much could he have taken out of petty cash?"

"He took a thousand dollars, which made him a felon."

"How come I didn't know this?" I asked. "Did he go to jail?"

"Actually he came forward and told the board," Mrs. Morgan said. "It seems that his father needed the money for surgery. Alex—Tori's father—didn't think the money would be missed. He was right. If he hadn't come forward and admitted what he had done, no one would have ever known."

"Why did he?"

"Come forward?" Mrs. O'Malley asked. "Alex wanted to pay them back. In order to do so, he had to pay them off slowly so he went to the board, admitted what he did and why, and then worked out a plan to pay them back with interest."

"That took a lot of guts," I said.

The women nodded. "Alex is a good man. The board agreed he could pay them back over four months and agreed not to prosecute if Alex promised to never steal again."

"He promised."

"In writing," Mrs. O'Malley said. "It's why everyone knows what he did."

"It doesn't make any sense to bring it up now. Why would Mrs. Smart tell Tori her father was embezzling?"

"She didn't," Mrs. O'Malley said. "She told Wanda Sikes who told Harriet Gross. Remember?"

"Still, why did Barbara bring it up now? Why did Wanda tell Harriet?"

"That's what we wondered," Mrs. Helmsworth said. "We don't know. Barbara was a mysterious creature full of plans and schemes. It's like she was purposefully goading Victoria."

"Or she wanted Victoria to be angry with Wanda," Mrs. O'Malley said. "Barbara always had an agenda of some sort. I guess we will never know what she was thinking now."

"But why? Isn't Barbara the one who called and asked Tori to come and plan the fund-raiser?"

"She is," Mrs. O'Malley said. "Strange. It's as if she lured the girl here and then ensured everyone saw her argue with her. It's as if she was setting her up for something."

"Which is why Victoria is a perfect suspect. She must have gotten wind of whatever Barbara was doing and told her to stop. The two fought and— bam!—she stabbed Barbara with a garden spade. That's where you walked in."

I rolled my eyes. "No, it takes time to die. When I got there, she was definitely dead. Poor Tori isn't used to finding dead people. Her first instinct was to try to pull out the trowel and stop the bleeding, but when she tried it was stuck in too tight. Then I showed up and told her to step away."

"Why are you defending the girl?" Mrs. Abernathy asked. "She hates you."

"Because she didn't do it," I said stubbornly. "And she doesn't hate me."

"If she didn't do it, who did?" Mrs. Abernathy asked.

"That's what I'm trying to find out," I said. "Do you know who Barbara hung out with?"

"Wanda Hewlett Sikes is or was Barbara's best friend," Mrs. Morgan said. "Poor dear is devastated. She couldn't even come for craft day."

"Wanda Sikes," I murmured. "She lives on First Street, right?"

"Yes, her family owns the Hewlett cottage and the clothing boutique on Main Street," Mrs. Morgan said. "She and Barbara grew up together. What terrors. They were always pranking people. You'd think they would outgrow that thing at our age."

"That's right," Mrs. O'Malley said. "Trouble was Barbara's middle name. Why, last year she had Marylou Spelt in tears thinking she had dementia."

"What? That's horrid."

"It seems Barbara and Wanda were upset because Marylou won the cookie contest at the center. So they set about a plan to tell her things she did that she wouldn't remember because she didn't really do them."

"They were diabolical," Mrs. Abernathy said.

"They had Marylou so convinced, she went to her doctor and they ran all the tests. It was after the third doctor didn't find anything that Marylou's daughter, Bridgett, became suspicious. You see, Marylou had no problem remembering things that happened with anyone else but Barbara and Wanda."

"Bridgett confronted them and they laughed and said it was all in good fun."

"Sounds like a few people had reasons to kill Barbara," I said.

"Indeed," Mrs. Morgan said. "Barbara Smart was a tricky one. She loved to manipulate people. She was always flirting with the men at the yacht club."

"It was rumored she had a new affair every year."

"She would pick a man, move in on him until he didn't know which way was up. She would have him following her around like a lost pup and then drop him like a hot potato at the end of the season."

"Indeed she was a soap opera rolled into one person."

"I heard she had liposuction and a tummy tuck."

"She had her forehead frozen with that inject-able poison and her lips and cheeks filled."

"She looked twenty years younger and had it all paid for by whichever man she was attaching herself to at the time."

"Then why would she have her lovers pay her doctor bills?"

"Well, you see, her mother-in-law, Ingrid Smart, was on to Barbara's ways early on and attached a codicil to her will. She allowed Barbara a monthly allowance. Her husband, Richard, was not allowed to give her any further support. When Richard died of cancer, everyone thought she would inherit, but Ingrid still holds the purse strings so to speak. Barbara might have had money coming but she couldn't get her hands on it until the old coot died."

"Wow—is Ingrid still alive?" I asked.

"Oh yes, she is ninety-eight years old and as sharp as a tack," Mrs. Helmsworth replied. "She would have had Richard divorce Barbara but he refused. Lovestruck the whole time, even though he knew of her affairs."

"Not very smart that one, despite his name," Mrs. Tunisian said.

"Barbara sounds like a nasty piece of work," I muttered.

"If you truly believe Victoria didn't kill her, then you are going to have trouble figuring out who did. There isn't a soul on the island who isn't a bit relieved to see her go."

"Except for Elmer, of course," Mrs. Abernathy said.

"Who's Elmer?"

"Elmer Hanson, Barbara's latest fling. Poor soul is devastated."

"He didn't come for his weekly pinochle game. We all know how devoted he is to his cards. Almost as devoted as he was to Barbara," Mrs. Morgan said.

I stood. "Thank you, ladies," I said. "You have given me a lot to think about."

"So you are sleuthing," Mrs. Abernathy said.

"Good. Do come back and update us on what you discover. We love a good puzzle."

"Yes, we'd sleuth ourselves if we were able to get around better," Mrs. Morgan said.

"I have a feeling you all get around pretty well," I said. "Thanks again for the information."

"Thank you for the fudge. Remember, dear, bring the pecan pie fudge next time."

"Emily, nuts will break your teeth."

"I'll chew slowly." She winked at me.

I left with a lot to think about. There were a couple of people I needed to see if I were to puzzle this thing out. The first would be Ingrid Smart. Then Wanda Sikes. Perhaps Wanda would be willing to tell me what Barbara's plans really were for my cousin.

Chapter 6

"I've booked a wedding party," Jenn said. "They are friends of mine from Chicago and they wanted a destination wedding."

"Wonderful," I said from my side of the office. Jenn and I worked facing each other in the center of the tiny room. I thought it was more collaborative than if we had put the two desks along the wall and had our backs to each other. "How big is the party and when are they coming?"

"They want to book the entire hotel," she said. "They have friends and family close by. I've got them booked for a sunset wedding at Arch Rock. It's going to be fabulous."

"The entire McMurphy? We have regulars that book every week of the season. How did Frances clear the hotel?"

"She's still working on that," Jenn said and put her chin in her hand and frowned at me. "Why all the negativity?"

"I'm not negative," I said. "I'm practical."

"You're hurt because Victoria hasn't come to

see you yet." Jenn knew me better than anyone. Sometimes I didn't like it.

"She insists on staying at her family cabin. I was in there. Everything is dust covered and I'm not even sure she has running water. She could stay here so much more comfortably."

"I heard through the grapevine that Victoria was running her own investigation into Barbara Smart."

"What?" That made me sit up. "Who told you that?"

"Mrs. Abernathy," Jenn said with a nod and studied me. "It seems you two are more alike than you realize."

"Except she seems to know everyone on the island better than I do," I said. "Which is why I don't understand how she could have let Barbara do this to her."

"Wait, what? Barbara is the victim here."

"Yes, I know," I said and waved it away. "I don't think she was supposed to be. There is something else going on."

"Why do you say that?"

"I went to the senior center looking for more information about Mrs. Smart. It seems she was a master manipulator. She has had more affairs and ruined more reputations than a Jane Austen villain."

"Really?"

"Yes," I said and put my hand in my chin. "Who would have thought that kind of psycho really existed? You should hear the stories they had to tell.

Apparently there wasn't a man on the island she didn't either seduce or attempt to seduce. It makes me wish Papa Liam was alive. He could tell me if she tried any of her tricks on him."

"Crazy."

"Oh, and it isn't just the men she went after. It seems she would decide she didn't like a woman and go about making things happen that would ruin her victim without actually making it look like she was involved. 'Diabolical' is what the ladies called her."

"Imagine having that kind of mind," Jenn said. "I mean in real life."

"I know, right? I'm so busy thinking up new candy recipes and figuring out how to pay bills, I don't have time to manipulate people. But apparently she started from nothing. Married Mr. Smart because he was incredibly rich but terribly dim-witted."

"She sounds like my kind of woman," Jenn said with a laugh. "Except of course, you know I like my men nerdy and scientific."

"She might sound cool, but it's something that got her killed. I'm sure her victims didn't think she was cool at all."

"I was just joking," Jenn said. "Sheesh—what will it take to get you to lighten up?"

"Figuring out who killed Barbara and why," I said. "And reconciling with my cousin."

"You should call Tori," Jenn suggested.

"That might not be a bad idea," I said and pulled out my cell phone. "If she is sleuthing, perhaps we can put our heads together and solve this murder."

I dialed Victoria's cell phone. Luckily I had gotten her number from my mother at Papa Liam's funeral. It was then that I realized I needed to keep in touch with my extended family. My parents didn't exactly speak to their cousins every day. It was a bad habit I needed to break. Especially because I had so few cousins. Mostly they were like Tori, second cousins. But family was family.

"Hello?"

"Hi, Tori," I said and raised a thumbs-up sign to Jenn as I stepped out of the office and into the tiny hallway that allowed access to the office and my apartment. "It's Allie."

There was a long-suffering sigh on the other end of the phone. "What do you want, Allie?"

I tried not to overreact. "I wanted to check on you and see how you're doing."

"I'm fine."

"I heard that you were questioned again about the murder. What happened?"

"Allie, I'm fine. Stay out of it. Okay?"

"I'm not going to do that, Victoria," I said. "You're my family and I won't let you go to jail for something you didn't do."

"I'm not going to jail," she said. "At least not yet."

"But you are the main suspect and I'm sorry for that."

"Stop. I'm not blaming you, Allie, okay? So just leave me alone."

"I didn't say you were blaming me. I said I wanted to help find the killer. Why don't you come for dinner? We can talk and put our heads together on this thing."

"Allie—"

"Hear me out, Tori. Please. Just come for dinner."

"Fine," she said. "What time?"

"We eat at seven."

"We?"

"My roommate, Jenn, and Frances, and Mr. Devaney. You remember Frances, right?"

"Sure, and did you say Mr. Devaney? The English teacher?"

"Yes, he's my new handyman and he's quite good at it."

"Okay, weird, but okay. I'll be there by seven."

"You can bring someone if you want."

"I don't have anyone here to bring, Allie," she said. "I'll be there. Just don't invite Liz McElroy, okay?"

"Sure, but why not?"

"She's making it sound like I murdered Barbara Smart," Tori said, her voice getting softer. "I didn't do it."

"Okay, no Liz. I'll see you at seven." I hung up the phone and went back into the office.

"So?" Jenn asked.

"She's coming to dinner."

She clapped her hands. "Good for you. Now what are we having for dinner?"

"I have no idea," I said and frowned then

brightened. "When we were kids she used to like sloppy joes. How about I fix those?"

"Oh my gosh, I haven't had those in ages. I'll make homemade fries to go with them and a nice green salad to round it out."

"Great. I guess I'm off to the grocery store to pick up the ground beef, the sauce fixings, and the hamburger buns."

"We can bake the fries so that they are healthier." Jenn popped up out of her chair. "This is so exciting. I get to meet another member of your family."

"You'll like her," I said. "As long as we don't talk about the murder or the McMurphy, everything will be fine."

"Good luck with that," Jenn said, her eyes twinkling. "You're going to need it."

Butter Pecan Fudge

Ingredients

½ cup of sugar
½ cup brown sugar
½ cup butter
½ cup heavy whipping cream
dash of salt
1 tsp. vanilla
1¾ cup sifted confectioners' sugar
1 cup toasted pecans, coarsely chopped

Directions

In a heavy saucepan, bring the sugar, brown sugar, butter, and heavy whipping cream to a rolling boil. Stir constantly and boil for 7-10 minutes until it hits softball stage. (Roughly 234 degrees on a candy thermometer.) Remove from heat. Add salt and vanilla. Do not stir—let cool in pan for roughly 30 minutes or until 110 degrees F. Then stir in confectioners' sugar until the fudge loses its gloss and is smooth. Add nuts. Blend. Pour into 8-inch square pan and let cool completely. Cut into 1-inch squares and enjoy!

Chapter 7

"I heard your cousin killed Barbara Smart." Mary Emery was the main cashier at the grocery store. She rarely spoke to anyone. So I was startled by her statement.

"I'm sorry, what?" I asked as I set my groceries on the counter for her to ring up.

"Your cousin is a murderer. That has to be tough on your business."

"My cousin is not a murderer," I said. "I wish people would stop saying that."

"But you found her kneeling over the body with the murder weapon in her hand, right?"

"Well, in a way, yes, but—"

"There's also an eyewitness to a heated argument between Barbara and your cousin. Wanda told me that Tori was hopping mad."

"It was just an argument," I said as I watched her bag my things. "All circumstantial."

"She had the look of a killer in her eyes," Mary

said. "Rex is going to put the pieces together and then Tori will go to jail."

"There isn't any real evidence she did anything wrong," I protested and gathered up my bags. "I wish you all would stop spreading such evil rumors."

"Oh, it's not a rumor," Mary said with a shake of her head. "Wanda wouldn't lie about a thing like that."

"Who is this Wanda anyway?"

"Wanda Sikes," Mary said. "She was Barbara's best friend."

"Oh, that Wanda. Well, Wanda is wrong." I left the shop in a huff. It wasn't very far from the grocer to the McMurphy as both were on Main Street. I negotiated the crowds of tourists with as much cheerfulness as I could muster. I didn't want to give anyone a bad impression.

The bells on the door to the McMurphy rang as I entered. Mal jumped up to greet me with a wag of her little stub tail.

"You look upset," Frances said from her perch at the receptionist desk.

"Mary Emery actually spoke to me again," I said.

"Why would that upset you?" Frances looked at me from over the top of her glasses.

"She told me that Wanda Sikes is the eyewitness to Tori's argument with Barbara."

"And that makes you angry because . . ."

"Because Wanda is telling everyone Tori killed Barbara in the heat of the moment."

"I didn't kill anyone," Victoria said from behind me. I turned on my heel. "I don't remember Wanda Sikes being anywhere near me when I argued with Barbara." Tori crossed her arms over her chest. "She's lying."

"I told Mary that you didn't do it." I started toward the stairs with my hands full. Mal trailed behind me, determined to get her welcoming pats.

"Thank you," Tori said. "I didn't do anything but try to save Barbara's life."

"Let's go upstairs," I said and started up. "It's better to have this conversation in private."

"I don't care who hears me," Tori said, raising her voice. "I didn't kill anyone."

"Fine," I said and blew out a long breath. "You're early."

"I was bored."

"Well, I'm going upstairs to put these groceries away and start dinner. I'm glad you came. You can keep me company."

Tori frowned at me suspiciously for a moment then followed me. My cousin was beautiful in a silky tank top and beach shorts. I could hear her flip-flops on the steps behind me. We walked up in silence. I unlocked the apartment door and Mella jumped up on the back of the couch to greet me. Mal barked at her, but the cat ignored the pup.

"What happened the night before last?" I asked. "Why were you arguing with Barbara?" I knew what the seniors had told me, but I wanted to hear from Tori why people would think she was mad enough to kill.

Tori looked around the apartment. "You haven't changed much. The place still looks like it did when Uncle Liam lived here. The décor is mid-century modern and run-down."

"Thanks," I said and started to take out the ingredients I needed for dinner. "I remodeled the lobby and guest rooms," I said. "There wasn't any money left to update the apartment."

"I noticed the remodel. The coffee bar and new wallpaper are nice touches."

I stopped for a moment. "Thanks."

"You're welcome."

"Would you like something to drink? I can pour us both a glass of wine. It seems like we need it."

"That works for me," Tori said as she slipped onto a bar stool and leaned her elbows on the island that separated the kitchen from the living area of the apartment. She was right. I hadn't put any thought into remodeling the space. It still had the green carpet with a raised leaf pattern. The walls were dark and partially paneled. The furniture was old. From Papa's beloved but ragtag easy chair to the mid-century modern couch with its faded avocado cushions. I was pretty sure the cushions weren't original, as Grammy liked to DIY her place.

I opened a bottle of red wine and poured us both some. "Look, I'm sorry that you didn't get a part of the McMurphy when Papa died. I had no idea you wanted it and I think it's a safe bet that Papa didn't know either."

"Oh, Uncle Liam knew," she said and raised her

glass to me in a mini salute. "He just didn't take the time to change his will. That's what has me stomping mad. That, and the fact that you took over without so much as asking how I felt about it. I'm a McMurphy, too."

"I'm sorry," I said again as sincerely as I could. "Truly sorry for not thinking past my own nose. I was so scared about doing this first season alone that I completely messed up."

"Well," she said with a short fast frown, "I suppose Uncle Liam didn't help by not putting me in his will."

"Funny how my dad and your mom didn't want anything to do with the place and here we are arguing over it. Please accept my apology."

"Fine," she said. "But it doesn't mean I'm going to stay here, Allie. My family's cottage is comfortable enough for now."

I started making the salad. I liked to make chopped salad by color starting with kale, arugula, and romaine. Then green things like cucumbers and green peppers. Next were red veggies like radishes, red peppers, and tomatoes; after that it was yellow peppers, yellow tomatoes, and then white onion and topped with black olives. I pulled out my chopping board and knife to begin the work. "Do you want me to have the lawyers draw up an agreement? We could split the profits eighty-twenty since I'm living here and doing the work."

"I suppose twenty percent is pretty generous. It's not about the money, though," she said. "It's about owning part of the family business. What if I get married and have kids someday and they want to run the hotel and fudge shop? I need to have a piece of it to ensure they can have a stake in it as well."

"Oh," I said and paused chopping for a moment. The scent of fresh cut pepper filled the air. "I hadn't thought about our children."

"Twenty percent is good," she said with a toast of the wineglass.

"That sounds fine to me." I stopped chopping and lifted my wineglass. "Here's to partnerships and family." We clinked glasses.

"Here, here," she said and we both drank.

Dinner was done and everyone had gathered after in the living room. I'd pulled out a chair from my bedroom. Frances and her fiancé, Mr. Devaney, sat on the couch. I sat in Papa's chair, Jenn lounged on a bar stool, and Tori sat in the chair I had added. I'd offered her Papa's chair but she refused.

"What did Rex say to you?" Frances asked Tori. "Are you okay?"

"I'm fine," she said. "Rex asked about what happened. I told him that I was supposed to meet Barbara to discuss the fund-raiser. I got to the Butterfly House and went inside. That's when I saw her lying there. I don't know why but my first reaction was to pull the hand trowel out. It looked painful. I knelt down and called her name. Then I put my hands on the handle, but when I tried to inch it out she bled even more. I stopped and that's when Allie came in and told me to step away from the body."

"That must have been horrible," Jenn said. "I don't know what I'd do if I had come across Barbara with a garden trowel in her chest."

"Rumor around town is that you are a person of interest in Barbara's death," Frances said and sipped her coffee.

"I'm sure it's just a rumor," I said. "Rex knows you wouldn't kill anyone."

"No," Tori said and curled up in the chair as if to protect herself. "I am a person of interest. I didn't do it, but I'm the most likely suspect."

"Is it because Wanda saw you arguing with Barbara the night before?"

"Yes," she said and sipped wine. "That, and Allie found me with my hand on the murder weapon and blood all over me."

"It's all circumstantial," I said. "No one saw you kill Barbara."

"It doesn't mean I didn't want to," Tori said softly. She looked up at us. "That woman was horrible, I swear. She had a way of manipulating people."

"What were you arguing about?" I asked, curious. "I mean, what could possibly be a motive for murder?"

"Barbara caught me just as I got off the ferry. She was hopping mad. It seems that Millie Hamm told her that I was bringing in my own catering group for the fund-raiser."

"Why would that make her mad?" Frances asked.

"She's the one who put you in charge in the first place."

"But she wanted to be in charge and I hadn't discussed anything with her yet. I planned on talking to her the morning I found her dead. You see, I have a good friend who has a catering service in St. Ignace and she offered to give us a good deal as long as she could deduct a portion from her taxes as charity."

"Sounds good," Jenn said.

"It took me a week to negotiate the thing with her. I figured Barbara would be fine with it."

"Sounds like you figured wrong."

"Hmm, she lit into me like I was a naughty schoolgirl. It got my back up. We were in public for goodness' sake and what I did didn't deserve that kind of talking to."

"How did you react?" I asked. "Were you physical? Did you threaten her?"

"No." Tori shook her head. "I just let her scream at me and stewed. I figured once she got it all out, I'd let her know in no uncertain terms that she couldn't treat me like that."

"That sounds reasonable," Frances said.

"I'm not good with confrontation," Tori said. "I usually think of all the good things to say the next day. So I've learned to just let people get things out of their system then I go see them later and let them know how wrong they are."

"So you said nothing during this?" I asked. "Because Wanda made it sound as if the argument gave you motive for murder. But what you are telling us sounds too tame and very different from what the seniors are telling me."

"The seniors?"

"My sources at the senior center," I said. "They told me that you started the argument with Barbara because she was spreading the rumor that your father was an embezzler."

"That's ridiculous."

"That's definitely two very different stories," Frances said. "Usually the senior gossip network is dead on."

"Not this time," Tori said. "My father? An embezzler?"

"They told me it was an old story. Your father took money out of the yacht club petty cash."

"He paid that back," Tori said, her expression one of confusion and disbelief. "That happened well before I was even born. Why bring that up again?"

"I don't know," I said. "The seniors didn't know either. They felt it was old hat. But the story is that you found out and lit into Barbara about it."

"Neither of those stories sound like motive for murder," Frances said.

"Perhaps it's just the fact that you argued that is contributing to you being a person of interest," Jenn suggested.

"If arguing is cause for murder then a lot of people could have done it," Frances said. "Barbara was known for causing trouble."

"I agree. That's not enough evidence to make you a person of interest," I said. "Whoever killed Barbara did so in the heat of the moment."

"How do you know that?" Mr. Devaney asked.

"They used a hand spade. It's not likely someone would come into the place intending to stab Barbara with such an unwieldy weapon. If it were a knife or a hatchet, maybe it was premeditated. But a trowel is spur of the moment. It was most likely lying around. I noticed that there were pads for kneeling nearby and a fresh bed of garden soil. Either Barbara was working on the garden or the killer was."

"The only other people who work in the gardens at the Butterfly House are Mrs. Gilmore and Ms. Scott," Frances said. "Oh, and a young man who was let go a few weeks ago. He wouldn't have been in the Butterfly House and Emma Scott was out sick with a summer cold."

"Well, someone has to have a motive for murder. I talked to the ladies at the senior center," I said. "They said that Barbara was very active in the community. They also told me that there were a lot of people with motives to kill her. It seems she had the reputation of being a bit of a mastermind when it comes to controlling people and outcomes."

"That part they got right," Frances said. "I'm afraid that Victoria isn't the only person to feel the sting of Barbara's tongue. That woman could manipulate things until you swore it was your idea to do it her way. Heaven help you if you were immune to that. Then she came down hard."

"That's what she did to me," Tori said. "I felt ambushed."

"And then someone ambushed Barbara at the Butterfly House," I said.

"Do you think it was someone who saw you arguing with Barbara on the dock?" Jenn asked.

"That could be anyone," Tori said. "She ambushed me in front of everyone who was docking."

"Besides, that would imply premeditation and like I said, I'm pretty sure if the murder were premeditated, the killer would have used something easier than a hand shovel."

"I bet they won't find any prints but yours on the handle," Mr. Devaney said. We all turned and looked at him. He shrugged. "If the murder was spur of the moment, the killer may have been gardening and would most likely be wearing garden gloves at the time of the murder."

"Oh," Tori said and put her hand on her mouth. "I wasn't wearing gloves."

"Exactly," Mr. Devaney said.

"That means the circumstantial evidence all points to me," Tori said. Her shoulders dropped and so did her expression. "No wonder Rex spent two hours questioning me." She looked up. "Do you think I need a lawyer?"

"I'll call my cousin," Frances said. "He worked out well when Allie was a suspect a few months ago."

"He's a good guy," I said. "He won't steer you wrong."

Tori ran her hand through her hair. "I can't believe I need a lawyer. I didn't do this."

"We can figure this out," I said and patted her hand.

"Allie's good at sleuthing," Jenn said.

"I'll help," Tori said. "I've got the most invested in this. The problem is that I need to plan this fund-raiser."

"We can help you with the fund-raiser," Jenn suggested.

"No." Victoria shook her head. "No, I don't need your help with that."

"Oh," Jenn said, clearly disappointed.

"It's not personal," Tori said. "I know more people on the island and the surrounding area. I can get things pulled together faster and with better results."

"Right," I said. "Well, good." I was a bit miffed at Tori for her refusing Jenn's offer. It got my back up that Victoria was considered a local and we weren't. There was a long awkward silence.

"I think it's time for me to get going," Frances said and got up. Mr. Devaney got up with her.

"I'll see you home," he said and put his hand on her shoulder.

Frances patted his hand. "Thank you, Douglas."

"I've got to go as well," Victoria said and stood. "Thanks for dinner, Allie. Now that I have a lawyer, I can put him to work drawing up the owner-ship papers on the McMurphy. If that still works for you."

"Do you think we need a lawyer?" I stood as well while Jenn continued to lounge and absently pet Mella the cat.

"I'm more comfortable with putting it in writ-ing," she replied.

"Sure," I said. It felt as if she didn't trust me.

Still, miffed or not, I was a person of my word. "That works. I'll just be sure that my lawyer is okay with the contract before I sign."

"I think you two have the same lawyer," Jenn pointed out with a raised eyebrow.

"I'll get a new one," I said. "My parents know a few in Detroit."

"Fine," Tori said.

"Good," I said and hugged my waist. "Thanks for coming over. You're welcome to come to dinner anytime."

"No thanks," she said and raised her chin. "But I'm good. I don't need your charity."

"Oh, for goodness' sake, it isn't charity when you're family," I said as I held the door open. "Frances, tell her it's not charity."

Frances looped her arm through Victoria's. "It's not charity. Douglas and I eat with Allie almost every night. Next time, you can bring dessert, okay? Now, come on. We'll see you home."

I closed the doors after our good-byes and turned to Jenn. Mal had gotten jealous of the kitty and sat on one side of Jenn nudging her hand for pets while Mella had the other side and batted Jenn's other hand. "That went well," I said with a hint of sarcasm.

"You can't expect one dinner to create harmony," Jenn said and got up to help me with the dishes. "I think it did go well considering."

"I'm insulted that she thinks we need a lawyer. We're family," I pointed out and filled the sink with soapy water.

"Inheritance is always a touchy subject. You probably should check with Papa Liam's lawyer and make sure the will allows you to share the McMurphy."

"Why wouldn't it?"

"I don't know." Jenn shrugged and picked up a towel to dry the dishes I'd washed. "I'm not all that good on the legality of things, but it seems to me there was a reason your papa left the McMurphy only to you. His lawyer might know a thing or two about it."

"You are pretty smart," I said.

"I know." Jenn grinned at me. "I know."

Chapter 8

The next day I had my rescheduled meeting with Mrs. Gilmore. I sat in her tiny jam-packed office. My chair was squished in between stacks of books and boxes that were clearly empty but marked RUSH.

"Thanks for coming in, Allie," Blake said. She sat at her desk. It was piled high with file folders and books on butterflies. The room was filled with bookshelves and a wide variety of books old and new. On the back wall was a scientific poster of a butterfly, its scientific name and the names of all its parts. "I'm so sorry about Barbara. If I hadn't asked you to meet me, you wouldn't have gotten involved."

"But then I wouldn't have known Victoria was on the island. Or that you were putting together a fund-raiser."

"I was going to tell you about the fund-raiser yesterday when we were supposed to meet. Victoria and the committee plan on bringing a lot of fudgies in and we would like to use the McMurphy as the hotel of choice for the fund-raiser."

"Well, thank you," I said and drew my eyebrows together. "What made you choose the McMurphy over the likes of the Grand or The Grander or even The Island House Hotel or one of the resorts?"

"We want them close to the Butterfly House and we want to give them a cheaper option than the Grand and others," Blake said. "You were the first we thought of. I know you have regular patrons and you seem to be doing well this season, but we thought it would help you and help us if the McMurphy was the hotel of choice for the fund-raiser."

"Okay," I said and pulled my phone out of my pocket to check the reservation calendar that I'd automated. "What dates are you considering?"

"The Thursday and Friday after Labor Day."

"That's after the season is over."

"Just after," Blake said. "We thought we could entice people to come and see that we are more than a summer island. Besides, the monarch butter-flies will be in their best shape that time of year."

"I see," I said, letting a frown cross my face. "I had promised my parents that I would visit them the week after Labor Day. Let me get back to you on the dates. I need to check with them and make sure they don't already have things planned for me to do."

"I understand," she said. "But don't take too long. We want to build flyers and other marketing pieces soon. We can't do anything without knowing the hotel."

"What kind of activities are you thinking?"

"Oh, Victoria is quite good at this. She has a complete package based on donation levels. The basic package is twelve hundred dollars for two. They get valet parking at the ferry, ferry to and from, hotel, a guided tour of the island by horse and carriage, a fancy dress ball dinner at the fort, and breakfast at the Island House the next morning. The packages will go up from there. The premium package will include private tours of the fort and the Butterfly House as well as the best parts of the parks. We hope to raise a quarter of a million dollars."

"That's a lot of money," I said.

"We need it for building repair and such. Now that I have a crime scene in the middle of the house we need it even more as I can't sell tickets until it is cleared and cleaned up. You would not believe how expensive it is to clean up a crime scene."

"Oh, I have some idea," I said. It had taken special crime scene cleaners to come in after they took away the body of my papa's archenemy that I found in my utility closet earlier this year.

"Oh that's right," Blake said. "I forgot about your crime scene. That seems a hundred years ago."

"It was April," I said. "I still have the card of the company who cleaned up, if you want the information. They did a great job in the McMurphy. You can't tell anything happened."

"Yes, please," Blake said. "That would help."

"Not a worry, I'll e-mail you their info when I get back." I made a note in my phone to remind me. "It sounds like a really big fund-raiser."

"Yes, that's our hope." Blake folded her hands on the top of her desk. "Victoria has it all in order. So we're good once you and the McMurphy are on board. That is if Victoria isn't arrested. If that happens, we're all in a pickle because she has everything in her head."

"She needs to write it down," I said. "Not that she's going to be arrested, but she could get sick, etc. It's always good to put your plans on paper."

"That's very true. Are you investigating the murder? Because, if that were solved, we could all go about our day not worrying over the fund-raiser."

"I'm sure Officer Manning has it all under control." I tried to put up a professional front. After all, I wasn't a law enforcement person. "Tell me, do you know why Barbara was in the Butterfly House that morning? I was told it was to meet Victoria and discuss the fund-raiser, but they could have done that anywhere."

"Oh, Victoria wanted to see the space and take measurements. We hoped to have a tour of the Butterfly House as one of the events."

"That explains why Tori was there, but why Barbara?"

Blake drew her brows together. "I thought because she wanted to talk details with Victoria."

"Barbara came down quite hard on Victoria the night before in front of a lot of people on the dock. Do you think she expected Victoria to forget about that?" I asked.

"Maybe she wanted to apologize. I know sometimes I fly off the handle and then realize later that an apology is needed."

"But everyone so far hasn't been surprised Barbara was there—even Victoria said they were meeting about the fund-raiser."

"I think you need to talk to Victoria about that," Blake said and waved off my question.

"You must have been there to open the door that morning," I said. "Did you hear anything? A fight? Anything?"

"Oh no, dear, I already told Rex that I opened the back door and let Barbara in and then I had to run to another meeting. By the time I got back it was all over."

"Who works in the gardens? Were they there that morning?"

"Emma works in the gardens," Blake said and tapped her fingers on her chin. "She has a cold and was off yesterday. She said she went to Mackinaw City to spend the day with her mother pampering her. Why do you ask?"

"I think the murder was a crime of opportunity," I said. "No one plans to kill someone with a garden trowel. I would imagine it's very difficult."

"I'm pretty sure Emma wasn't there." Blake frowned. "But if she wasn't there, then the hand spade should have been put away. We have a storage place that holds a workbench and everything has its place. I like to be meticulous in that way."

"Can I see the space?"

"Sure," Blake said. We both got up and I followed her through the Butterfly House. The
butterflies floated around the flowers and plants,
landing on the crime scene tape as if it were just
another part of the exhibit. I was careful where I
stepped. We passed through the vinyl flaps at
the back to a shed just outside the greenhouse.
She opened the door and turned on the light. The
place was anything but neat as a pin. Someone
had come in and clearly searched it—pots were
overturned, hand hoes were scattered around the
floor, a watering can sat on its side on the floor.
Bags of mulch were torn open and so were bags of
dirt. The dirt and mulch were scattered around
the concrete floor in piles. "I don't understand,"
Blake said. "Who would do this?"

I reached for my phone and speed-dialed Rex.

"Manning," he said in his clear baritone that
always slid pleasantly over my skin.

"Hi, Rex, it's Allie."

"Is there another body?"

Why was that always the first question out of
everyone's mouth when I called? I did a silent
eye roll. "No, but I'm at the Butterfly House with
Mrs. Gilmore and someone has trashed her work
shed. It looks like they were looking for something.
I think it may be connected to Barbara's murder."

"Don't touch anything," Rex said sternly. "I'll be
right there."

I hung up the phone and looked at Blake. "He
said not to touch anything."

"All right," she agreed.

I stepped into the shed and looked around. "What do you suppose they were looking for? I mean, why open mulch and soil and dump it out?"

"I'm not sure," Blake said. "Maybe they were angry."

I glanced at her over my shoulder. "Do you know of anyone who is upset with the Butterfly House?"

"Goodness, no," she said.

"Did you get a shipment of anything rare or expensive lately? Maybe they were looking to steal it."

"We did get a box of rare chrysalises from Africa just a few days ago. Because of their rarity, I didn't put them in the chrysalis box at the front of the house. Instead I put them in a viewing box in our second office. Then I put a camera on it to stream it so that people can watch the butterflies emerge on-line."

"How rare are they?"

"They cost a thousand dollars each and there were four."

"Wow, I didn't know it cost so much to have butterflies."

"Curating rare breeds is an art and a science," she said, her tone proud. "Do you think that's what they were looking for?"

"Maybe," I said. "Maybe they came in looking for that and when they didn't find it they got mad and trashed the shed. If Barbara surprised them, then they could have picked up what was handy and stabbed her."

"That's a good theory," Rex said behind me. "But there is no proof of anything other than someone clearly was looking for something they thought was hidden in the shed." He pulled out his flashlight and hit my eyes. "I thought I told you not to touch anything."

"I didn't," I said and put my hand up to block the light. "I just took two steps inside."

"Now you can take two steps outside," he said. "Please."

"Fine." I did what he said and watched as he took his flashlight and looked around. The light was on so I didn't think he needed the flashlight, but it did illuminate dark corners and really exposed the extent of damage done. I turned to Blake. "Have you checked on the rare butterflies lately?"

"No," she said. "Surely whoever did this would know that the rare butterflies are on camera. We would catch anyone who tried to make off with them."

"Maybe they didn't know the butterflies were being taped," I suggested.

"Have you checked on them?" Rex asked.

"I'm sure it's fine," Blake said. "I was just in there before the murder."

"We'd better check it out," I said.

"Don't go anywhere in here without me," Rex warned. He stepped out of the shed. "Maybe you two should stay outside."

"No," Blake said. "This is my place, my office. If someone stole from the Butterfly House, I want to know."

"Fine," Rex said. "But stay behind me and don't touch anything."

He took us back through the Butterfly House around the crime scene and into the lobby area where you bought tickets. The offices were down the hall to the left of the ticket booth. Blake unlocked the door to the second office and pushed it open.

Inside was a huge mess. It was immediately clear that someone had come in and tossed the room. Blake gasped at the mess. I stuck my head in and noticed the glass box with the heat lamp and chrysalises was intact. Whatever they were looking for, it wasn't exotic butterflies.

"Stay back, ladies," Rex warned and pushed past us. He hit his walkie-talkie and called in reinforcements.

"What the devil were they looking for?" Blake asked.

"Whoever did it had to have a key to this office," I said and studied the door. "You unlocked it, so the lock wasn't left open." I ran my fingers along the wood. "It doesn't appear to be broken either."

"I'm the only one who has a key to this office," Blake said and put her hand on her mouth. "How could they get in and do all this damage without a key?"

"They must have made a copy of it. Where do you put the key when it's not in use?"

"I keep it on my key chain with my house keys. That is in my purse and my purse I keep locked in a filing cabinet." Blake looked unsettled. "I don't know how they would have gotten ahold of the key, but, if they copied it, then they must have copies of my house keys as well." She grabbed her cell phone. "I'm going to get my locks changed right now."

"Wait," Rex said. "Let me send a patrol over to your house and see if there has been a break-in. If so, we'll have to process it before you change the locks."

"I'm going to head over there right now," Blake said. "I may be the only one who knows if something is missing."

"Wait for the officers before you go in."

"Oh"—Blake put her hand on her throat—"do you think whoever did this could still be in my house?"

"I'd rather not take any chances."

"This is all too much." Blake sat down hard in a chair in the hallway.

"Let me get you some water," I said and went off to locate the vending machine near the entrance to the exhibit. I put in my money and listened to the kerthump of the bottle hitting the bottom of the machine and I pulled it out, to come face-to-face with Rex. "Oh! You startled me."

"Not my intention," he said. His gorgeous blue gaze was very close. "Listen, go with her, will you? Try to get her to tell you about how and where she keeps her keys. Get her mind off this."

"Sure thing," I said with a nod. "Do you think this is related to the murder? Or just an opportunity seized by thieves?"

"If Blake is right, they left the most valuable thing in her office."

"So not an opportunity for theft."

"I'm ruling it out for now."

A thought occurred to me. "Do you think Blake Gilmore was the intended victim?"

"Who would want to kill me?" Blake said behind Rex.

I winced at being overheard.

Rex turned on his heel. "The two things are most likely not connected," he said gently. "But I've asked Allie to spend some time with you while we get a better handle on the situation."

"I hope that's okay," I said and handed her the bottle of water. "I know I wouldn't want to be alone right now if I were you."

She swallowed visibly. A bead of sweat formed on her forehead. "Yes, yes, I will feel better if I'm not alone. I still can't figure out how they got copies of my keys." She opened the water and took a long swig. "Wait, that means that they could have been inside the Butterfly House before I opened it the morning of the murder." She shivered. "I could have walked right past a killer and not even known it."

I patted her hand as she swayed at the thought. "You're safe now," I said.

"You see this stuff on TV, but you never imagine it could happen in real life."

"I know," I said. "Come on. Let's go check out your home. Perhaps they left it untouched."

"I'm still changing the locks," she said as I drew her toward the outside. "It's too creepy to think that someone could have copies of my keys. I will have a hard enough time falling asleep as it is."

"I'm sure Rex can have a patrol come by your home the next few days, can't you, Rex?" I asked.

"You bet," he said. "The patrolmen are at your house now. Please go. And Mrs. Gilmore . . ."

"Yes?"

"I'm sorry about this."

"Thank you, young man. I am, too."

Chapter 9

Officer Brent Pulaski and Officer Lasko were at Mrs. Gilmore's small cottage when we arrived. Their patrol bikes were parked outside and Officer Lasko walked the perimeter and Officer Pulaski waited for us by the door.

"I tried the handle, and it's locked," he said. "I knew you were on your way so I didn't break in."

"Thank you," Blake said and handed me her nearly empty water bottle. She pulled out the keys. Her hands shook as she unlocked her door and let it swing open. "I can't look," she said and stepped aside, closing her eyes.

Brent went in with his flashlight on and his gun drawn. I stayed outside, but peered into the living area. The living area was cluttered and dusty as if it was well lived in, but nothing was tossed like it was in the Butterfly House. Officer Lasko glared at me and brushed past.

I have no idea why she didn't like me. But it

seemed that ever since she first laid eyes on me she was upset that I was on the island. I guess sometimes you just don't like a person right off. I never felt that way, but Jenn assured me that it can happen. So I took Officer Lasko's dislike as a quirk of her personality.

"I don't think they're in your home," I said. "It looks pretty normal from here."

The older woman opened her eyes and peered inside. "Oh, thank goodness!" She went to take a step in, but I stopped her.

"We have to wait until they clear the entire place. The living room looks fine but that doesn't mean it's safe yet."

"Right," she said with a sigh. I gave her back her water bottle and patted her hand. She clenched the water bottle. "I just don't understand how they could have made a copy of my keys. They are usually on my person."

"Do you have a place you keep them when you are home? Or in your office?"

"I keep them in the side pocket of my purse," she said.

"And where do you keep your purse?"

"On the hall tree. As soon as I enter, I set it down and take off my shoes."

"So, right here by the door."

"Yes."

"Has anyone been in your house lately? A visitor or a worker?"

"I did have a cable company worker in two days ago. He had to replace my Wi-Fi modem. The thing was acting up. But when he replaced it, it still wasn't right, so he went outside and replaced the cable to the main line. It's worked ever since."

"Do you remember if he was near your purse?" I asked.

"He could have been," she said. "We stood and talked in the foyer."

"So he could have taken your keys when he was inside, gone and made copies, then returned them when he came back to tell you he changed the main line and had you sign off on the work."

"Oh my, yes, he could have." She frowned. "Why would Sean Grady want my keys? What is he looking for in the Butterfly House?"

"Sean Grady was the cable guy?"

"Yes," she said. "It's a small island. I've known Sean since he was knee high to a grasshopper."

"The place is clear," Officer Pulaski said as he came out of the house. "It looks like they didn't touch anything. Why don't you come in, Mrs. Gilmore, and take a look around just to be sure?"

"I'll go right in," Blake said and stepped inside. Her nervousness had settled a bit.

Officer Lasko came and stood by the door. I stepped past Officer Lasko with a grim smile. "Do you think they only wanted something at the Butterfly House?"

"You need to leave the investigating to the professionals," the officer growled at me and gave me the stink eye.

"Hey, Rex told me to walk her over here." I

studied the living room. It was a bit dusty and cluttered but I'm pretty sure it wasn't tossed.

"My rings!" I heard Blake shout from her bedroom. She came out with a ring box in her hand. "Someone was here. They took my heirloom diamond rings. I had two of them." She lifted the box to show us it was empty.

Office Pulaski slipped on some gloves and took the box from her. He pulled an evidence bag out of his back pocket and slipped the ring box into it. "We'll have Shane dust it for prints. Let me suggest that Allie take you to the McMurphy for the afternoon. We'll have Shane come out and go over your home for prints and such."

"But how will he know what else is missing? I mean, they didn't search my home like they searched the Butterfly House."

"Here, put on these gloves and booties," he said to Mrs. Gilmore. "Officer Lasko will walk you through the house. And make a list of things you find missing." He turned to me as Blake put on the booties and gloves. "Allie, you should go. I don't want to contaminate the crime scene any more than I need to."

"Okay," I said. "Blake, come to the McMurphy after you are done here. Frances will get you a soothing cup of tea and you can use the Wi-Fi while the officers go over your house."

"Okay, Allie," she said and went back into her bedroom. Officer Pulaski walked me out to the small porch.

"Thanks for bringing her by, Allie," he said. "I

understand the shed in the Butterfly House was pretty bad off."

"Whatever they were looking for, I'm not sure they found it," I said. "It doesn't feel the same as this." I nodded toward the house. "This feels careful and calculated. I mean, only Mrs. Gilmore could tell they were even in her home. Meanwhile the Butterfly House was torn apart and left as if they didn't care one bit if they got caught."

"Did she give you any idea who might have done such a thing?"

"She has no idea. She keeps the keys in her purse and only the cable guy has been in her home."

"What about when she is at the Butterfly House?"

"She keeps her purse locked in a file cabinet."

"Unfortunately keys are very easy to copy these days," Brent said. "You need to keep that in mind."

"You mean the whole wax mold thing?"

"No, now they have software that can recreate a key from a photo of it," he said.

"Wow, that's not good for me and the McMurphy. We use the old-fashioned keys for our guest rooms."

"I know it has charm, but I'd suggest you get a computer system with the magnetic cards for the safety of your guests."

I sighed. My money was going to go to a major roof overhaul this fall after the season. To add a new keying system would make things even more expensive. I needed that tour group for the event.

"I'll see you," I said and headed down the street. I made a quick cell phone call to Frances.

"Frances, where can you go to get new keys made on the island?"

"There's only one place," she said. "McGregor's Hardware Store on Market Street. Why?"

"Someone got into the Butterfly House searching for something. Then we went to Mrs. Gilmore's home and she found things stolen as well. We suspect someone copied her keys."

"Do you think this has anything to do with the murder?"

"There's no real link yet," I said. "But it seems odd that around the time of the murder, someone was searching for something at the Butterfly House and now things have been stolen from Mrs. Gilmore. The thing is . . ."

"What?"

"They didn't take the expensive butterflies. Mrs. Gilmore told me those butterflies were the most expensive thing in her office."

"That is interesting. I wonder what else they were looking for? Do you think Barbara caught them in the act and they killed her?"

"There's a chance," I said. "The killer could have already been in the Butterfly House when Mrs. Gilmore opened it. We didn't check the shed until today so it could have been tossed that day."

"Why didn't they check the shed? I mean they should have cleared the entire area when they processed it."

"Apparently they thought they had the killer."

"You mean Victoria."

"Yes," I said. "Listen, I'm going to the hardware. Do we need anything?"

"Some WD-40, the guests told me today that the closet door in two-zero-one has a squeak and Douglas mentioned he was out of the good stuff."

"Okay, tell him I'll pick it up."

"You're going to ask about the keys, aren't you?"

"You know me too well," I said and smiled. "See you soon."

Could it be as easy as asking who made a copy of Blake's keys?

California Mission Fig and Fudge Cookies

Ingredients

2 eggs
2 cups sugar
1/2 tsp. vanilla
4 tbsp. of butter, melted
9 tbsp. of cocoa powder

¾ cup of flour
1 tsp. baking powder
dash of salt

16 dried California Mission Figs—divided,
    8 chopped, 8 thinly sliced
½ cup powdered sugar

Directions

In a large bowl, whisk eggs, granulated sugar, and vanilla until lemon yellow. Slowly add melted butter. Then sift together cocoa, flour, baking powder and salt—add to egg mixture along with 8 coarsely chopped figs. Beat until smooth. Chill until firm.

Use a tablespoon to scoop out dough—roll into a ball and roll ball into powdered sugar. Place on parchment-lined cookie sheet. Garnish with a thin slice of fig. Bake at 325 for 15 minutes. Cool on baking sheet and dust with additional powdered sugar. Serve.

Chapter 10

"I'll be with you in a minute," a gruff voice said from the back corner of the hardware store when I entered.

"Okay," I answered and searched the aisles until I found the WD-40 and then went back to the key-cutting area.

"Can I help you?" an older man with a thick mustache and gray hair asked. I had a moment of pause because he sort of looked like that old cowboy actor Sam Elliott. He wore a denim shirt and jeans.

"Hi. Yes," I said and tried to remember what I was doing. "Um, I have a question about keys."

"Okay."

"I'm Allie McMurphy from the Historic McMurphy Hotel." I held out my hand.

"Ian McGregor," he said and shook it. "You have the look of your grandma Alice."

"Thanks." I smiled. It was hard to think straight. He had that sort of masculine aura about him.

"You wanted to know about keys?"

"Oh yes," I said and felt the heat of a blush rush over my cheeks. "Do you make keys from wax mold copies?"

"No."

"Oh, um, okay. What about 3D printed keys. Do you copy those?"

"I suppose we could, but I've never had that come up. What's this all about?"

"Someone burglarized the Butterfly House and Mrs. Gilmore's home, but there's no sign of a break-in. We think her keys might have been copied. Did anyone come in and make a new set of keys in the last week?"

"We make keys all the time, young lady."

"Oh."

"All the hotels and bed and breakfasts on the island use old-fashioned keys. You'd be surprised how often keys get lost. Don't they get lost or accidently taken home at your place?"

"Yes," I said with a frown. "But these would be home keys."

"Uh-huh, and what do the keys to your rooms look like?"

"House keys," I said and tapped my chin. "I see the predicament. Let me ask you this. Has Sean Grady come in and made any keys lately?"

"He came in three days ago and made a set for his grandmother. Why?"

"No reason," I said. "Thanks. All I need is this WD-40." I handed him the oil and he walked me to the register.

"Wait. You don't think he copied Mrs. Gilmore's keys, do you?" he asked and rang up my purchase.

"I intend to find out," I said and paid him. "Thanks for the information."

"Keep me posted," he said as I walked away. "His grandma has dementia and loses her keys at least once a week. If he's copying keys that aren't his, I need to know."

"I'll keep you posted."

I had to get back to the McMurphy for a fudge making demonstration. Then I was going to pay Mr. Sean Grady a visit.

"You can't just go up to Sean Grady and ask him if he's been taking things from people's homes," Frances said.

"Why not?"

"Because he might panic at getting caught and hurt you," Jenn said.

We stood around the reception desk. The demonstration had been a hit and we had sold quite a bit of fudge. Now Sandy was using the kitchen to put together her latest piece for The Island House Hotel.

"I'll bring Mal," I said. The pup perked up at the mention of her name and came over to jump up to beg for attention.

"I have a better idea," Frances said. "Go see Grady's grandma."

"But she has dementia," I said. "At least that is

what the hardware guy said so it has to be true. The island is too small to keep a lie for very long."

"Go visit her," Frances said. "Ask her about the keys. You never know. She might give you enough information that you can take it to Rex and have him confront Grady."

"Okay, I guess that makes the most sense."

"Take Mal," Jenn suggested. "Puppies can lift the spirits of people with memory problems."

"I will," I said. "I'll take Mrs. Grady a basket of fudge. I've found bribes often help, too."

"Here's her address," Frances said and pushed a note toward me. "Don't stay too late or Grady might get suspicious."

"I won't," I promised, then ran upstairs, changed out of my candy making polo and black slacks, put on a sundress, combed my hair and fixed my ponytail, then leashed Mal, and headed out.

Mrs. Grady lived in a tiny cottage by the airport. I opened the short, picket fence gate and walked up to the door with a basket of fudge in my hands. I knocked and could hear someone moving about inside. An elderly lady pulled her lace curtain aside and looked out at me. I waved. "Hello. We brought fudge."

Her gaze went to Mal who stood on her back legs and waved her front paws.

There was some more noise as she came over to the door and opened it a crack. "Who are you?"

"Hi, I'm Allie McMurphy. I run the McMurphy Hotel and Fudge Shop," I said. "You used to know my papa Liam."

"Papa Liam?" Her voice was weak and shaky. "You mean Liam McMurphy?"

"Yes," I said. "Can we come in?"

"I'm not supposed to let strangers in," she said.

"Oh," I said. "Yes, I understand. I brought you fudge." I held the basket up and the crack between the door and the jamb widened. "Can you come out and talk with me?"

She opened the door wide enough to take the fudge. "I can't leave the porch."

"We can sit on your lovely swing," I said and pointed to the porch swing. "Mal would love to show you her tricks. I imagine you could use a little company."

She was silent for a moment and then seemed to make a decision. Her chin rose as if in defiance of the rules she lived under. "I'll be right out. Wait for me."

"We will," I said.

I sat on the creaky old porch swing. The house clearly needed to be painted. The chain on the swing was rusted and the swing itself was peeling. I wondered if her grandson even thought about caring for the house. But then I couldn't judge. It was my understanding from listening to the seniors at the senior center talk that taking care of someone with dementia was a full-time job and I knew that Grady worked at the cable company as well.

Mal sat under the swing in the spot of shade. Soon Mrs. Grady came out with two glasses of cold lemonade in her hands. She was a tiny woman, slightly bent from osteoporosis. She wore a cotton flowered blouse and a striped skirt. On her ankle was a monitor. Her feet were stuffed into slippers.

"I hope you like lemonade," she said and handed me a glass before she sat down beside me. I took the glass and held the swing as she settled down beside me in a cloud of White Shoulders perfume. I recognized the scent because my Grammy Alice used to wear it.

"I do. Thank you," I said. "Cheers." I lifted my glass to her and made a small toast. Then took a sip. It was so sour, I had to turn away until my eye quit scrunching. "Yum," I choked out and put the glass on the porch rail.

"So, you are Liam's daughter," Mrs. Grady said.

"His granddaughter," I corrected. "My dad is Papa Liam's only child."

"I didn't know he had a daughter. I thought he only had that boy of his. Big britches that one. Thought he was too good to live on the island." She sipped her drink and didn't seem to have any trouble with the flavor. "Lives in Detroit now, I hear." She looked at me. "You look like your mother."

"Grand—" I paused. "Thank you."

"So how are your parents?"

"They are gone now."

"Where'd they go?" Her blue eyes crinkled in misunderstanding. Her gray hair was short and curled.

"On vacation," I said.

"Funny to go on vacation when we live on the

perfect vacation spot," she said and took another sip of lemonade.

I wondered if I would be able to get any information out of her that was accurate. Mal jumped up in my lap and smiled at the old woman.

"Well, who's this?" she asked and patted Mal's head.

"This is Mal," I said. "Mal, this is Mrs. Grady." Mal held up her paw for a shake.

"Well, look at that," Mrs. Grady said and shook Mal's paw. "Clever doggie."

"Would you like to see her tricks?"

"She does tricks?"

"Sure." I put Mal down and ran her through her tricks of up, twirl, sit, shake, sit pretty, down, and roll over. Then I slipped her a treat. Mrs. Grady laughed and clapped.

"Wonderful," she said. "So, Miss Allie McMurphy, what really brings you out to visit an old woman?" Her eyes were suddenly clear and bright. It made the hair on the back of my neck stand on end.

"I was wondering about your house keys," I said. "Mr. McGregor at the hardware store tells me that your grandson Sean has to make new keys for you nearly once a week. Where do all those keys go?"

"I don't lose my keys," she said and frowned. "I'm not allowed to leave the house so why would I carry keys?"

"You have a leg monitor," I said gently. "Do you wander off?"

"One time," she said with a sigh. "I got a pail

and went berry picking like we did as kids and couldn't find my way back out of the woods. Sean got the monitor. He said it was for my own good. I'm on house arrest."

"I'm sorry you feel that way," I said. "It must get lonely. If you want, Mal and I can come over more often."

"Why would you?" she asked with a knitted brow. "Don't you have a fudge shop to run?" Her blue eyes had glazed over a bit.

"I do," I said and stood. "Mal and I like to take walks every day. We can swing by here once a week if you don't mind."

"The doggie will come?" she asked and gave Mal pats on the head.

"Yes," I said. "But we have to go now. Thanks for the lemonade."

She stood. "I can't be outside." She picked up the glasses and we watched her go into the house. I heard the scrape of a lock and, knowing she was secure, I left.

I wasn't sure if anything she told me was accurate. She seemed to have lucid moments. And she was right; if she was not allowed to leave the house, why would she lose her keys? It was a question for Sean.

"Hey, who are you and what are you doing here?" a man in his early thirties asked me as I closed the picket gate behind me.

"Oh, do you live here?"

"Yes, in the carriage house. My grandmother is

not allowed to speak to strangers," he said and frowned at me. "She has dementia."

"I'm sorry to hear that," I said and held out my hand. "I'm Allie McMurphy."

He looked at my hand but didn't take it. His arms remained crossed. He had a plastic grocery bag in one hand and fisted the other. "You're that girl who keeps finding dead people."

"I guess you could say that," I admitted and Mal jumped on her back legs and twirled to try to impress him. "Are you Sean Grady?"

"What if I am?"

"I heard you install cable," I said and tried to act innocently. "I own the—"

"McMurphy," he finished for me. "Are you having cable problems?"

"One of the guest rooms may need to be re-wired," I said. It wasn't a lie. Room 205 had spotty cable. "I wondered if you can give me a quote."

"Oh." He adjusted his stance to a more relaxed position. "Sure. I charge fifty dollars an hour. Only one room you said?"

"Yes," I replied.

"I could probably do it in two hours so about a hundred dollars would do it."

"Thanks," I said. "I can't do it right now, but I definitely plan to fix it once the season is over." I stepped around him. "It was nice to meet you." Mal took the hint and pulled me down the sidewalk.

"Call me if you need it sooner. It's best to get it done sooner rather than later."

"I'll keep that in mind," I said over my shoulder. Mal and I made our escape down the sidewalk back to the safety of the McMurphy. If Sean was copying keys and breaking into homes, I didn't want him anywhere near the McMurphy. Not that we had anything valuable enough to steal. But I wanted to make sure to keep my guests safe. I didn't want anyone to end up like Barbara Smart.

Chapter 11

"It doesn't prove anything," Rex said. He sat behind his desk and shook his head at me. "The fact is Mrs. Grady has Alzheimer's. There's no predicting what they will do from one moment to the next. She might take the keys and hide them from Grady out of spite for being left alone in the house."

"That doesn't make any sense," I said. "Seriously, you need to look into this. Has there been a string of robberies lately?"

"One or two," he said with a shrug. "You get them with so many people packing into the island. The locals tend to leave their doors unlocked." He held up his hand before I could speak. "Which means there isn't much reason for Sean to copy the keys anyway."

"But you will look into it, won't you?"

"I will look into it," he said with a nod. "If Sean

Grady is stealing from people, I'll bring him in and prosecute to the highest level."

"It should be simple to figure out," I said. "Just overlap a map of where Sean worked and where the latest burglaries took place. If they overlap, that should be enough cause to bring him in."

"Are you telling me how to do my job?" He tilted his head and gave me a look.

"I—no," I said. "No, I'm not telling you how to do your job. I just think that you should at least talk to Sean. Something is fishy when a guy copies a set of keys a week."

"I'll talk to him, but he hasn't broken any laws. Not that I can prove anyway."

"I'd talk to him, but he didn't seem like the type to talk things through with."

"Allie, stay out of it, okay? For your own safety."

"But someone broke into Mrs. Gilmore's home and took her diamond rings. That same someone may have broken into the Butterfly House and murdered Barbara Smart. It seems to me that Sean Grady is your best suspect right now." I paced in front of his desk.

"Oh, I see," he said and crossed his arms, leaning back into his chair. "You think Sean murdered Barbara."

"Yes," I said and stopped in the middle of the room. "He could have been in the middle of a burglary and Barbara caught him. So he killed her. I mean, it takes a lot of force to stab someone to death with a garden trowel." I made a stabbing motion with my arm then stopped. "Hey, has Shane looked at the direction of the wound? I mean, can't he tell the height of the killer by the entry wound?"

"You have been watching too many whodunits on television," Rex said and leaned forward. "To begin with, the autopsy results are still pending. The coroner's office is backed up. Then, the angle of the weapon thrust depends on the position of the arm at the time of the thrust," he said. "If it was an overhead thrust, the angle would be different than an underhanded thrust."

"But they could still estimate the height and force needed," I said.

"Yes, but it will be next year before we could get those results. The county doesn't have gelatinous test dummies lying around to test angles and force on. Life is not like the movies, kiddo."

"Don't call me kiddo," I bristled. "I'm a grown woman."

"With a vivid imagination," he said and leaned back. "Look, I know you're trying to save your cousin from this, but right now she is my best suspect. Until I have concrete evidence otherwise, she will stay my best suspect."

I crossed my arms and frowned at him. "But you are going to look into Sean, right?"

"I'll look into it," he said. "But, Allie, even if Sean did take Mrs. Gilmore's diamond rings, it doesn't mean he killed Barbara Smart."

"I agree," I said. "But it could mean he did. If he was there, he could have even seen who did it."

"What if he points the finger at Victoria?"

"He won't," I said with more confidence than I could muster. "If he did, it would all be circumstantial, right? I mean eyewitnesses are known to make mistakes."

"Allie, you're arguing yourself in circles. Now get out of my office."

I frowned at him. "Fine."

"Good," he replied and pointed to the door.

I walked to it and stopped. "But what if—"

"Out!"

I skulked out. He had said it loud enough for everyone in the building to hear. Fine. If Rex wouldn't listen to me about the suspicious Sean Grady, then maybe Liz would. I headed straight for the newspaper office, which was a block or so past the administration building on Market Street. It was strange not to have Mal with me, but I had left her behind to take a nap in her bed beside Frances. Our journey out to the Grady home wiped her out.

I pushed open the door to the newspaper and was greeted with a groan.

"Oh no, here comes trouble, and I left my lucky rabbit's foot at home." This was said by Mr. McElroy, Liz's grandfather and current owner/publisher of the newspaper. He teased me that he needed the rabbit's foot to feel safe around me since I found so many old people dead.

"It seems to work from a distance since you are alive and kicking," I said. "How are you today?"

"Better if I had my rabbit's foot," he grumbled. Mr. McElroy had white hair and a white beard and was a little round in the belly and soft in the jaw from sitting behind a desk his whole life. "What do you want?"

"Is Liz around?"

"Why?"

"I might have a solid lead for her."

He studied me from the vantage point of his creaky wooden desk chair. "What kind of lead?"

"I'm only going to tell Liz," I said. "Is she around?"

"Now that seems to be for me to know and you to figure out on your own. Especially if you won't share leads with me. I'm still a darn fine journalist if you ask me. Might be old, but I can still get around."

"Fine," I said with a roll of my eyes, and leaned on the bar height railing that separated the work space from the public space. "What do you know about Sean Grady?"

"The cable guy?" Liz asked as she walked in from the back room. At one time they had a printing press in the back that actually printed the papers daily. Now they sent out the work to a printer in Mackinaw City. The hard copy of the paper came out once a week while daily news was written and put up online.

"Yes," I said.

Liz shrugged. "Not much. He was one of the crowd of jocks at school who had more brawn than brains. Why?"

"I think he may be stealing from people."

"What? Why?"

"Well, someone broke into the shed at the Butterfly House. And then went on to break into the second office. They were looking for something and didn't find it."

Liz grabbed a piece of paper and a pen and started taking notes. "And you think Sean was behind this?"

"Well, whoever broke into the Butterfly House had a key. Mrs. Gilmore said she is the only one with a key which she keeps in her purse. Her purse is either locked up at the Butterfly House or set near the door of her home—which was also broken into, by the way."

"So let me get this straight." Liz pointed the top of her pen at me. "Someone broke into the Butterfly House looking for something they didn't find and then burglarized Mrs. Gilmore?"

"Yes, and there was no evidence of a forced entry at either place."

"So we can assume someone has a key to both places."

"And Mrs. Gilmore said that Sean was in her home a few days ago fixing her Internet."

"You think he took her keys and made copies," Liz said. "I think that would kind of stand out in Mr. McGregor's mind."

"That's what I thought."

"So you went to see him?"

"Yes, I went to see him to see if he knew who might have copied the keys. He told me that Sean Grady copies keys almost weekly because his grandmother—who has dementia—keeps losing the keys."

"So Mr. McGregor didn't think anything was out of the ordinary about Sean making quick copies of keys."

"Exactly," I said. "I took this to Rex, but he says there is no proof, only conjecture, and he has a murder to solve."

"You said the Butterfly House was tossed," Mr. McElroy said. "Did they do the same thing to Mrs. Gilmore's home?"

"No." I shook my head. "Oddly her place appeared untouched. The only way we even knew something was stolen was her diamond rings were missing."

"This is a good lead, Allie," Liz said.

"I told Rex he should cross-check where Sean was working on cable with who might have stuff missing."

"You think he's been doing this a long time?" Mr. McElroy asked.

"Maybe." I shrugged. "I thought it might be something for an investigative reporter to look into."

"Good choice," Liz said with a grin. "I'll do a little legwork on this and see what happens."

"Thanks," I said. "I think maybe Barbara saw Sean going through things at the Butterfly House and confronted him."

"And he stabbed her?" Liz tapped the pen against her cheek. "That might work. The real question in all of this is what the heck was he looking for at the Butterfly House?"

"I don't know. Nothing was missing. He just made a mess of the office and the back shed."

"Two places that are rarely connected," Liz pointed out.

"Mrs. Gilmore said she had nothing of value at the Butterfly House but the latest shipment of rare chrysalises and those were the only things left untouched."

"Why would he leave them?"

I shrugged again. "Maybe because they were on camera and he didn't want to get caught."

"That would explain it, I guess," Liz said. "Still, it is a weak argument. My bet is that Sean Grady wasn't looking for valuables. He was looking for something else."

"What?" I asked.

"That's the question of the day," Liz said.

"Well, whatever it was, if we can prove that Sean was there at the time of the murder, then Rex will have to consider him a person of interest."

"It still doesn't take the suspicion away from your cousin," Liz said.

"Maybe not yet," I replied. "But it does cast reasonable doubt on Tori being the only one to have murdered Barbara."

"Two stories to investigate," Liz said with a grin. "I love a good news day."

I stuck my hands in my back pockets. "Let me know what you find out, okay? I know Tori didn't do it. I just need help proving it."

"Will do," Liz said.

My thoughts were all over the place as I left the newspaper office. There had to be something more I could do. It was tough leaving things in other people's hands. They weren't as invested in the investigation as I was. Would they really look into a possible connection between Sean and the robberies? Maybe there was something I could do. A thought struck me and I hurried back to the McMurphy.

Chapter 12

"We can set up a sting operation," I said. It was after dinner and my crew was gathered in my living room.

"That sounds interesting," Jenn said. "I'm in."

"It sounds dangerous," Frances said. "You should really leave this to Rex."

"Rex said he doesn't have enough evidence to even bring Sean in for questioning." I sipped my wine. "We can give him that evidence."

"How exactly?" Mr. Devaney asked.

"I ran into Sean today," I said.

"You ran into him? How did you know it was him?" Frances asked.

"Where did you meet him?" Jenn asked.

"I went to see his grandmother," I said. "I had to see for myself whether she was bad enough to lose keys weekly."

"Was she?" Jenn asked.

"I'm not sure," I said. "What I do know is that she isn't allowed outside the house."

"So she wouldn't have any need for keys," Frances interpreted.

"Exactly," I said. "Plus Sean was pretty upset when he saw me leaving his grandmother's property. It's suspicious if you ask me."

"Maybe he's protective of his grandmother," Mr. Devaney said. "If she has dementia, then anyone can come to the door and scam her."

"Oh," I said, deflated. "I guess that makes sense." I pursed my lips in thought. "Still, I don't want to just give him the benefit of the doubt. "

"What do you have in mind?" Jenn asked.

"Do you know how room 205 has an issue with the cable? I was thinking we could hire Sean to come in and work on the cable. I would 'Trust'"—I made air quotes—"him with the master key. Then see if he goes outside to check the line."

"And makes a copy?" Jenn asked.

"Yes."

"How will you know he did?"

"Mr. Devaney can stake out the hardware store, and if Sean makes a copy of a key, confiscate it. Bring it back here and test it to see if it is a copy of the master key. Then we will have proof."

"Sounds dangerous," Frances said. "I'm not sure if I like it."

"Mr. Devaney"—I looked at him—"would you be willing to do it?"

He scowled at me. "What if he doesn't leave the McMurphy? Am I supposed to hang around McGregor's Hardware all morning?"

"We can have Frances text you if he finishes without leaving," Jenn suggested.

"Really, you only have to ask him for the key he just copied, bring it back here, and compare it to the master."

"If he just copied it, then he'd have the master key on him."

"Right," I said. "You can compare it there."

"But there wouldn't be any proof it was the McMurphy master key," Jenn pointed out.

"I'll paint a bit of red nail polish on the end of the key."

"Then if you see him copying the red marked key you can ask Mr. McGregor for the keys, and when they match you can call Rex."

"Maybe we should call Rex and have him waiting at the hardware store," Frances suggested.

"No," I said. "That would tip Sean off. I mean, I doubt he would be so bold as to copy a key in front of a police officer."

"You never know," Frances said.

"Ugh," I said and tugged at my hair. "Why is everything so complicated?"

"I'll do it," Mr. Devaney said. "If it will make you feel better to know for sure if this guy is copying keys and breaking and entering, then I'll do it."

"Yes!" I said and nearly bounced out of my chair. "Thank you!" I hugged him. He went stiff under my enthusiasm. Mr. Devaney was a curmudgeon and not much for displays of affection unless it came to Frances. She, of course, had stolen his heart.

"Now that that's cleared up," Jenn said and turned to Frances, "have you picked a date for the wedding?"

Frances blushed. "No."

"Why not?" I asked.

"Because I want to get married tomorrow if possible and she wants to have a ceremony," Mr. Devaney said gently.

"I need time to plan a nice little party and Douglas doesn't want to wait," Frances said.

"Well, we can do both," Jenn said.

"We can?" Frances turned to her. "I heard you have to book your venue six months in advance at least."

"Not if you have an outdoor wedding," Jenn said. "We could have a pretty trestle set up and folding chairs with flowers on each row and candles if you want it at sunset. It would be awesome."

"Can we do it this week?" Mr. Devaney asked.

"Douglas!"

"Yes," Jenn said. "I've planned a few weddings on the island. I have an in with many of the vendors. All you need to do is pick a date."

"Tomorrow."

"Sunday," They spoke at the same time.

"It's Wednesday," I said. "Can we pull off a wedding in less than four days?"

"Yes!" Jenn said with pride. "Mr. Devaney, can you wait a few days?"

He looked at Frances who had a hopeful expression on her face. "Yes," he said. "I can wait a few days if it makes Frances happy." He looked at us and frowned. "Keep it small. I don't have any family or friends I need to have there. Frances?"

"My family is right here except, of course, Maggs, my best friend, my cousin, the lawyer and his family, and then there are my friends from the senior center, and the girls will want to bring dates."

"I said small," Mr. Devaney grumbled.

"Now I'm sure you want to declare your love for Frances to the entire world," Jenn pointed out. "So a few close friends and relatives aren't going to make it too big. Right?"

"Douglas?" Frances looked at him and he crumbled.

"Whatever you want as long as I get my Sunday wedding."

"Yay!" Jenn clapped her hands. She got up and pulled Frances into the kitchen where she pulled a pen and paper out of the junk drawer. "Now let's list who all you want to invite. Do you have a dress? Oh, Allie, we have to go dress shopping."

"I'm in," I said and grinned at Mr. Devaney. "Do you have a suit?"

"I have a gray suit."

"There you have it," Jenn said. "One of the colors will be gray. Now, speaking of colors, what colors will you want your bridesmaids to wear? You will have bridesmaids, right?"

"We should call Maggs," Frances said. "She wants to be invited and she will be my maid of honor. You girls can be bridesmaids if that's okay?"

"Okay? Sounds perfect!" Jenn said.

I had to smile. Nothing brought out the leader in Jenn like a good wedding to plan. Meanwhile I had a sting operation to plan. It was pretty simple: get Sean to come do the cable work and see if he takes the bait. What could possibly go wrong?

* * *

The next morning after the first fudge making demonstration, Victoria came barreling into the McMurphy. "What is this I hear that you suspect Sean Grady of murdering Barbara?"

"Sheesh," I said and took her arm, pulling her over to Frances. "Keep it down."

"Why should I whisper?" Tori asked. "Liz is writing an exposé about it."

"We don't have anything concrete," I said. "So we are pulling off a sting operation."

"A what?"

"I called Sean earlier. He'll be here at one this afternoon to fix the cable."

"We're going to give him a master key," Frances said low.

"You think he'll take it?" Tori asked. Today she wore blue shorts and a blue and white striped shirt that buttoned down the middle. Her hair was pulled back into a high ponytail. She looked like Malibu Barbie.

"We hope so," I said.

"How will you know if he copies it?"

"We'll have someone at McGregor's to watch for him and then confront him."

"Oh, this is bad." Tori shook her head. "I hope you aren't doing this in some silly way of trying to save me."

"What do you mean 'silly'?" Talk about insult.

"I mean you don't need to defend me. I can take care of myself." She put her hands on her hips.

"Really? Because not thinking clearly in an

emergency is what got you into this mess in the first place."

"Don't get me started on not thinking clearly," Tori said. Her eyes flashed with emotion. "What are you going to do if someone gets hurt in this little sting of yours? Hmm? Does your insurance cover that? You'd better not get sued and lose the McMurphy."

"This sting is not going to cause me to lose the McMurphy. Don't worry. You'll get your percent of the inheritance."

"What sting?" Sean Grady asked as he walked in.

I glanced at my watch. "You're early."

"Yeah, I figured I had the time right now so I came on over. It's okay, right? I mean usually people are happy when I come early."

"I'm okay with you being early," I said and sent my cousin a sharp look. "Let me get you the master key and show you the room that is having a problem."

"Sure, but you said something about a sting and she said it could cost you money. Do you have a wasp problem? Are there bees in the walls? Because those are things I need to know before I go messing around with the cable."

"No, we don't have wasps or bees. Everything is fine. My cousin is just overprotective."

"Okay," he said and adjusted his tool belt. "I have some wasp spray in my kit if you need it."

"I won't be needing it." I grabbed the master key from the wall behind the receptionist desk. "Frances, can you let Mr. Devaney know I need that errand done now."

"Sure," Frances said.

"Good," I replied. "It's room 205," I told Sean. "Come right this way."

He lifted the box of wire and gadgets he had in his hand. "After you." He waved toward the stairs.

I walked up with him and glanced over my shoulder to see Frances on the phone to Mr. Devaney and Victoria giving me the stink eye. I smiled at her and took Sean to the room. "Now this is the master key," I said and opened the door. "I'll leave it with you so that you can get into any closets or other rooms that you might need to check."

"Cool." He took the key, pocketed it, and went over to the television set on the top of the chest of drawers. "What exactly is the problem?" He turned on the TV.

"The cable is fuzzy and comes and goes. It's most likely just the wire itself."

The television reception was indeed wacky. I figured if nothing else I would get the cable in the room repaired. Tori could stick that in her pipe and smoke it.

"I see."

"Well, I'll let you get to it. Got to go upstairs and do some paperwork. A hotel owner's job is never done."

"Okay." He had his back to me and was flipping through the channels.

"Just leave the key with Frances when you're done."

"Got it," he said. "Wait, who's Frances?"

"She's the older lady at the receptionist desk."

"Cool."

I walked out and crossed my fingers. *With any luck, he'll take the bait and try to make a copy of the key.*

Fig Fudge Balls

Ingredients

1½ cups cashews
2 cups figs with stems removed
3 tbsp. shredded coconut
1 tsp. vanilla
1 tbsp. honey
4 tbsp. cocoa powder
1 tsp. coarse sea salt

Directions

Mix figs and cashews in food processor on high until you get a paste. Add remaining ingredients and process on high until well mixed. Taste for salt—you may add more or less to taste. Once well mixed, roll into small balls. Top with a sprinkle of coarse sea salt. Enjoy!

Chapter 13

I paced impatiently in my office as I waited for Sean to take the bait. So far, nothing. "If it's not him, it's not him," I muttered. "No harm done. Cable fixed and all will continue as before." I hated the sneaky feeling that Victoria might be right. That this little sting might prove to be a bad idea.

The phone rang and I jumped. "McMurphy Hotel and Fudge Shop," I said. "Allie speaking. How can I help you?"

"Hi. Yes, this is Patricia down at the bridal shop. Your friend Jenn booked you an emergency appointment to get fitted for a bridesmaid dress."

"Oh right," I said and glanced at my watch. "What time was that again?"

"Right now," she said. "If you can't make it, I have another opening next week."

"No, no." I chewed my bottom lip. "I'll be there. I need the dress for Sunday."

"All right. I can wait another few minutes."

"Thanks!" I hung up the phone and hesitated

for a second. The sting would go on without me. But it didn't make it any easier to leave the McMurphy. I grabbed my purse and keys and hurried down the stairs.

"Where are you off to?" Frances asked. She looked surprised.

"I've got that appointment to get fitted for the bridesmaid dress," I said. "You and Mr. Devaney have this covered, right?"

"I suppose so," she said. "Shouldn't you go up and let him know you're leaving?"

"Another good idea," I replied and backtracked back up the stairs and into room 205. The room was in a state of disarray as Sean had pulled the chest of drawers away from the wall and was currently on his knees shining a flashlight into the hole in the wall where the cable used to be. "Sean."

"Yeah." He glanced up at me.

"I have to go. Frances will help you if you have any questions."

"Cool," he said. "By the way, I don't see anything with a stinger nearby. You can tell your cousin that she doesn't have to worry about losing the McMurphy."

"Oh, thanks."

"Also, this wiring is old. I'm going to have to go out and check the line from the box outside. No extra charge, of course."

"Okay, sure," I said, pretending that my heart wasn't trying to beat its way out of my chest. Was the sting actually working? "Like I said, take any questions to Frances. She can also sign for the bill."

"Cool," he said and went back to work.

I hurried down the stairs. Frances gave me a questioning gaze. I shrugged. "He wants to check the outside line."

"Got it," she said. "Have fun with the dress!"

I sent her a salute and headed outside. Within minutes I was at the dress shop on Main Street across from the hardware store. *Oh, best timing ever,* I thought. Inside, Jenn was waiting along with a sour-faced salesgirl.

"You're really late."

"Sorry," I said and put down my purse on the nearest striped comfy chair. The whole place was an explosion of pink and white and smelled like the inside of a flower bouquet. Soft music played overhead. "The cable guy arrived early." I sent Jenn a look and her eyes grew wide.

"Oh, that's happening now?"

"He told me he needed to check the outside line," I said and glanced over to the window.

"Come on, no dawdling," the salesgirl said. "Let's get you into the dress."

"I'll watch the window for you," Jenn reassured me.

I let the salesgirl whose name tag said BRITTANY drag me into a fitting room where a pale blue, midi-length dress awaited. I stripped out of my clothes and pulled the spaghetti-strap dress over my head. It fit like a glove. I whirled in front of the mirror for a moment. The hem of the chiffon lifted and played around my calves.

"How's the fit?" the salesgirl asked. She poked her head in. "Oh, it looks great." For the first time her face lit up in a smile. She pulled me out to the three-way mirror.

"Oh, you look gorgeous!" Jenn said and stood beside me, her expression filled with joy. "I do know how to pick a dress, don't I?"

I was a bit embarrassed by all the attention. "Yes," I said. "It's perfect." I did a little twirl to show off the floaty skirt. "It's going to be pretty outside."

"That's what I thought," Jenn said.

"What color is your dress?" I asked Jenn,

"A pale lavender," the salesgirl said and smiled at me. "It's going to look so good in pictures."

I noticed the window in the mirror. Crowds of fudgies wandered by. "Any sighting of you know who?" I asked.

"No." Jenn frowned. "He must have gone out the back."

"I'll call Mr. Devaney and see if there's been a sighting."

"No, don't do it. A ringing phone will bring attention to Mr. Devaney," Jenn pointed out. "We need to wait now."

Just then Sean walked down the street with his box of tools. I looked from him to Jenn and back. "Why would he take his tools?" I rushed out of the dress shop to see what direction he was going. Sean walked in the opposite direction of the hardware store.

"Miss, miss!" The salesgirl took me by the arm. "You have to pay for the dress."

"Right," I said. Disappointment filled my chest. I let her bring me back into the shop. Ten minutes later, I was back in my usual black slacks and white polo. The dress was neatly hung and zippered into a garment bag.

"He didn't go into the hardware store," Jenn said.

"Is there anywhere else to get a key copied?"

"I don't think so."

"Well, darn it. He didn't take the bait." We walked down the alley and into the McMurphy.

"How's your dress?" Frances asked.

"It fits like a glove," Jenn said.

"Did Sean leave for good?" I asked.

"Yes," Frances said. "He left a bill and said we shouldn't have any more trouble."

"But he never went into the hardware store," I said. "We would have seen him."

"He didn't take the bait," Frances said.

"I guess not. Maybe he figured out that it was a trap," I said. "He did hear us mention *sting*, but I thought I deflected it well."

"I'll call Douglas back and let him know it didn't work."

I sighed and leaned against the receptionist's desk. "I could have sworn he was the one."

"This doesn't prove he isn't," Jenn said and took the dress from me. "All it proves is that he didn't copy your key."

"That we know," I said. "He could still have made an impression or taken a photo for 3D printing."

"Now you are reaching," Frances said with a tsk of her tongue. "It's time for a fudge demonstration. We'll worry about solving the murder later."

"By the way," I said. "What was it Tori wanted earlier?"

"She came to see if Sandy would do chocolate sculptures for the Butterfly House fund-raiser's formal event."

"Oh well, good for Sandy to get more business."

"I offered the McMurphy as a sponsor," Frances said. "She liked the idea."

"What do we have to do to sponsor the event?"

"Pay a thousand dollars," Frances said and I gulped. "But you get two free tickets to the formal affair and access to all the people coming in. Besides, if they are going to fill the McMurphy with the group then we need to pay it forward."

"Right," I said. "How is that going? Were you able to rearrange the reservations so that we can have those days for the fund-raiser?"

Mella took that moment to leap up on the bar-height desk and come over to be petted. Frances stroked her absently and the cat rubbed her face on Frances's flowered blouse.

"Lucky for us, it's after Labor Day," Frances said. "We had two regulars who come in then, but when I mentioned the fund-raiser, they called Sandy and signed up."

"So they keep their spots in the McMurphy."

"Yes," Frances said.

"Brilliant."

"I agree." She smiled.

I grabbed an apron to start the fudge for the next demonstration. So the sting failed. We still had no proof that Sean Grady was copying keys and stealing. My thoughts ran rampant as I searched for a clue to help Victoria. What was I missing? If Sean wasn't the one to take the keys, then who was?

I decided that after the fudge demonstration I would go see Blake Gilmore again. Maybe there was someone else who had access to her keys.

I knocked on Blake Gilmore's door with a basket of homemade chocolate chip cookies in my hand.

"I'll be right there," I heard Blake call from behind her door. The front window curtains moved as she peered out to see who it was. Then she opened the door. "Allie, what a surprise. What brings you here?"

"I made you some cookies," I said. "I wanted to check on you and make sure you were okay."

"Come on in," she said and closed and locked the door behind me. "Goodness, I've been a little on the nervous side since the burglary. It feels like such a violation. I lost my trust in the island."

"I'm so sorry," I said and handed her the cookies. "Was anything else taken?"

"Please sit and I'll make us some tea."

"So there was more."

"I hate to think about it," she said and left to make tea. While she was gone I went over to the foyer and noticed she no longer kept her purse on the hall tree. I frowned. Who would do such a thing? The door looked untouched.

"I changed the locks," she said as she came out of the kitchen carrying a tray with a tea set on it.

"I see you don't keep your purse here anymore."

I followed her into the living room and sat in a floral-print covered chair.

"Lesson learned," she replied and poured the tea. "Cream, sugar?"

"Just cream."

"To answer your earlier question, they also took my good silver and the money out of the small box I kept in my underwear drawer for emergencies." She handed me a cup and saucer.

I picked up a spoon and stirred. "The loss must be devastating," I said.

"I can't stand to think that a stranger went through my drawers. I threw everything out and ordered all new."

"I can understand that reaction," I said. "Did the police dust for fingerprints?"

"They did. What a mess that was. That Shane boy—the one with the glasses—he told me the best way to clean it was with vinegar and water." She sipped her cup. "It took me all night last night."

"I certainly hope they catch the thief."

"I had to change the locks on the Butterfly House. I simply don't know what they were looking for there to make such a mess of things. Why, they even poked around inside Insect World. I hadn't noticed before, but some of the displays were slightly off center. It's as if they were looking behind the hanging cases filled with insects on display."

"Oh no," I said. "That means they were even more likely to have been in the greenhouse area where Barbara was killed. She might have discovered them."

"Well, that's an interesting theory," Blake said. "But I thought Victoria was a serious person of interest. Whoever took my key was looking for something and could have been gone a long time before I let Barbara into the Butterfly House."

"Right," I said. "Do you have any idea what they might have been looking for?"

"No idea whatsoever. Really, the only valuable things in the Butterfly House are the butterflies themselves. Everyone on the island knows that."

"So there would be no real reason for Sean Grady to copy your keys," I said.

She seemed startled by that idea. "I hadn't thought of that. Do you think it was done by someone outside the island?"

"How would they get access to your keys?"

"That is the question of the day," she said and sipped her tea. She picked up a cookie and bit into it and talked as she chewed. "These are good." She swallowed. "As I told Officer Manning, Sean is the only one who came inside my home last week. Except for my mahjong ladies, of course."

"Your mahjong ladies?"

"Yes, Irene Hammerstein, Wanda Sikes, Paula Abbot, and I meet to play mahjong. They wouldn't take my keys," she said. "Why would they? If they want anything, all they had to do was ask me. We've known each other for years."

"How often do you see them?"

"Oh, once a week," she replied. "We meet on Mondays."

"Do you mind if I talk to your friends?"

"Why would you do that?"

"To see if they remember anything or anyone who might have needed your keys or might have hidden something in the Butterfly House."

"You think someone might have hidden something in the Butterfly House and the killer or thief knows about it?"

"That's what I'm thinking," I said.

"Well, you can certainly talk to the ladies, but I'm sure they don't know any more than I do about what is what."

"What about the girls who work at the Butterfly House?" I asked. "You know besides Emma?"

"My assistants? You can certainly talk to them if you wish, but I already spoke to them and so did Officer Manning. They were as appalled as I was about the rummaging at the Butterfly House. They don't have any idea who would trash the House or what they would be looking for."

"Can I have their names?"

"Catlin Jones, Ashley Hicks, and Holly Johnson." She finished her cookie and picked the crumbs off her shirt front. "Holly is out on vacation this week, but Catlin and Ashley are around. In fact, they will be in tomorrow to help me restore the Butterfly House to visitor-ready status. The new African chrysalises have hatched. We expect visitors to come out to see them."

"What time do they come in in the mornings?"

"They come in at nine AM. We open at ten so we have an hour to finish cleaning up and release the new butterflies."

"I'll be there as soon as I can get away," I said and stood. "Thank you for the tea."

"Thank you for the cookies," she said and walked me out. "Don't bring the dog," she warned me. "I don't want her to snap at the butterflies."

"Okay," I said. "But she doesn't snap."

"They are thousand-dollar butterflies," she said and opened the door.

"I'll be sure to leave Mal at home."

"Thank you. See you later."

I left and took the street beside the Butterfly House then cut in front of it. It was still closed but a big sign said they would be reopening tomorrow. I wondered if the people would flock there to see the new butterflies or catch a glimpse of where Barbara Smart was murdered.

Chapter 14

I called Irene Hammerstein first. "Hi, Irene, this is Allie McMurphy. How are you today?"

"I'm well. What do you need, young lady?"

"I understand that you play mahjong with Blake Gilmore once a week."

"Why, yes, we do every Monday. Why? Are you wanting to join a group? Because ours is very competitive. We play for quarters of course, but the members who play with us expect a certain level of expertise."

"Oh no, I don't know how to play. I was wondering if you heard about Blake's burglary?"

"Honey, everyone's heard about poor Blake's break-in. I suppose it wasn't really a break-in if nothing was broken, but you know what I mean. Her poor rings, good silver, and the money. I've started locking my place up tight whenever I go out now. Such a shame we have to do that. It's not like the old days, you know."

"I know," I agreed. "I was wondering if you have any idea who might have taken Blake's keys?"

"You are the third person asking me that," she said.

"Really? Other people are asking?"

"Oh yes. Officer Manning asked me the same thing and your cousin Victoria. I'm afraid I wasn't much help to either of them."

Rex asking, I understood, but why was Tori inquiring? I had a vague memory about someone saying she was also investigating. I'd have to have a talk with her. We should put our heads together on this. That is if she let me.

"I see. Well, what about the other ladies in your group?"

"Oh, they are all holding on as best we can. Poor Wanda. She was Barbara's best friend her entire life. I'm afraid she is devastated."

"Oh that's right," I said. "I would be devastated if I lost my best friend. The funeral is tomorrow. Perhaps I'll make her a casserole and bring it to her."

"That might be a good idea. Everyone is thinking about Barbara's family, but Wanda was as much a part of their family as anyone."

"How about Paula?"

"Oh, she's fine," Irene said. "I just talked to her last night. We are skipping mahjong this week and meeting at Wanda's for wine and ladies' night after the funeral. Sort of a small wake. You can come if you want and bring your friends. It might be nice to show Wanda that the community supports her."

"That would make it more than a small wake," I said.

"It's okay. I already invited the entire female portion of the senior center. I just worry that Wanda feels abandoned."

"I'll take her that casserole."

"You are a good person, Allie," Irene said. "I don't know why your cousin doesn't like you."

I cringed. "Neither do I."

I called Paula Abbot and got pretty much the same story. Paula also invited me, Jenn, and Frances to the wake. I figured it wouldn't hurt to show up. Maybe I could get Tori to come with us.

After the final fudge demonstration of the day—today's special was peanut butter cup fudge—I went upstairs to make Grammy Alice's funeral casserole. I found the recipe in her recipe box in the cupboard. I smiled at the fact that she actually titled it "Funeral Casserole." It must be what she took to anyone who was facing the loss of a family member.

The recipe was pretty simple. An easy take on lasagna, it consisted of ground beef, ricotta and egg filling, pasta and mozzarella cheese. The pasta was elbow macaroni and it was mixed with the sauce and meat. Then alternated with the ricotta mixture and cheese. Grammy made a note that it tastes best when it sits a day, so when it was done I covered it and put it in the fridge. I would bring it over to Wanda after the funeral tomorrow.

"Hey." Jenn came bounding into the apartment. "What smells so good?"

"Grammy Alice's funeral casserole. I made some to take over to Wanda Sikes. She was Barbara's best friend. I thought she might need a meal after the funeral."

"Gosh, I hadn't thought about what it might be like to lose your best friend." Jenn came over and gave me a hug. "I would be devastated if I lost you."

"I feel the same about you," I said and hugged her back. "Irene told me they were friends her entire life. So it must be like losing a sister."

"Who's Irene?"

"Irene Hammerstein. She's one of Mrs. Gilmore's mahjong group. I called them today to see if they knew anything helpful about who might have stolen Blake's rings. Also, her silver, and the money out of her underwear drawer."

"Yikes, creepy to think of someone going through your underwear drawer. It had to be someone who knew where the rings and cash were kept."

"That's what I was thinking," I said. "I'm not sure Sean Grady would know where to find the items."

"You know my grandma kept cash in her underwear drawer. If you search enough houses you must get good at finding cash fast."

"Now that's a creepy thought," I said with a shudder.

"Let's talk about happy news," Jenn said and poured us both some wine then went and plopped on the couch. "Frances picked out her wedding dress today."

"Oh that is wonderful news. Can I see it?"

"I took pictures on my phone." Jenn pulled out

her cell and quickly thumbed her way through the pictures. She held the phone up for me to see.

Frances had picked a dress with a lace bodice and three-quarter-length sleeves in an ice blue. Underneath was an off-white strapless gown that was tight to the waist and then flared out into a ball gown skirt. "Oh, it's lovely. She will look so pretty."

"I know, right? The minute I saw it I knew it was the one. It's going to blow Mr. Devaney's socks off. Once he sees this he'll understand why it took a few days to plan a ceremony."

"How's that going?"

"Great," she said and sipped her wine.

I picked up my wineglass and settled into a side chair. "I'm sure you have it well in hand. What are the flowers?"

"We picked pale blue peonies and white hydrangeas. I've got a trellis and permission to have the wedding in Turtle Park. I've rented fifty folding chairs in white and we will have ribbon bouquets in her colors at the aisle ends. A white carpet for her to walk down and Pastor Neuveau will officiate. Maggs is matron of honor. You and I are bridesmaids. Mr. Devaney has his friend Ted for his best man and Rex and Shane as his groomsmen."

"And if it rains?"

"I have a white awning tent rented and ready to be set up in case of rain. It has four plastic sides so that the wind can't drive any rain in."

"Sounds perfect."

"I know. I'm pretty good at this," Jenn said with a laugh, her eyes flashing.

I threw a blue pillow at her. She ducked and it barely missed her wineglass as we laughed.

There was a knock at the door. We both froze. I looked at Jenn. "Are you expecting anyone?"

"No. You?"

"No." I got up when the knock came again.

I opened the door to find Tori standing there with her suitcase in hand. "The power is out at the cottage. You said I could stay with you."

"Yes, of course. Come on in." I opened the door wide.

"I didn't mean to interrupt," Tori said.

"No interruption." Jenn welcomed her in with a come-in wave. "We were just having wine and talking about what an awesome wedding planner I am."

Tori dragged her suitcase over to the sofa and I poured her a glass of wine. "Wedding? Who's getting married?"

"Frances, and Douglas Devaney," Jenn and I said at the same time. "Jinx."

We both laughed and I handed my sober cousin a glass of wine. "Take your shoes off and stay a while."

"Okay," she said and slipped off her shoes. She wore a pair of linen shorts and a scooped-neck T-shirt. Her blond Barbie hair was in a ponytail and she wore little makeup. She didn't need it to be stunningly gorgeous. She crossed her legs underneath her as she sat and sipped the wine. "When is this awesome wedding?"

"Sunday," Jenn said. "You're invited."

"Oh, I didn't mean to beg an invitation."

"No, no, you are really invited. The invitations went out in today's mail. I suppose they didn't get to you yet. You should see it in the morning. Except I sent it to the cottage."

"I'll pick up the mail at the post office," Tori said. "Thanks. Smells good in here."

"Thanks. It's Grammy's recipe for funeral casserole. I'm taking it over to Wanda Sikes after the funeral tomorrow. Irene Hammerstein told me Wanda was taking Barbara's death pretty hard."

"No big dinner tonight?"

"No, it's just us girls tonight. Want to get a pizza?"

We did just that. The night flew by with pizza and wine and girl talk. The McMurphy was full so Tori was sleeping in my apartment. Jenn tried to give up her bed but Tori was having none of it and ended up on the couch.

I got to bed late, but it was worth it as I felt like Victoria was finally warming up to me again. I had been so busy with the fudge shop and the investigation, I hadn't had time to contact the lawyer yet. I decided to make it a priority tomorrow.

At two AM I woke up with a start. The intruder alarm I had installed after I found a guy living in my attic was going off. I jumped out of bed and grabbed a baseball bat I kept in the corner. Mal jumped up with me and barked.

"Hush!"

Slipping on a robe, I checked my cell phone. When the motion sensors were installed, the alarm was set to send a signal to my cell phone. I touched on the application and up popped a window with a grainy camera. It was a picture of the lobby. At first it appeared empty. My heart was racing and I stumbled out of the bedroom. Mal was barking at me and wagging her tail as if we were playing a game. Then I saw the figure of a man stealthily going through the mailbox slots behind the receptionist's desk.

"What's going on?" Jenn asked as she came out of her room with her hair piled messily on her head, wearing a short nightgown and bathrobe and tying the belt around her waist.

She startled me and I gasped and nearly dropped my phone. "Someone's downstairs," I whispered.

"No sense in whispering," Victoria said and turned on a light. "I'm awake."

"Sorry," I said as Mal raced over and jumped up on the couch, pinning Tori down with puppy kisses. "The motion sensor alarm is going off downstairs."

"You have a bat," Tori said. "Are you going down there alone?"

"You should call Rex," Jenn said.

"What if it's just a guest who is drunk or sleepwalking?" I asked. "No, I need to check it out first."

"And the bat?" Tori asked and pointed to the wooden baseball bat I clung to.

"It's just in case."

"You're not going down there alone," Jenn said. "I'm going with you."

"You need to stay here," I said, "where it's safe."

Tori got up. She wore pajama pants and a

button-down pajama top. She grabbed her robe and slipped her arms into it. "I'm going, too."

Mal barked and twirled in the air as if she were going, too. But the last thing I needed was a puppy getting involved. "Mal, not you. Kennel," I ordered.

She dipped her head and slunk over to her crate. I gave her a dog treat from the dish on top of the bar and closed her in tight. The alarm on my app sounded again. This time, whoever it was, was in the fudge shop attempting to open the cash register.

"Jenn, call Rex," I said as I headed to the door. "I don't think this is a guest."

"Right," Jenn said and her fingers flew over her cell phone. I opened the apartment door and tiptoed out.

Victoria was behind me with my chef's knife in hand.

"You can seriously hurt someone with that," I whispered.

"That's the point," she said.

I rolled my eyes. Jenn came up behind us when we got to the top of the stairs. She had a hammer in her hand. We definitely looked like we planned on hurting someone. I would hate for any of our guests to step out of their rooms as we crept down the stairs.

Luckily we got to the landing before the last stair without incident. I flipped on the light and the male figure froze in place. "Don't move!" I said. "We have weapons and we will use them." The guy didn't respond but he didn't run. "Put your hands where we can see them."

None of us was willing to take those last ten steps down into the lobby to get close to this guy. My heart beat fast and my hands shook as I held the bat. The guy raised his hands slowly. His hands were full of bills. We usually kept four hundred dollars in the cash register every day to handle the crowds.

I felt anger rise up within me. He was violating my home and ruining my business.

"Move up against the wall!" I ordered and took those last steps down. He glanced around to see what weapon I had. It was then that I wish I had gotten Papa's double-barrel shotgun. It seemed a woman in her pajamas holding a bat was not enough to terrify the guy.

He sprinted toward the front door.

"Stop him," I shouted and chased after him. The girls came down the stairs. I swung the bat at his knees and he dropped to the floor just in front of the door. Tori straddled him, grabbed him by the hair, and stuck the point of her knife into his neck.

"Try to move," she said.

"I'll get some rope," Jenn said as I picked up my bat and came around to see the man's face. It was Sean Grady.

"Sean Grady!" I glanced at the door; it didn't show any sign of breakage. "You copied my master key."

"Of course I did," he said. "You don't think I'd be so stupid as to go to the hardware store and make a metal copy, do you? I knew what you were talking about when you said you were working a sting."

"But you got inside."

"You don't need to make a metal copy anymore," he said.

"So what exactly did you use? Wax?"

Tori poked his throat with her knife. "Tell us."

"Okay, okay, I took a picture of it and then had it 3D printed by a friend of mine."

"That's just plain scary," I said. Just then the door to the street swung open behind me. Startled, I gasped and turned with my bat raised.

"Whoa there. It's me, Rex. Put down the weapon."

I lowered my bat and Rex took his hand away from his gun until he saw Victoria. Then he pulled his weapon out of the holster and pointed it at Tori. "Put down the knife!"

Tori let the knife fall to the ground.

"Put your hands in the air and get off of him right now!"

"Rex, she was just—"

"Up against the wall," he ordered. "Spread your legs." He patted Victoria down.

"Rex, she didn't do anything." I put my foot on Sean's back and kept the bat where he could see it.

"What is going on?" Jenn asked as she walked in with a round of clothesline rope in her hands.

"Rex is arresting the wrong person," I said.

"Rex, get the guy. He's the one who broke into the McMurphy."

Rex cuffed Victoria and turned her around. "One at a time," he said. He hit the squawk box on his shoulder. "Charlene, I need back-up at the McMurphy."

"Officer Pulaski is on his way." Charlene's voice echoed through the lobby.

"What do you mean 'one at a time'?" I demanded and put my hands on my hips. "Victoria was helping us catch Sean. He broke into the McMurphy. We were defending ourselves."

"We were," Jenn agreed as Rex cuffed Sean and pulled him to his feet.

"I don't know what these women are talking about," Sean said with a straight face. "I didn't break into anything. They left the door open."

"Then why is there money all over the floor?" I said. "I bet there is cash in your pockets."

"That's tip money I earned putting in cable. I only stopped by to see if the cable was still working for you."

"At two AM?" Jenn said with her hands on her hips, mirroring me.

"The door was open. You make fudge. I figured someone was up."

"He copied our master key," I said and pointed at him. "He's been copying keys and coming back later to steal things."

"How would I copy it?" he jeered. "I didn't take it out of the McMurphy."

"He told us he took a picture and made a 3D printed key from it," Jenn said.

I glanced at Tori who was silent but glaring at

me as if her being in handcuffs was all my fault.
Which it was, sort of. . . . "Check him for the key,"
I said.

"I'll check him when I get them both down to
the station," Rex said. He turned to Tori. "I told
you to stay out of trouble."

"I was. Ask Allie." Victoria spit out my name.
Her eyes flashed.

"I told you that knife was dangerous," I said.

"And I told you that giving Sean Grady a master
key was dangerous," she said.

"You gave him the master key?" Rex asked me.

"Yes, we wanted to prove that he'd been making
copies of the keys and breaking in and stealing
things. The fact that he's here now is proof it was
him. He's the one who broke into Mrs. Gilmore's
home and the Butterfly House."

"These girls attacked me," Sean said when Officer Pulaski came through the door. "That one had
a knife to my throat." He nodded toward Tori. "I
want to press assault charges."

"Oh, for goodness' sake," Jenn said. "He broke
into the McMurphy and was stealing from the cash
register."

"I have video to prove it," I said and held up my
cell phone.

Guests from the rooms upstairs had started to
gather on the landing. "Is everything okay?" an
older gentleman with thick glasses and a pointy
beard asked.

"Everything is fine," I said and went over to
the small crowd. "You are safe. The officers have

everything under control. You can go back to your rooms."

"Officers?" a middle-aged woman asked. She was standing there in a nightgown with matching robe.

"Everything is okay," Rex repeated. "Please, go on to bed now. Officer Lasko will be here shortly and she will remain in the lobby to ensure your safety."

"All right, Edith," the older man said and put his hand on the woman's arm. "Let's go back to bed."

"I want you girls to get dressed and come down to the station to give a statement," Rex instructed. "We'll sort this all out then."

"Jenn, can you bring me some clothes?" Tori asked.

"I can do that," I offered.

"Jenn, please tell your friend that I'm no longer speaking to her."

I rolled my eyes. "Oh, for Pete's sake. Rex, let her go. She was defending the McMurphy. I had a baseball bat. We were both armed."

"You are not a murder suspect," Rex said. "And I didn't walk in to see you sitting on a man with a knife to his throat."

"But that's ridiculous," I protested.

"Let's get these two out of here," Rex said to Brent.

Officer Lasko opened the door and sneered at the sight of me. "What's up, boss?" she asked Rex.

"There's been an incident," Rex said. "Brent and I are taking these two to the station. I need you to hang out here and ensure nothing further happens this evening."

"Great," she said and gave me the side eye. "Babysitting duty."

"Just see that no one else gets hurt," he said. "Come on, Brent, let's go." Rex took Tori by the arm and took her out first. Brent hauled Sean Grady out behind Tori. I turned on my heel and rushed up the stairs to get dressed. Jenn wasn't far behind me.

"I can't believe he arrested Victoria," I said.

"She's not very happy with you right now."

"I know, and we were just starting to trust each other."

"Can you believe the chutzpah of Sean Grady claiming that he was the innocent party?"

"I know. Right?" I said and rushed into my bedroom to tear off my pajamas and pull on jeans and a T-shirt. I stuffed my feet into my shoes and came out to find Jenn had put on a sundress and a pair of sandals. Jenn had let Mal out of her kennel. My pup was running between the two of us and jumping up at my hand. "No, we aren't going for a walk," I said. Mal stopped, sat, and gave me sad puppy eyes. "No sad eyes. I have to go fix things with Victoria and I can't take you into the police department again."

Mal didn't seem to understand so I grabbed another treat off the counter. "Do your tricks," I said and we went through her repertoire while Jenn pulled out clothes and shoes from Tori's suitcase near the couch. Mella came over to where I was and rubbed against me. "Okay, treats for you, too." I grabbed a handful of kitty snacks and put them on the counter. Mella jumped up and delicately ate them one by one.

"I want to kill that Sean Grady," Jenn said. "He not only burglarized and terrorized us and Mrs. Gilmore—"

"And who knows how many others?" I continued.

"But he has Tori under even more suspicion."

"I wish I had never set up that sting. Tori told me that something bad would happen and she was right. She has every reason to hate me now."

"She won't hate you," Jenn said. "Rex overreacted. We'll go down and get this sorted out."

"Rex better listen," I said as we headed down the stairs.

"He will." Jenn was more confident than I was. "Then Tori will forgive you and everything will be all right."

"I certainly hope so."

"After all," Jenn said, "what more could go wrong?"

Chapter 15

"Rex Manning is a real jerk," Tori said as she stormed into the apartment. It had taken three hours of talking before Rex let her go. It helped that he found the plastic master key in Sean Grady's pocket.

"I agree," I said. "He should have never arrested you."

"Don't talk to me," she said and packed up her stuff.

"Where are you going?"

"I have friends on the island. I don't need you around, you know."

"I don't think you need me," I said and took out clothes as fast as she put them in her suitcase. "Maybe I need you."

"You don't need me. You have your life all together, owning the McMurphy and making fudge. You even have friends working with you."

"Come on, there's no reason you can't have these things, too. Please stay."

We fought over the clothes until she growled and grabbed them out of my hands. "Stop. Just stop. I have never been investigated before you. Now I was even arrested. Arrested! And threatened with the charge of battery. Not only that, I was arrested in my pajamas for crying out loud." She closed up her suitcase and looked right at me. "Who in their right mind would stay with you after that?"

"I'm sorry," I said. "I can't apologize enough. You were right. The sting was dangerous. Sean could have hurt someone if you didn't help me catch him. Your help is what got you in trouble. For that I owe you."

"You owe me so big it isn't even funny."

"Then let me pay you back. Please stay."

"It's not safe around you, Allie," she said and picked up her suitcase. "You aren't good for me." She walked out and I bit my lip closed. Mal chased after her and down the stairs. Frances had come in already and I was behind on making fudge.

"You had to let her go," Jenn said as she stepped inside the apartment. "I think after a few good nights of rest she will come to her senses."

"Where will she stay?" I asked.

"She knows a lot of people on the island. In fact, Paige Jessop was one of her best friends growing up. She'll probably stay there."

"How do you know that?" I asked, exhausted and frustrated that everyone seemed to know more about my cousin than I did.

"Frances told me."

"Fine," I said and tossed up my hands. "I'm done trying to be nice. It's not getting me anywhere."

"Listen, you only got two hours of sleep last night," Jenn said. "Frances has called Sandy and she will come in and do the morning fudge and the demonstration so that you can get some sleep. Hot sugar and exhaustion don't mix."

"Fine," I conceded and turned toward my room. "But you get some sleep as well."

"Don't worry," Jenn said. "I'll be napping longer than you. Saving the McMurphy is hard work."

"Helping my cousin Tori is even harder. Don't forget the funeral is today at two PM."

"I'll be dressed and ready."

I went to bed and pulled a sleep mask over my eyes. I drifted off into an unsettled sleep, listening to the clip-clop of the horses pulling carts and people on the roads outside. It seemed like no matter what I did to help my cousin, things only got worse. Maybe she was right. Maybe this time it was best if I just stayed out of it.

The funeral was well attended. We left my part time assistant, Megan, at the front desk and closed the fudge shop out of respect. Afterward I hugged Barbara's family and gave them my condolences. It was a bit awkward as everyone knew I had been at the Butterfly House and found the body. Everyone suspected my cousin Tori of killing Barbara. No matter how much I protested, the theory that

Tori killed Barbara remained. The problem was I was the witness who found Tori kneeling over Barbara.

Tori wasn't at the funeral. I didn't expect her to be even though she knew the Smarts better than I did. I went home afterward and opened the fudge shop. I created dark chocolate chunk fudge for the evening demonstration and we sold out of the fudge that we had.

I closed up the shop when Rex came in to see me. He took off his police hat as he entered the lobby. "Hey, Allie."

"Hi, Rex. What can I do for you?"

"I wanted to apologize for jumping to conclusions this morning and arresting your cousin. You have to understand that when I came in, she was the one with the deadly weapon at a guy's throat."

"It's because he robbed me and we were trying to stop him."

"I realize that," he said. His gorgeous blue eyes ringed with thick black lashes were solemn. His square jaw was tight. "I don't take to apologizing very well, but when I'm wrong. I say I'm wrong."

Mal came racing down the stairs and with a short bark she leapt up into Rex's arms. "Well, hello," he said and she gave him kisses on the face.

"Someone likes you," I said. "You can put her down. She needs to learn to greet people with a little more politeness and a little less enthusiasm."

"I don't know, I kind of like enthusiasm," he said in a way that had my cheeks warming. "How are things with Trent?"

"Trent's been out of town on business," I said with a shrug. "It's the price you pay, I guess."

"It's not all that a good a price if you ask me," Rex said.

"You could turn the week around for me."

"Oh? How's that?"

"Tell Tori you know she didn't kill Barbara."

"Well, now, I can't do that. Despite the break-in at the Butterfly House, she is still my best suspect."

"She blames me," I said with a sigh and went over to the coffee bar to make myself a cup of thick coffee. I was still exhausted from the lack of sleep the night before. "She wasn't even able to attend Barbara's funeral."

"I understand your frustration, Allie," Rex said. I turned to find him unnervingly close behind me. "Coffee."

"Help yourself," I said and sidestepped him. "If you understand, then let her go."

"She's still my best suspect."

"What about Sean Grady? I'm sure you figured out that he has been stealing things from all over."

"Yes." Rex nodded. "We found quite a few stolen goods in his home. You were right there. He was copying keys and scoping out valuables while he was working on the cable system. Then he'd go back at night or when no one was home and take things. Some of the things the owners didn't even realize were missing."

"Then he is the best candidate for Barbara's murder."

"No, he isn't," Rex said and sipped his coffee.

"Sean was always sure to not leave a trace that he'd been in the house. In fact, you wouldn't have even known he was here if you didn't have the motion alarm set up downstairs."

"I would have when I opened the register and discovered the missing cash."

"But you wouldn't be able to prove it was Sean. You got lucky."

"Maybe," I said. "Or maybe I made my own luck. Aren't you going to thank me?"

"For what exactly?"

"For catching a thief? I'm sure that Liz will make you out to be a hero returning all those people's things. What was he doing with the stuff anyway?"

"He has connections in the south and they were selling the things on-line," he said. "Sean admitted to keeping the cash."

"So see, my little sting operation wasn't all bad."

"It wasn't safe," Rex said. "Just for the record. I did believe you when you said you suspected Sean. I was working on finding evidence on him. Listen, Allie, you have to trust me to do my job."

"I do trust you."

"Really? Because you are in over your head on investigating who killed Barbara Smart."

"But you are wrong," I said. "I know in my heart that Victoria didn't do it."

"I can't work from my heart," he said, and suddenly the double meaning made the air thick around us. "I can only work with the evidence I find." He reached over and pushed a stray lock of hair behind my ear. "Right now I only have evidence on Victoria."

I could hear the unspoken words, that he only had evidence I wanted to date Trent. Trent who was still away from the island on business. Who sometimes seemed to be more off the island than on it. Trent who had shut me out when his family was in trouble.

"I'm always here, Allie," Rex said. "It's my job and my pleasure to protect you and the people of the island. I take it very seriously."

Oh man. My heart rate picked up and I walked away. "You want me to quit actively investigating."

"Yes."

I turned toward him once there was enough space between us to cool my thundering heart. "Tori isn't exactly happy with me right now. I feel responsible for her and I think you know how that feels. Would you stop if it were me under suspicion?"

"Allie—"

"I can't stop, Rex. I need to fix the rift between us."

He ran his hand over his bald head and looked at me with a hint of understanding and a whole lot of aggravation. "Then at least promise me you'll be safe. No more sting operations."

"I'll be as safe as I can be," I said. "No more sting operations. I promise." Mella, the cat, hopped down from her sleeping place on the striped chair and wound her way around Rex's legs. He put down his coffee and picked her up to pet her.

My gaze went to his hands and my wayward
thoughts wondered what it would be like to have
Rex's hands stroke me like that. Jeez. I broke my
gaze and went to the reception desk. Frances
hadn't come back from the funeral yet. I looked
at all the keys to the rooms. My part-time assistant,
Megan, was on her break. "I guess I need to rekey
the hotel," I said changing the subject. "If Sean
has a copy of the master key he might have shared
it with whomever he was working with."

"I agree," Rex said. "You should update to one
of those new computer systems—they are not so
easy to hack."

I gave a half laugh. "I'll add it to the list of
things to spend money on when I have it." I
paused for a moment. "Wait, if Sean is arrested
who is looking after his grandmother?"

"Social Services is taking her into senior care
for dementia." Rex put the cat down and took a
step toward me. "She will be fine. Listen, I have to
get back to work. Please, Allie, try not to get into
any more trouble."

I sent him a half smile. "I thought *trouble* was my
middle name."

When Megan got off her break, Frances and
Jenn let me know they were headed back to the
hotel from their trip to find the perfect wedding
cake. I got the casserole out and put it in a basket
and biked over to Wanda Sikes's place. She lived
half a block from Barbara Smart. While people still

came and went from the Smart home, Wanda's home was quiet. My heart was heavy for her. I walked up to the two-story Victorian and rang the doorbell.

Wanda opened the door. "Yes?"

"Hi, Wanda, I'm Allie McMurphy."

"Oh, what do you want?"

I lifted the pan of funeral casserole. "I brought you a casserole."

She scrunched up her face in confusion. "For me?"

"Yes," I said. "I'd hate to think about what it must be like to lose your best friend. I figured you needed the casserole more than the Smarts." I nodded toward the Smarts' home where people were still coming with food in their hands.

"Oh, right. Sure," she said. "Please come in."

I followed her into the heavily paneled foyer. The wood paneling was from the turn of the last century and was well cared for as it shone with a warm patina.

"Please have a seat. I'll bring out some coffee," she said as she took the casserole from me and pointed to the living room.

The house was decorated comfortably with a padded floral couch and wingback chairs that were modern yet reflected the style of the home. Wanda's family was clearly not poor. The fireplace was tiled in green and gold and on the mantel were framed pictures of Wanda and her husband, Fred. They looked happy golfing together. Playing tennis in another picture and at a dance in a third.

There were three pictures of Wanda and Barbara. One where they were sitting on the Grand Hotel's veranda sipping mimosas. Another of the two of them receiving an award for a fund-raiser, and a third where they were clearly on vacation together.

"She was like a sister to me," Wanda said. She was a tall woman with broad shoulders and shoulder-length hair dyed a golden blond. She had a patrician nose and wore a silk blouse and pressed linen pants in black and charcoal. She came into the room with a tray containing a coffee carafe, two mugs, and cream and sugar. "I still can't believe she is gone."

"My condolences," I said and took a seat on the couch across from her. "I can't imagine."

"I think I'm still in shock," she said and poured the coffee. "Cream and sugar?"

"Just cream," I said. "Thanks." I took the mug from Wanda. "Do you have any idea who might have done this terrible thing?"

"I've been thinking a lot about that lately." She sat back and held her mug between her fingers. She wore a diamond wedding ring that was at least a full carat. It was clear she'd had work done on her face to keep up her youthful look. Everything about her screamed money and a lifetime of privilege. "I really can't be sure."

"From what I understand, you two were quite tight," I said. "You must have some inkling of what Barbara was thinking. I understand she had an argument with Victoria the night before she died. But then wanted to meet with her the next morning."

"Oh, Barbara was always good at getting over slights," Wanda said. "Seriously she could be mad at you one minute and totally forgive you the next. It was a quirk of her nature that I admired."

I noticed Wanda's hands shook a little. "Tell me about one of the good times with her." I hoped to draw Wanda out a little bit and let her talk about her friend. Sometimes listening was the best thing you could do to help people who were grieving.

"She was always so generous." Wanda sipped her coffee. "She worked on nearly every fund-raiser. We always put together the spring formal. It's held at the end of May when all the cottages begin to open. The yacht club has a formal to fund-raise for the chamber of commerce to help promote the island." Wanda gave a dreamy smile. "Barbara was in true form. She flitted from couple to couple, ensuring everyone was having a good time. Flirting with all the men." Wanda sent me a look. "She was good at that. She could make any man feel like the king of the world."

"I bet that was great for fund-raising," I said.

"Yes." Wanda smiled. "When Barbara was on, men and women alike opened their wallets."

"Blake told me she had a way with men," I said.

Wanda's eyes flashed. "She could have any man she wanted. I don't know how she did it. I am so in love with Fred that I could never think about looking elsewhere."

"Do you think she made any enemies with her affairs?"

"Oh, yes, she had several people who were

sending her e-mails that they were upset about her flirting with their husbands. Wanda would just shrug it off and say it wasn't her fault their husbands were attracted to her attention. She thought if women gave their husbands more attention they wouldn't stray."

"She would shift the blame from her affairs on the wives? That must have made her quite a few enemies."

"The thing about Barbara is she really didn't care. She did what she wanted and that was the way she lived her life."

"I see you two won an award together for volunteering."

"Yes." She smiled at the memory. "Like I said, we did everything together."

"Are you working on the Butterfly House fundraiser?"

"Yes, I was co-chair with Barbara. In fact, I was the one who suggested your cousin as the planner."

"What made you think of Victoria?"

"Her mother is a friend of mine. She said Victoria was in a bad relationship and needed a change of environment for a while. I remembered that Victoria put together her class reunion last year and then I suggested her helping with the Butterfly House."

"Oh, so were you meeting with Tori that morning?"

"I was supposed to," she said and tears came to her eyes. "But my husband was sick and I couldn't go. I worry if only I had been there I might have saved Barbara. She might still be alive today."

I patted her knee. "Or you could be dead as well," I said. "I believe she caught someone in the act of rummaging through the Butterfly House. They panicked and killed her. Whoever it was was pretty strong and would most likely have harmed you as well."

"Why did I survive and not Barbara?" She hung her head.

"Try your best to think of it as meant to be. There was nothing you could have done to save her and you could have been killed as well."

She put her hand on her heart. "That's a frightening thought."

"Do you know anyone who might have wanted Barbara dead?"

"You think your cousin didn't do it?"

"I was there when Tori tried to help her. So no, I don't think my cousin killed Barbara."

She reached for a tissue from the box and dabbed at her eyes. "Good, because I would hate to lose my friendship with Victoria's mother as well as my best friend."

I squeezed her hand. "It's going to be all right. I'm going to figure out who did this."

"You are?" She looked me in the eye. "Are you sure?"

"I'm certain that whoever was rummaging through the Butterfly House was the one who did it. All I have to do is figure out what they were looking for and who they were."

"Ah, here you are." Fred Sikes entered the room. He was dressed in black slacks and a white dress shirt. Wanda straightened at the sound of his voice. "I thought I heard voices. Hello," he said to me and stuck out his hand. "Fred Sikes."

"Allie McMurphy," I said and shook his hand.

Wanda stood. "Allie brought us a casserole. She was worried about me losing my best friend."

"Is that right?" He looked from her to me. "I'm sure she's going to be just fine."

I stood at the sound of finality in his voice. Wanda put her hands on his arm and looked up at him. "Yes, I'll be fine." She turned to me. "Thank you for coming over and for the casserole."

"You're most welcome. I can see myself out."

"Allie," she called after me.

I turned. "Yes?"

"Don't be a stranger. I appreciate your thoughtfulness."

I noticed the strained expression on Fred Sikes's face, but wasn't able to understand the reason behind it. "I won't. I promise." I meant every word. Something was going on with the Sikeses and it felt suspicious. Maybe Fred Sikes had a reason to kill Barbara. It was something worth investigating.

Fast Fudge

Ingredients

14 oz. of sweetened condensed milk
2 cups of dark chocolate chips
1 tsp. of vanilla

Directions

In a 2-quart microwave-safe bowl, microwave the sweetened condensed milk and chocolate chips on high for 1 minute. Let sit for 1 minute and stir. (If chips are not all melted, microwave another 30 seconds.) Add vanilla and pour into a buttered 8-inch square pan. Cool completely. Cut into 1-inch squares and enjoy!

Chapter 16

"Yay, you're back," Jenn said when I walked into the apartment. She and Frances and Douglas were all sitting around the kitchen bar. "We're cake tasting and we can use your expert opinion."

"I don't know how much of an expert I am," I demurred and put my purse down.

"We have orange blossom with chocolate ganache and chocolate butter cream. Classic white almond with strawberry filling and vanilla bean butter cream and a chocolate cake with salted caramel filling and dark chocolate butter cream."

They all sat with three plates in front of them and I could tell they were enjoying the tasting. "Chocolate is certainly unconventional for a wedding," I said and pulled up a bar stool.

"Because it's a second wedding for us both we thought we could have whatever cake we wanted," Frances said. "But Heather Lakeland, the baker, included the almond cake in case we decided that we were traditionalists after all."

"Heather Lakeland?" I asked as I cut a small piece from each taster cake.

"She's a baker over at Mackinac Island Cakes. She made these three cakes and gave us a sample of decoration as well. Aren't they pretty?"

"They are." The orange cake had fondant orange blossoms strewn across it. The chocolate was frosted in art deco geometric frosting with white chocolate fan shapes. The white cake was decorated with real flowers in Frances's colors of lavender and blue.

"Which one are you favoring?" I asked.

"I like the chocolate orange," Frances said. "Douglas likes the traditional white."

I forked up some of the chocolate orange. It was light with good sponge and tasted like a chocolate orange Christmas candy. "It's good." Then I forked up a bit of the white cake; it was moist with a lighter sponge and the flavor was subtle and not as bright.

"I like the salted caramel," Jenn said and took another bite of her favorite. "But I don't get a vote."

"We're stuck," Frances said. "What do you think?"

"Mr. Devaney, why do you prefer the white cake?"

"It's not so sweet and I like the real flowers on it."

"And, Frances, why do you like the chocolate orange cake?"

"It's bright and citrusy with the mystery of chocolate."

"Which decorations do you prefer?"

"I like the real flowers," Frances said.

"So do I," Mr. Devaney agreed.

"Then why don't you ask Heather to make you a chocolate layer and a white layer with an orange filling and white frosting?"

"You are genius!" Frances said and clapped her hands. "That way we have both."

"And the citrus of the orange filling will cut the sweetness of the chocolate cake," Jenn said. "That's a good idea. I knew Allie could solve this little dilemma."

"I'm glad to help," I said.

"How'd it go taking the casserole over to Wanda Sikes?"

"Wanda seemed pretty broken up at the loss," I said. "She told me she was supposed to go with Barbara that morning but her husband was sick so she called off."

"Oh wow," Jenn said and put down her fork. "Talk about guilt trip."

"What do you mean?" Frances asked.

"Well, Wanda feels that if she had gone that morning, Barbara might still be alive," I said. "She has survivor's remorse."

"Poor thing," Frances said and took a sip of her coffee.

"What do you know about Mr. Sikes?" I asked.

"He's wealthy," Frances said. "I think his family runs a shipping business. They own several warehouses and barges that ship through the straits and move goods from Detroit to Chicago and Green Bay."

"Have they always been a member of island society?"

"Yes, they are one of the prominent families," Frances said. "Why?"

"Do you know any reason why Mr. Sikes might want to get Barbara out of Wanda's life?"

"That's a pretty serious accusation," Mr. Devaney said.

"It's just he came in while I was visiting and didn't seem at all happy I was there," I explained. "It was as if he didn't want me talking to Wanda. After introducing himself, he had Wanda basically show me the door."

"That is odd," Frances said. "I've always found Fred to be a rather accommodating gentleman."

"Perhaps he was still not feeling well," Mr. Devaney said. "I know I can get grumpy when I'm ill."

"She did say she missed meeting with Barbara because Fred was sick."

"I don't know," I said. "Something feels off. Do you think Wanda is covering for Fred?"

"Why would Fred Sikes want to kill Barbara?" Mr. Devaney asked.

"I don't know," I said. "But he didn't seem sick to me."

"I wouldn't mention this theory until you get more evidence. The Sikeses have a lot of influence, and a misstep in handling them can lead to a social disaster," Frances said.

I frowned. "I suppose it makes sense that Wanda would marry as well as Barbara did. The only difference is Barbara's husband died young and Wanda's didn't."

"That left Barbara to have as many affairs as she wanted," Jenn said. "I understand she was notorious. Maybe one of her jilted lovers killed her."

"That's ridiculous," I said. "Barbara was in her late sixties. If a jilted lover was going to kill her, he would have done it when she was younger. Don't you think?"

"I don't know," Frances said. "Barbara took very good care of herself. It was no secret that she had a little work done here and there. She still had men at the social club fawning over her."

"So you think it might have been a jilted lover who killed her?" I waved my fork in the air.

Frances shook her head. "I'm only saying that you can't rule it out just because of her age." She forked up more cake. "People fall in love at all ages."

Yikes. I felt that little dig. "I didn't mean that she was too old for a jealous lover."

"What did you mean?" Mr. Devaney looked at me.

I felt the heat of a blush rush over my face. "I meant that it is much more likely that whoever broke into the Butterfly House killed Barbara than a jilted lover."

"She might have had a stalker," Jenn said with a bit of glee. "I heard a rumor that she posted a formal complaint about someone following her."

"So Rex would know if she had a stalker."

"He might," Jenn said. "You should ask him. If she did have a stalker, he could have followed her that morning, saw she was alone when she went into the Butterfly House, and confronted her there. They fought and Barbara threatened to go to the police."

"So he picks up a gardening spade and stabs her?" I shook my head. "Why would he stab the object of his obsession? Then she is gone forever."

"It was most likely an accident," Frances said. "You said that it had to be a crime of passion. The garden trowel was a weapon of opportunity."

"I suppose she could have rejected her stalker's advances. He got angry and stabbed her." I bit my bottom lip thoughtfully. "So our list of possible suspects grows. I'm going to have a talk with Liz. She would know if the rumor about a stalker is true and who it might be."

"Why not ask Rex?" Jenn asked.

I made a face. "He doesn't want me to investigate."

"That hasn't stopped you before," Frances said. "You have three possible scenarios, well, four if you count Victoria."

"I'm not counting Victoria as a killer."

"Then you have whoever broke into the Butterfly House, the possible stalker, and a jilted lover," Frances said and counted them on her fingers. "But these are just theories. You have no names and no proof. I think you're really reaching."

"I know," I agreed and rested my elbow on the bar and my chin on my hand. "But I've made such a mess of things for Victoria. I really feel if I can prove someone else did it, then Rex will have to apologize to Victoria and she will see that I care about her."

"That's a lot of work for a cousin who still may not like you," Mr. Devaney said.

"I know, but I feel as if Papa Liam would want me and Victoria to be friends again."

"Getting her arrested twice is hardly the way to win over her friendship," Jenn teased.

"See," I insisted. "I feel responsible."

"Don't feel responsible. You didn't do anything wrong. Anyone who thinks otherwise is not thinking straight."

The next morning, I walked Mal by the newspaper office on our morning walk. Liz was outside opening up the door and sweeping the stoop. "Hey, Liz," I said with a wave.

"Good morning, Allie."

I let Mal pull me up the walk to greet Liz. Mal jumped up and did a little twirl.

"Aren't you in good form today, puppy?" Liz said and petted Mal.

"Did you find out any more on Sean Grady?" I asked. "Rex said he found all kinds of stolen goods in Sean's place."

"It was a great lead you gave me," Liz agreed. "From what Rex told me, people have been coming forward to collect their things back. Sadly a good bit of it was already sold off."

"Listen, I heard a rumor that Barbara had filed a complaint about someone who was following her and harassing her. Do you know anything about that?"

"Yes," Liz said. "According to Bruce at the police

desk, Barbara came in the week before she died and filed a formal harassment charge against Henry Potts. Potts was one of Barbara's lovers. When she told him it was over, he took it badly."

"Do you think he took it badly enough to want to kill her?"

"It was something I considered," Liz said, "but Henry has an alibi. He was visiting his sister in Manistee the morning Barbara was killed. I have confirmation from the diner where they ate breakfast."

"There were witnesses besides his sister," I said.

"Yes. That's why Rex ruled him out."

"Well, darn."

Liz rubbed Mal's ears. "Does this mean you are still investigating Barbara's murder?"

"Yes. I just don't understand why Rex keeps insisting Victoria is guilty."

"She's his best candidate," Liz explained. "I hear he arrested her for battery the other night."

I rolled my eyes and blew out a long sigh. "It was all a case of mistaken identity. Sean Grady broke into the McMurphy. Tori was helping me catch him and hold him until Rex could get there."

"I heard she had a knife to his throat."

"None of us had a gun," I said. "I already used my baseball bat to take him down."

"How?"

"I threw it at him," I said. "It hit his knees and knocked him over."

"Sounds daring. Can I write about it?"

"Only if you talk about Sean being the bad guy and Tori being a hero. You can ask her. She'll tell you she was only trying to help me hold Sean until the police arrived."

"VICTORIA ANDREWS, HERO," Liz said. "I do like the headline, or even better—HERO ARRESTED FOR NABBING BURGLAR: THE TRUE STORY OF HOW SEAN GRADY WAS CAPTURED. Yes, I like that. Thanks for the lead. I'll get right on the story."

I smiled. And Mal did a little dance before she pulled me away to continue our walk. I may never be able to make things up to Victoria, but it didn't mean I wasn't going to try.

Chapter 17

Our walk took us by the stables on the way to Main Street. The scent of horses filled the air and the sound of their shoes clomping on the pavement was comforting. The stables belonged to Trent's family, and he usually smelled of expensive cologne with a hint of horse and leather from the saddles and gear. The stables offered horse rides around the island. I'd never tried it. My horseman skills were sub-par at best. I was a baker, not an equestrian.

I glanced inside to see Victoria talking to someone. As I got closer, I paused. She was talking to Trent. I didn't even know he was back on the island. They seemed to be in a serious conversation. That's when it happened. She kissed him.

I froze. He put his arms around her and kissed her back. My boyfriend was kissing my cousin! That was not good. Mal saw Trent and pulled me toward him with great enthusiasm and I tugged her back. "No, Mal," I said.

It was then that Trent saw me. "Allie."

"Come on, Mal, we need to go home." I pulled my dog away from the stables and down the street.

"Allie, wait!"

No, I wasn't waiting. It was one thing to want to take a portion of the McMurphy from me. But it was a whole other thing to hit on my boyfriend. That was it. I was done with Victoria, and right at the moment I was done with Trent.

"Allie!" he called behind me, but I let the crowds of tourists slow him down as I practically ran to the McMurphy and slammed the door on him. I let Mal off her leash and stormed past Frances.

"What's going on?"

"Tell Trent Jessop that I'm not talking to him."

"What happened?" she asked as I hurried up the stairs. I didn't take the time to answer because the door to the McMurphy opened and Mal went to greet her friend. Traitor.

I was trembling mad when I got to my apartment door. Maybe Rex was right; maybe it was Tori all along. I locked the door behind me and took two steps before Trent pounded on it. "Allie, let me in. It wasn't what you think."

"Go away, Trent."

"Allie, please."

"I'm not doing this right now," I said.

"Allie, Tori and I—"

I stormed into my bedroom and closed the door, put on headphones, and listened to soothing music as I paced the length of my room. I figured it would take all of fifteen minutes before he had a business call that he would have to answer.

Trent Jessop was a busy man. Too busy to let me know he was back on the island and too busy kissing my cousin to kiss me. I wanted to stomp my feet and kick something. Back in Chicago when things made me mad I would go to the gym and work the emotion off. I didn't have time for a gym here. I had taken to doing workout videos.

So I popped in a kickboxing video, put on my gloves, and spent the next forty minutes air punching Trent's face.

"I can't believe he kissed her," Frances said. "He seems like such a genuine guy."

I made a face. "How do I know that all these business trips of his aren't him dating some woman in Chicago or Detroit?"

"I don't think so," Frances said. "He doesn't have a history of running around like that."

I was in the fudge shop making the last batch of fudges for the day. Trent was long gone. Frances said he left after twenty minutes. Good. I figured he didn't have much time to waste. Tears welled up in my eyes and I dashed them away. I was pathetic. I should have known he was losing interest. A few weeks ago he shut me out of an investigation involving his sister. He swore things were different now, but after today I wasn't so sure.

"Well, at least I don't have to worry about trying to save Tori anymore. As far as I'm concerned, she can save herself. And if she believes for one moment I'm going to go through with giving her a share in the McMurphy, she has another think coming."

"Allie, I just heard about what happened with Trent," Jenn came rushing in. "Are you okay?"

"No, I'm not okay," I said. "Would you be?"

"No. If I caught someone kissing Shane, I would have to punch them in the nose."

"I restrained myself," I said, "but only because I had Mal with me and she didn't need to see me get violent."

The pup perked up at the sound of her name and came over to the glass wall that separated the kitchen from the rest of the lobby.

"Perhaps you should have heard him out," Frances said softly. "It might not have been what you think."

"What I think is I saw my cousin kiss Trent and Trent kissed her back."

"Rumor has it they dated in high school," Jenn said. "I guess you never get over your first love."

"That's not helpful," I said and put my back into stirring the hot sugar cocoa base for the fudge.

"Sorry," Jenn said. "He should be shot."

"That's better," I said. "Can you grab an apron and help me pour the fudge on the table?"

"Sure." Jenn put an apron on over her capris and short-sleeve blouse. Then we both put hot pads on our hands and lifted the big copper kettle. We poured the hot fudge onto the marble cooling table. The scent of sweet dark chocolate filled the air. I got a scraper, while Jenn held the kettle, and I scraped out the last bits of fudge.

Then I began the process of stirring the fudge with a long-handled spatula.

It was hard work that I needed to distract me from the myriad of emotions that ran through me. Right now I didn't care if I ever saw my cousin again. I wish I hadn't given Liz the information for the article to make up for Rex arresting her. After all, it wasn't my fault. How was I to know that Sean would try to run, that Tori would use the knife to stop him, or that Rex would see it as a threat and arrest Tori?

My head hurt.

Jenn watched me in silence for a moment. "There's no excuse for what happened."

"None."

"Let's talk about happier things," Frances suggested.

"Like the wedding." Jenn perked up. "We have the gown. Magg's has approved her dress so we have the bridesmaids' dresses, and Heather confirmed the cake. I've sent out handwritten invitations to the fifty people you want there. So far, ten have RSVP'd that they will come."

"That's fine," Frances said and crossed her arms. "I sent out fifty hoping for twenty people to come. If it were up to Douglas, only you girls and Sandy would be there."

Sandy was busy setting up centerpieces for another wedding right now and had yet to hear the news about Trent and Tori. I wondered what she would say. Sandy was pretty reserved. It seemed she was as calm and unfazed by emotions as any human being could be. It was times like now that I wish I had less Irish in me and more Ottawa. Sandy always seemed to be the calm eye in a storm.

The door to the McMurphy opened and a porter carrying a giant vase of purple hyacinths walked in. Behind him was another porter carrying a box with a clear lid that also held flowers.

"Delivery for Allie McMurphy," the first porter said.

"I'll get them," Jenn said. She signed for the flowers, gave the porters a tip, and put the vase of purple hyacinths on the reception desk and opened the box to show me a bouquet of white orchids. "Oh, this guy knows his flowers."

"Why?" I asked as I rounded the table. The fudge had started to set up and I switched to a short hand scraper. I poured chopped cherries, raisins, and pecans in the center of the fudge and began the process of hand folding it in.

"Both of these flowers mean 'I'm sorry,'" Jenn said.

"Sorry doesn't cut it, bub," I muttered.

"Can I put the orchids in water?" Jenn asked.

"I don't care what you do with them," I said. "I'm not in the mood for flowers."

The door to the McMurphy opened and Fred Sikes walked in. He stopped and glanced around then made a beeline for the fudge counter. "Ms. McMurphy," he said and put my casserole dish on top of the glass candy counter.

"Hello, Mr. Sikes," I said. "How is Wanda doing?"

"She's fine," he said, his mouth a straight line. "Listen. I know you have a reputation of solving murders and finding killers and such nonsense, but I want you to stay away from Wanda."

"What?"

"She is having a tough enough time without you coming by and giving her false hopes. We appreciate the effort with the casserole, but frankly, stay away from my family. Most importantly, keep your nose out of my business."

"Okay," I said out of reflex, and I stopped and studied him.

"Do I make myself clear?" he asked. He wore a thousand-dollar Italian suit and looked like something out of *GQ*.

"Crystal," I said.

"Good. Good day." He turned on his heel and walked back out of the McMurphy.

I looked at Jenn and she looked at me.

"What the heck was that all about?" Jenn asked.

"I think he wants me to stay away from Wanda," I said.

"Clearly, but why?" Jenn asked. "I mean; doesn't that seem suspicious to you?"

"Yeah," I said. "It does. Not that it matters, because I'm no longer investigating Barbara's murder. Tori can look out for herself."

"Still, that was highly suspicious," Jenn said and picked up the casserole pan. "Didn't you say that you thought Mr. Sikes was hiding something?"

"Yes," I said and cut the fudge into one pound pieces and placed them on a tray.

"Hmm," Jenn said. "Very interesting."

I put the tray in the candy display case. "You are

not going to investigate him," I said. "Seriously, I'm done trying to help Victoria. Don't you start."

"Oh, I'm not going to start to help Victoria after what she did," Jenn said. "But that doesn't mean I don't find Mr. Sikes's behavior odd."

"It seems everyone is acting strangely today."

Victoria walked into the McMurphy.

"Oh no," I said and pointed to the door. "You need to get out."

"Allie, I came to apologize. I didn't know that you were dating Trent."

"I don't care what you knew or didn't know," I said. "You need to leave."

"Fine. Look, Trent asked me to come in and explain."

"You are still seeing him after I discovered you two kissing? Really. Get out now or I'll have Mr. Devaney throw you out."

"But, Allie."

"Out!" The tone of my voice had Mal running for her bed beside Frances and the reception desk. Mella, the cat, stood up from her sleep on the desk, arched her back, and jumped down to get a closer look at what was going on.

"Allie—"

I tore off my apron, hung it on the coat rack in the corner of the shop, and went upstairs.

"You're being unreasonable," Tori said from the bottom of the stairs.

I didn't reply. Instead I went up to the office to work on bills. When I sat down at my desk, I noticed that Jenn had put the orchids in a fluted, clear vase in the center of our two desks. I scowled at the flowers. There was a tiny card in its envelope on my desk. I blew out a long sigh and opened it. *I'm flying back to Chicago. The merger goes through today. Please forgive me. The kiss meant nothing. Trent*

Right, I thought. And tossed the card in the trash. He didn't even tell me he was on the island and now he was gone again. He was here long enough to kiss Victoria, though. I put my head in my hands and closed my eyes. Why was I dating a guy who spent so much time away from me?

Maybe, just maybe, I needed to rethink my relationship status.

Mr. Sikes was in the shipping business. The thought had me sitting up straight. I had fallen asleep at my desk; a small patch of drool on my desktop calendar proved it. I glanced at the clock. It was eight AM. I dialed Blake Gilmore.

"Butterfly House, this is Blake. How can I help you?"

"Hi, Blake, it's Allie," I said.

"Hi, Allie, how are you doing? I heard about Trent and Victoria. What a scoundrel. Are you doing okay?"

I cringed, filled with embarrassment over the fact that my love life was common knowledge on the small island. "I'm fine," I said. "Listen, I have a quick question."

"Sure. Anything, dear."

"When did you receive the last shipment of chrysalises? Did you tell me they were from Africa?"

"Oh, I got them in the day before the murder

and yes, they are from Africa. They have come out of their shells completely and are now flying around the greenhouse if you want to see them."

"Oh, I'd love to," I said. "I'll be right over."

"Great, see you soon."

I got up, washed my face, and combed my hair before I took the back stairs down to the alley. It had cooled considerably outside. Even though the sun didn't set until after eight PM, I still shivered. I should have brought a jacket with me. I cut through the alley and walked up Main Street past the church and over to the Butterfly House. Blake was working the admissions desk when I arrived.

"Hey, Allie, that was fast." She came around and gave me a hug. "How are you holding up?"

"I'm fine," I said with a brush of my hand. "Blake, can you tell me again how you get the butterflies?"

"Sure. We get around three hundred and fifty chrysalises every week. The day of the shipment we got about fifty, but ten of them were the highly prized ones from Africa. They appear to glow in the dark. It's really the light reflecting off their tiny green feathers."

"And you said these butterflies are expensive?"

"Yes, bigger chrysalises can cost upwards three thousand dollars."

"How do you get them? Can you walk me through the process?"

"Well, they are delivered to us via FedEx. They are carefully wrapped in cotton. So we remove them from the batting and inspect and pin them to these foam rods then put them in emergence cages and display them up front." She took me through the vinyl slats that hung in each doorway to keep the butterflies from escaping. There was a small room before you got to the greenhouse where one wall was devoted to chrysalises. "This is the emergence box. People get to see the week's chrysalises and if they are lucky they will see a butterfly emerge."

"But you didn't put the special butterflies in here with the others," I pointed out.

"No, I made them their own emergence box. They are a brand-new breed and highly prized. I put them in here." She took me out of the second room, to the office that had been trashed. "I set it up under a camera to allow people to live stream it."

"And it was while they were in here that the room got tossed."

"Yes."

"So walk me back through the process. How do they get to you?"

"They are flown in via the FedEx plane and brought over here by the FedEx porters on their bicycles."

"That doesn't bounce them around or damage them?"

"Oh no. They are carefully wrapped and specially packaged. Let me show you today's shipment." She pulled a box over and, using a box cutter, opened it. Inside, carefully rolled in cotton and protected by extra cardboard pieces and batting, were twenty chrysalises.

"I see," I said, and carefully examined the cotton.

"What do you do with the cotton and cardboard afterward?"

"We generally isolate it in the back shed to ensure we don't have any stowaway insects in them."

"Can I see?"

"Sure." She took me through Insect World and out the back of the greenhouse to the shed. This time it was locked with a heavy paddle lock.

"I see you have an extra measure of protection."

"We do," she said and opened the paddle lock. "I felt it was prudent considering. I know they didn't take anything, but they could have and I thought extra caution was in order." It was dusk and so she turned on the inside light, which consisted of a single bulb hanging from the ceiling. "We put the packaging inside these sealed trash containers for seventy-two hours to ensure nothing else hatches."

She went over to three bins with reinforced lids that were held down with metal clamps.

"Why do you go through so much trouble?"

"Well, with insects being shipped from all over the world, we have to be careful not to introduce any non-native varieties to the island. They are sneaky little suckers after all."

"So that's it."

"Yes, pretty simple."

"I have a question."

"What, dear?"

"So you think whoever tossed the Butterfly House could have been looking for something that was smuggled in with the rare butterflies?"

She seemed startled by the idea. "Who would smuggle something in, and how?"

"That's a good question," I said. "Did you put the latest bit of packaging in the bins?"

"No," she said and shook her head. "The delivery came later than usual and I had a dinner party. So I was in a bit of a hurry." She blushed at the thought. "I was careful with the chrysalises, but put the packaging in my tote. I meant to put it in the bins the next morning but, well, Barbara was murdered and things just went crazy."

"Is it still in your tote?"

She colored a deeper red. "Yes," she said. "I didn't dispose of it correctly. I'm certain that there were no stowaway bugs. My tote is zippered so they would be in the tote and not out."

"It's not the stowaways that have me worried," I said. "It's your safety. Where is the tote?"

"Here, behind the ticket desk." She walked me back through the greenhouse to the tall ticket desk near the front door. "I didn't want to take it home in case there was a stowaway." She pulled out a striped beach tote that was filled to rounded.

"Can we open it?"

"Of course," she said. "Let's do it in the staging area in case a stowaway insect emerges."

We walked into the small room where the customers came between the greenhouse and the front door. This room was blocked off with vinyl strips as well. Once inside, she opened the tote carefully under a fluorescent light to ensure nothing flew out. Once safe she showed me the box and batting the chrysalises came in. I carefully pulled at the batting, feeling my way through it. Sure enough, there was what felt like a small bag of rocks. I pulled the batting away to lift up a bag of what appeared to be diamonds.

"Oh dear." Blake looked at me. "Do you think those are real?"

"Yes," I said and got out my cell phone and pressed Contacts, calling Rex.

"Manning," he said.

"Hi, Rex, it's Allie. I'm at the Butterfly House and we have something you need to see."

"Allie, I told you not to investigate any further."

"I wasn't investigating the murder," I said. "Please come."

"I'll be right there."

I hung up and looked at Blake. "We need to stay right here."

"Okay," she said. "Lucky for us, the Butterfly House is closing. Do you think this is what the thief was looking for?"

"I do," I said. "And I don't think that thief was Sean Grady."

"Oh no, you think someone else has a copy of the key to the building?"

"You had the locks changed, right?" I asked, suddenly feeling as if I needed to look over my shoulder.

"Yes," she said. "Do you think this is the only time they have smuggled something in through us?"

"I have no idea," I said. "If not, then why search the Butterfly House? Why not extract it in the usual manner? Didn't you fire someone recently?"

"Dan Jones," she said. "He worked as a part-time gardener in the greenhouse."

"Did you tell Rex about Dan?"

"No, I fired Dan two weeks ago. It didn't seem relevant. Besides, Dan never had access to my keys."

"How long did he work here?"

"Since May," she said. "I fired him because he wasn't doing a good job. He was rather lackadaisical in his work and I counseled him about it, but he didn't get better. That seems typical for young men these days, but that didn't mean I had to like it."

"Was he mad or scared when you fired him?"

"He did seem quite upset. But I figured it was because he lost his job. Do you think he was the one smuggling things in?"

"No," I said. "If he was young and lackadaisical, as you said, then I imagine he worked for someone with the connections to smuggle things in."

There was a knock at the door and we both jumped. "That must be Rex," I said. "Let's go together so that we have proof that none of the diamonds were taken."

"Okay," she said. "Good thinking. I would have just walked out and left you alone with them."

"I don't want anyone to accuse me of pocketing anything that isn't mine." We both walked out into the entrance and Blake let Rex inside.

"What is so darn important that I needed to come right away?" he asked as he took off his hat and wiped his feet on the welcome mat.

"We found diamonds," Blake blurted.

I held up the small bag of sparkling rocks. "They were inside the batting from the African shipment."

"Well, that explains a lot," he said and took the bag from me. He lifted it in the light and whistled low. "There must be a million dollars' worth here."

"Or more," I said. "I wanted you to witness. Come into the staging area." We walked through the vinyl and Blake and I took him step by step through the process of how she left the tote, where we opened it, and showed him the spot on the ground where the tote and box and batting was as proof.

"I'll call Shane in," he said. "All of this is evidence."

"What about Dan Jones?" I asked. "You should go see him."

"I'll send Brent over." He called dispatch and had Brent go over to Dan Jones's apartment. The call came in within twenty minutes. When Dan didn't answer his door, Brent broke it down and found the young man dead face down on his kitchen floor.

Rex looked at me. "Things just got a whole lot worse."

Chapter 18

"Wait, you found a bag of diamonds?" Jenn said, astounded. "Did you dump them into your palm? I would have totally dumped them into my palm to see if it looked like it does on TV when they find them."

"What made you think to look in the batting?" Frances asked.

"I was thinking about why someone would search through everything at the Butterfly House. It wasn't how Sean acted when he stole things. Then I realized that she just received a shipment from Africa and since they didn't take the butterflies, maybe there was something else in the shipment. It occurred to me when I was thinking about Mr. Sikes being in the import/export shipping business."

"Do you suspect Mr. Sikes is the big boss behind this?" Jenn asked.

We sat on the patio of a local bar. It was Frances's bachelorette party. We made her wear a

sash that said BRIDE and a crown. She glowed with
happiness and embarrassment. She had agreed to
the attention as long as we didn't hire a stripper.
Jenn had pouted with disappointment but I was
secretly glad not to have that at the party either.
My own love life was pretty messed up right now
and I didn't need to make things worse.

"Oh, I hadn't thought of that," I said. "There
are so many people who own summer homes
here who could be involved."

"That's right," Frances said. "There's Randal
Hunter, who has a packaging company. Thad
Beaumont, who owns the airline company FedEx
uses, and John Eves, who runs the butterfly import/
export business."

I sipped my margarita. "Diamonds are marked
with a serial number. I'm sure Shane will figure
out where they came from. It might take a while,
but they will be able to find out who was smuggling them into the area. The real question is, was
Barbara's death part of this?"

"So you're still investigating," Jenn said.

"No." I shook my head. "No more investigating
for me. I have a dear friend with a wedding tomorrow." I raised my glass. "To Frances and Douglas,
may they find their happy ever after."

"Here, here," the other ladies said. There were
four of us: Frances, me, Jenn, and Sandy. We had
left Megan in charge of the McMurphy with strict
instructions to notify us if she needed anything.
We had a table at a noisy bar that faced the water.
Tomorrow evening was Frances's wedding. Jenn

had done a great job of planning and executing everything Frances wanted. There was even to be a harp player playing as she went down the aisle. My friends were happy and healthy and made me proud.

My thoughts turned to Wanda who had lost her best friend. After the wedding I would go check on her again. Mr. Sikes wasn't too receptive, but if I ran into him I would reassure him that I was definitely off this case. As far as I was concerned, Victoria could do her own investigating.

Two hours into the party, I got up to use the restroom. I wound my way inside and noticed that Mr. Sikes was here, talking to another man I didn't recognize. They were arguing over something. I wasn't close enough to hear, but was close enough that he looked up and spotted me. He gave me a hair-curling glare and turned his back on me.

It was almost as if he blamed me for Barbara's death. Which was just plain silly. Maybe he was afraid I would uncover the truth. Maybe he killed Barbara. Maybe Frances was right. He could have easily been working with Dan Jones to smuggle diamonds into the U.S. Mackinac Island was pretty close to Canada.

"Hey, Allie." Liz intercepted me on my way back from the bathroom. "How are things going?"

"Fine," I said. "We're here for Frances's bachelorette party. You should stop by and have a drink in her honor."

"My pleasure. But first I need you to talk to me about Dan Jones's murder."

I paused and grabbed an empty bar-height chair and climbed up. Liz sat across from me and took out her pen and notepad. "What do you want to know?"

"I need details. Rex is being pretty close-mouthed about this one."

"I'll do what I can. What do you not know?"

"It's better that I tell you what I do know," she said and flipped open her pad. "Dan Jones was found dead by Officer Pulaski. He got a call from Rex asking him to check in on Dan. When he got there the door was locked and it seemed no one was home. Brent entered the apartment to find Dan dead on the floor."

"Yes, that sounds about right to me," I said.

"Why did Rex call Brent to check on Dan? Do you know?" Liz asked.

"Rex didn't tell you?"

"He said it was an ongoing investigation." Liz frowned.

"I don't know if it's okay to say anything on the record," I said. "But then again, Rex didn't tell me to keep it to myself."

"What happened?"

I told Liz the story of finding the diamonds and how Dan was our first suspect because he was recently fired.

"Wow, that is a great story," Liz said.

"Hey, Allie, there you are," Jenn said as she came in from the patio. "We were wondering what happened to you. Hi, Liz, why don't you come out and have a drink with us?"

"Sure."

We went back to the patio and chatted about girl things, but my mind was on Trent and Victoria. Even if she was the one to kiss him first, I saw him kiss her back. It didn't help that they had been high school sweethearts. You never do forget your first love. I didn't like it. Not one bit.

"So, Allie"—Liz turned to me—"I hear that you got flowers yesterday and today. Sounds like someone's either in love or in trouble."

"Trouble," I grumbled.

"Oh no, what happened?"

"I saw Trent and Victoria kissing. I didn't even know he was on the island and now he's gone again." I crossed my arms as tears welled up.

"Well, that certainly sounds fishy to me."

"Me, too," I said. "Do you want any flowers?"

Everyone at the table laughed. It was late and we all had had enough excitement. Especially the bride. She looked about ready to fall out of her chair. So we said our good-byes to Liz and walked Frances home, made sure she got into her condo, and tucked her into bed before we left.

The McMurphy was a short walk home. The scent of night on the island filled my senses. Warm air, lake breezes, horses, and the lingering scent of fudge and candy surrounded us. Main Street was empty of tourists. The ferries didn't run this late at night and most people who stayed on the island overnight were at their hotels, swimming in the pools or sitting outside on the lawns toasting marshmallows.

"I'm sorry about Trent," Jenn said. "You have every reason to be mad at him."

"Thanks. It really hurts that Victoria knew he was on the island and I didn't. I have no idea why."

"Maybe you should hear him out."

"No, I'm still too mad."

"What you need is a distraction."

"You mean a wedding and running my fudge shop isn't enough distraction?"

"Clearly not, as you weren't in the room with us tonight. We were celebrating Frances."

"Ugh," I said and slumped my shoulders. "I'm sorry."

"You have to do better tomorrow. You are a bridesmaid. You should be focused on Frances."

"I'll be focused," I said. We cut through the back alley to go up the steps that led to my apartment on the top floor. When I first moved in, the back alley entrance was a fire escape with only a ladder. I had installed stairs and now we used it to take Mal out of the apartment. It became more of a front door of sorts so that locals didn't have to go through the McMurphy at night to visit.

Trent stood on the landing waiting for us. He had flowers in hand. Gerbera daisies, one of my favorites.

"Hi, Trent," Jenn said.

"Jenn, Allie."

I was stuck. I had to get by him to get into my home and he knew it.

"Well, I'll leave you two alone." Jenn opened the door and slipped inside. I stood as far from Trent as I could. My arms were crossed.

"I came to apologize," he said and held out the flowers.

"I really am not sure I'm ready to hear you out."

"I hate that you're this angry," he said. "If you would let me explain."

"Explain why you were back on the island and didn't tell me. Explain why I saw you kissing my cousin. I understand that she was your first love. If you were going to cheat on me, you should have broken up with me first."

"It wasn't anything like that." He pulled the flowers back when I refused to take them. "Look, Victoria contacted me."

"And you came running back. Meanwhile I'm left waiting for you. I thought you were in Chicago."

"I was in Chicago," he said. "Please listen."

"How do I know you weren't in Chicago with some other girl?"

"Allie, that's crazy."

"I saw you with my own eyes."

He shoved his hand through his thick preppy hair. "I'm buying horses and I have a couple that are for sale. They have done good work and now should be given homes where they can be out to pasture."

"What does that have to do with anything?"

"I had a buyer for the horses but he wanted to see them. So I flew him up on the company jet."

"Why didn't I see this buyer?"

"Most likely because he was looking at the horses. Victoria came into the stables and pulled me aside."

"So you could kiss her."

"She kissed me."

"You kissed her back."

"Allie—"

"Why didn't you text me that you were coming? We could have gotten lunch or at the very least I could have been the one kissing you."

"I know how busy you are with the McMurphy and we were only here for two hours."

"So you flew a buyer up here, looked at horses, kissed my cousin, and flew back. All in too short a time to tell me you were coming."

"I know it sounds ridiculous," he said.

"And."

"And I'm sorry," he said. "It won't happen again."

"No, it won't because I'm pretty sure we're over."

"Allie, I don't want us to be over."

"What did Tori want with you anyway?"

"She's investigating Barbara Smart's murder and she had a death threat."

"Why tell you? Why not go to Rex?"

"She doesn't trust Rex after he arrested her."

"So she had a death threat and wanted you to run to save her." I hated the indignation in the tone of my voice.

"She wanted to know if I knew who might have figured out she was investigating Barbara's murder."

"Why would you know something like that?"

"Because I hear things," he said. "It's a small island. I know that you are investigating who broke into the Butterfly House. I know you found diamonds in the packing."

"That means everyone knows I was the one who found diamonds in the packing."

"Yes," Trent said. "It's another reason I came back. I don't want to see you get hurt."

"But I'm no longer investigating Barbara's murder," I said. "And I didn't get a death threat. So don't change the subject on me. You were kissing Tori—"

"She kissed me."

"Because she had a death threat?"

"Because I sent a locksmith out to change the locks on her cottage."

"What is my boyfriend doing sending a locksmith out to another woman's house? Did Tori ask for that?"

"No, she didn't have to. She's my friend, Allie."

"A friend you kiss. How many such friends do you have? Here I was thinking I was the only one. But I guess I was wrong."

"It was a thank you," he said. "That's all."

"Nice thank you."

"It didn't mean anything."

"I'm sorry if I'm not ready to accept that just yet."

He frowned and pushed the flowers at me. "I don't know what more I can do to satisfy you."

"Give me time," I said. "Time to work things out."

"Just know while you're taking this time, Allie, that I only have eyes for you."

"And my cousin."

"Who's my childhood friend."

"You mean first love."

"We aren't getting anywhere." He tugged on his hair. "Just take the flowers." He pressed them against me and placed a kiss on my cheek. "Think of me when you look at them." He let go and I grabbed them before they could fall to my feet. "I'm not going anywhere until you know how much you mean to me."

"You can't camp out at my doorstep."

"No, but I won't be leaving the island," he said. "I don't care about business. It means nothing if I lose you."

I felt he was being overdramatic. I lifted the corner of my mouth in disbelief. "Please just give me some time. Okay? I can't unsee you kissing Tori."

"Tori kissed me."

"You kissed her back." It was my turn to sigh. "Good-bye, Trent."

"I'll call you tomorrow."

"Don't be too surprised if I don't answer."

"Allie?"

"Frances is marrying Douglas," I said. "I'm going to be busy."

"Wait, why wasn't I invited? Or Paige or my mom?"

"It's very small," I said. "I'm in the wedding party so if I brought you as my plus one, you would spend a lot of time alone. Besides you've been off the island a lot lately, I didn't think you had the time."

"Oh, that's not fair."

"Isn't it? And Paige and your mom are off the

island this week as well. I checked with your housekeeper. Frances didn't want you all to feel obligated to send a present. In fact, she has asked for no presents, only our presence."

"She can't have my presence if I don't know about it."

"I think it's best if you and Tori stay away. This is Frances's day. I don't want any drama."

"Fine."

"Good."

"Good night, Allie." He turned and went down the stairs, leaving me in the soft starlight with a bouquet of flowers in my hand wondering who to believe.

Chapter 19

The next morning, I made extra batches of fudge and canceled the demonstrations. This was one day I would take off and devote to my friends. Jenn and I met Frances and Maggs at the Island Salon for manicures, pedicures, and to have our hair done.

"I heard that you and Trent are on the outs because he kissed your cousin Victoria," Sally Jenkins said as she started my manicure.

"Let's not talk about that today, okay?" I said. "It's Frances's big day."

"Got it." She sent me an exaggerated wink.

I tried hard not to let her see me roll my eyes. "Frances, Jenn has everything setting up in the park by four PM. That gives us a couple of hours to get gussied up and then Jenn and I will escort you out to the park in a special carriage. The men will be there a few minutes before us and will be up front."

"Maybe we should have had a rehearsal," Frances fretted.

"We didn't need one," Jenn reminded her. "It's very simple. You've done this before. There is a small, short aisle. I'll walk down, then Allie, then Maggs, and you. You will stand beside Douglas and the preacher will say a few words. Do you have your vows ready?"

"I do," Frances said and blushed. "Do you want to hear them?"

"Yes," I said.

Frances opened her mouth to give us her vows when the door to the salon opened and Rex came in. He took his hat off and came straight over to me. "Excuse me, ladies, I need to talk to Allie."

"What is it?" I asked.

"I know you all are prepping for the wedding, but I have some bad news."

"Now you're scaring me."

"Your cousin Victoria is missing," he said. "She was supposed to meet Irene Hammerstein for coffee. When she didn't show, Irene contacted her mother and her mother called the police. Brent went over to your uncle's cabin. The door was wide open and it looks as if there was a struggle."

"I don't understand," I said, stunned. My toenails were done and drying. We were only on the first layer of polish on my fingers. I pulled my hands away and stood. "Tori is missing?"

"We believe she's missing," Rex said. "I'm sorry, but I have to ask you some questions."

"Of course," I said and sat back down.

"Did you want to go somewhere private?"

"No." I shook my head. "There isn't anything you could ask that Frances, Maggs, and Jenn couldn't hear." I looked at Sally. "Sally, could you get us all a cup of coffee?"

"Oh, right." She got up and went around the corner to the coffee station there.

"Ask away."

"When was the last time you saw Victoria?"

"Two days ago," I said. "She came into the McMurphy but I told her to get out."

"Why?"

"I saw her kissing Trent in the stable," I said and felt my chest tighten in anger over the memory. "I haven't seen her since. Why do you suspect she's missing?"

"Her mother called me to say she missed her daily phone call and Irene said she missed an appointment. I sent Brent over to check on the house and the door was wide open. Did she mention leaving the island?"

"No," I said. "Like I said, we really didn't talk. Did you find her suitcase? She said something about the power to the cabin being out and she spent the night at our place the night you wrongly arrested her for assault."

"So she's at the McMurphy?"

"No." I shook my head. "She blamed me for getting her arrested twice and stormed out. The next time I saw her she was kissing Trent. The last time I saw her she tried to talk to me about the kiss and I kicked her out."

"She said something about staying with a friend," Jenn said.

Rex looked at Jenn. "When?"

"When she took her suitcase and left the McMurphy she said she was going to stay with friends. Maybe she's still with one of them."

"I've talked to all of her friends," Rex said. "No one's seen her."

"Maybe she left the island because you keep arresting her," I said.

"I told her she wasn't to leave until I figured out who killed Barbara."

"You mean until you had enough evidence to really arrest her," I said.

"Until I had enough evidence to exclude her," Rex said. His hands played with the brim of his hat. "I don't think she did it, but I can't have people talking about my letting her go back to California without proving she was innocent."

"I thought you were innocent until proven guilty."

"Not in the court of public opinion," Rex said. "I asked her to stick around. Besides, she was working on putting together that fund-raiser for the Butterfly House."

I chewed on my bottom lip. "You think something bad has happened to her?"

"At this point I'm just looking for her. But things aren't looking good."

"Trent told me that Tori was investigating Barbara's murder," I said. "Do you know if that was true? Is that why you suspect she is missing and hasn't just left?"

"She told me she was," Rex confirmed. "She's a lot like you, Allie."

"Except it seems she has better connections in the community," I groused. Then a thought came to mind and I glanced at Rex with horror. I swallowed hard. "Trent said that Tori was thanking him for having his locksmith go over and change the locks on the cottage."

"Why would she need to have the locks changed?" Frances asked.

"Because Tori had a death threat," I said, looking from Frances to Rex. "This is bad. This is very bad."

"I have one more question for you, Allie," Rex said.

"What?"

"Where were you yesterday afternoon?"

"I was making fudge."

"Do you have witnesses to prove it?"

"What is this, Rex? Do you think I would threaten and hurt my own cousin?"

"Everyone knew you were hopping mad, Allie. I have to rule you out."

"You can rule her out," Frances said and raised her chin. "She was with me."

"What do you know about that death threat?" Jenn asked. "If Victoria is like Allie, she kept investigating, threat or no threat. Do you have any idea who threatened her?"

"No," Rex said. "I had no idea she was threatened."

"Talk to Trent," I said. "He can tell you what Tori told him. He's on the island now."

"I'll do that," Rex said. He paused and looked at Frances. "I'm sorry, Frances, but I can't make the wedding. With Victoria missing, every minute counts. Ladies, don't go anywhere until this is worked out."

"I fully understand," Frances said. "I'll talk to Douglas." She picked up her cell phone and looked at me and Jenn. "We can postpone this thing until Victoria is found safe."

Maggs patted Frances's hand. We all knew what a sacrifice this was for her and Mr. Devaney.

"Thank you, Frances," Rex said. "Stay safe, ladies. Don't go anywhere alone until we figure this thing out. Okay?"

"We won't," Jenn said.

Rex put on his hat and walked out.

"I'm so glad you said that," I said as Sally walked back in with coffees on a tray. "Sally, we're postponing the wedding."

"I understand," Sally said. "We can finish your nails and do your hair after you find Victoria."

I sent her a smile and paid her for the work she had done, along with a big tip. "If you hear anything about Victoria, don't hesitate to give me a call."

"I won't, dear," Sally said. "Go find her."

We gathered up our stuff as Frances got off the phone with Mr. Devaney. "Douglas agrees that we must find Victoria."

"I'm glad," I said. "I know he didn't want to wait this long."

"He's a good man," Frances said. "He'll wait as long as it takes." The two older women walked ahead of Jenn and me.

"What's the plan?" Jenn asked. "I can call and

postpone all the vendors, but we really need to find Victoria."

"Let's go to the cottage and see if we can figure out what happened," I said. "We need to trace Victoria's steps, talk to whomever she talked to, and see what leads she dug up."

"Find the leads, catch the killer," Jenn said.

"Find Victoria," I said. "Before it's too late."

Chapter 20

The cottage looked much different with police inside than it did when I picked up Tori's clothes that first day. The sheets were off all the furniture, which was worn with love and reminded me of family gatherings. In the summer I used to come to the cottage to play with Victoria when I stayed with Grammy Alice and Papa Liam. We would play dolls in her bedroom.

"You can't be in here," Officer Lasko said when we entered the house. The cottage kitchen was clean. There were dishes in the drying rack. It was obvious that Tori had made herself at home over the last week.

"This is my uncle's house," I said. "He asked me to look inside." I had called my aunt and uncle on the way over. They were on their way to the island and asked that I do my best to find Victoria.

"This is an active crime scene."

Shane stepped out of the bedroom with his evidence collection kit in his hand. "Allie, Jenn, what are you doing here?"

"Tori's parents asked us to come here and keep on top of the investigation," I said. "Have you found anything?"

"Her suitcase is here," Shane said. "I don't think she went missing on purpose."

"So she wasn't staying with friends," Jenn said.

"Why would she stay with friends?" Shane asked.

"She told us the power was out," I said.

"I noticed that," Shane said and flipped the kitchen light switch on and off. "I thought she didn't have it turned on. There are candles in the bedroom and candles in the kitchen."

I noticed that he was right. Tori had been using candles to see when it was dark. That would make it easier for someone to surprise her. I frowned. "She had power when I came that day to get her clothes." I went outside.

"What are you doing?" Officer Lasko followed me out.

"Checking something," I said and went to the side of the cottage where the power entered the home. Sure enough, the wires were cut. I showed the officer without touching the dangling hot wire. "Looks like someone deliberately cut her power."

"Why didn't Victoria notice this?" Officer Lasko asked me.

"I don't know," I said. "Maybe because she didn't think that anyone on the island would do such a thing."

Officer Lasko scowled at me. "It's because she's local."

"And I'm not," I said. "I get it. Is that why you don't like me?"

"No," she said and crossed her arms. "I don't like you because you are a nosy busybody who doesn't leave things to the professionals. You didn't spend eight weeks at police boot camp. What makes you think you are better at solving things than we are?"

"I don't," I said. "I'm only trying to help."

"The best way for you to help is to stay out of things."

"If I had, you wouldn't have checked to see if anyone cut the wires to the cottage," I pointed out. "Was the door broken into?"

"No," Officer Lasko said as I went around to the door to check. The new lock was shiny and solid. No one had broken it or crashed the door in. I frowned. How had they gotten in?

"Shane says they think she let her kidnappers in," Jenn said as she stepped out of the house. "That means she knew and trusted whoever took her."

"So it was someone she knew."

"That's the theory," Jenn said.

"Someone cut the wires to the power," I said. "Let's walk the perimeter and see if maybe they went in through the windows."

I started around the opposite side of the cottage from where Officer Lasko watched over the cut wires. The windows all seemed locked up tight.

"Shane says there's no evidence that anyone forcibly opened a window."

"Yes, but without power, my guess is that Tori

slept with the window open to let the lake breeze in to cool off at night."

We walked past the first bedroom to the bathroom where a transom window was half cracked but up at the six foot mark it would have been difficult to squeeze through. Next was her bedroom in the back. It had windows on two sides. I tried the first and it pulled right up. "She had them both open," I said and went over to the other wall and opened the window. "It made a nice cross breeze over the bed."

"I bet she thought she was safe with the screens." Jenn pointed to the screens, which were popped out and set beside the house.

"Why didn't the police see this?" I asked.

"We haven't gotten that far is all," Brent said as he came toward us. "Allie, you have to give us time. We couldn't come out and check until we confirmed that Tori was missing."

"So this is a missing persons case."

"Yes," he said. "Rex told us that you said Tori had a death threat."

"That's what Trent told me," I said. "She had the locks changed."

Jenn frowned. "Why would she have the locks changed and then sleep with the windows open? It doesn't make sense."

"You're right," I said. "I know I would sleep with the windows closed and locked—heat or no heat, if I was worried enough to change the locks."

"This might be a decoy," Brent said. "Someone may want us to think that Jenn was kidnapped through the window."

"Why?" I asked.

"To cover up that she let them in through the front," Rex said. "Allie, I told you to stay out of this."

"I'm sorry, but you brought me into it when you came to see me. I called Tori's parents. They are on their way."

"I know," Rex said. "Allie, I'm going to ask you to leave. This is police business and I don't want to have to arrest you for impeding an investigation."

"Fine."

"Good."

"Come on, Jenn," I said and threaded my arm through hers. "Let's go home."

Jenn let me pull her away out of reach of the police. "You're going to give up just like that?"

"Please," I said. "You know me better than that."

Jenn grinned. "So where to now?"

"Well," I said, "Let's backtrack. Rex said Tori was supposed to meet Irene Hammerstein and didn't."

"Okay."

"I happen to know that Blake Gilmore has a mahjong group that meets on Monday nights. I happen to know they were meeting tonight instead of Monday to give Barbara a bit of a wake. We were invited but weren't going because of the wedding. Maybe we should go now—someone in the group might know something."

Jenn looked at her watch. It was seven PM. "I say we call Blake and see if we can't meet with the group."

I thought about the time. Frances and Douglas

were supposed to be getting married right now. But the flowers were in cool storage in the basement of the McMurphy and everything was put on hold. My heart squeezed. If Tori went missing on purpose I just might have to hurt her myself.

"I'll call."

The phone call was well received. Irene had told the group that Tori was missing and they were eager to help in any way they could. Jenn and I showed up to find the ladies gathered around Blake's kitchen table sipping margaritas. Their mood was somber. They were remembering things about Barbara. Mourning the loss of a friend was difficult. Right now, I didn't want to think about mourning my cousin.

"Welcome, girls," Blake said. "Can I get you a drink?"

"I'll take a margarita," Jenn said.

"Water is good for me," I said. I wanted to keep a clear mind when it came to finding Victoria.

"Water and a margarita coming up," Blake said.

We took our seats around the table. "I'm sorry your cousin is missing," Irene said. "Do they suspect foul play?"

"I'm afraid so," I said. "The power to her cabin was purposefully cut and her suitcase is still in the bedroom."

"No one leaves without their suitcase," Wanda Sikes said. "Still it seems strange that it would be connected to Barbara's murder."

"I know," I said. "I think it may be connected but Rex is still on the fence."

"Why do you think it's connected?" Blake came out of the kitchen with my ice water and Jenn's drink in her hands. She put them down in front of us.

"Because Trent told me that Tori received a death threat. He sent a locksmith out to change the locks on the cabin."

"Oh, probably because everyone knew where the spare key was," Blake said. "We all know now how easy it is to copy a key, but in her case they didn't even need to copy it to get in."

"I know Tori was investigating Barbara's murder. Did she share her death threat with any of you?"

"She told me that someone tacked a note to her door," Irene said. "The door was left open with the spare key in the lock and the note was scrawled on the door."

"Creepy," Jenn said.

"What exactly did the note say? Do you know?"

"Tori told me it said to stop investigating or she would be the next person to end up dead."

"Yikes," I said. "No wonder Trent had her locks changed."

"Was she kidnapped?" Blake asked. "Because that would mean a change in the way the killer operated."

"Her bedroom windows were left open and the screens on the ground," I said. "Someone wanted it to look like a kidnapping, but no ransom demands have been made yet."

"She had to have gotten too close to the killer," Blake said. "Maybe she's in hiding."

"I certainly hope not," I said. "Her parents and I have put our lives on hold for her."

"What can you ladies tell us about what Victoria asked and perhaps what she found out?"

"Victoria was asking about Barbara's affairs," Irene said.

"What kind of affairs?" I asked.

"Her lovers," Wanda said. "Barbara had several lovers." She said the word with disgust in her tone.

"You didn't like her having lovers?"

"Barbara slept with men for many reasons," Irene said. "One was to blackmail them. We knew what she was doing, but couldn't prove she ever got anything more than presents from the men."

"It was one of those secrets that everyone knew but no one could prove," Blake said. "Barbara liked the attention."

"If everyone knew that she had the propensity to blackmail her lovers, why would any of the men sleep with her?"

"Barbara had a magnetic personality," Irene said. "Men couldn't help themselves."

"Are you implying that she could make them do things they didn't want to do?"

"The men certainly believed it," Wanda said. "It was not one of Barbara's best traits."

"Did she brag about her conquests?"

"Yes," Wanda said. "She thought it was hilarious how easy it was to seduce anyone's husband or lover."

"No one was safe but the mahjong group," Irene

said. "Since we knew her secrets, she swore never to go after our husbands."

"What would you do if she did?" I had to ask.

"She never did," Wanda said. "She knew we would kick her out of the group and she would lose the only friends she had left on the island."

"Barbara was a pathological liar," Blake said. "But my husband is dead. Irene's is deaf, and Wanda's is too busy to fall for Barbara's tricks."

"Mine is too smart to fall for anything Barbara said," Paula Abbot said.

"Can I ask why you remained friends if she was so bad?"

"Entertainment," Irene said. "Our lives are rather boring. We behave in all the proper ways. But not Barbara. She was always ready to rebel. Breaking the social rules was her way of staying young, I guess."

"So you kept her in the group for entertainment?"

"And to keep an eye on her," Wanda said. "Trust me, the last thing you wanted was to make an enemy out of Barbara. If you think it was bad that she took lovers and then blackmailed them, you should see what she did when someone crossed her."

I looked at Jenn and she looked at me. "She had dirt on each of you ladies, didn't she?" It was a statement not a question.

There was a moment of silence as everyone avoided looking at each other.

"She had dirt on a lot of people," Paula piped

up. "It was a shock when she was killed, but not too much of a surprise."

"Do you think Tori figured out who all Barbara was blackmailing?" I asked.

"Maybe," Blake said. "But it could be anyone on the island. Barbara's reach was far."

"Who all was she blackmailing?" Jenn asked.

"There were so many over the years that it could be anyone who attended the funeral," Irene said and sipped her drink. "I think we were all there to ensure the old witch was really dead and buried."

"I don't understand," I said. "Why would so many people have done something that Barbara could blackmail them for?"

"Because she manipulated things," Wanda said. "She made it seem as if things were all aboveboard and you would do her a favor or listen to her advice and then bam! She would show you the errors of your ways and hold it over you. She was a master manipulator."

"Why are you all telling me this now and not before?"

"It didn't matter before," Irene said. "But now that Victoria is missing, it matters a great deal."

"One final thing," I said and turned to Blake. "Does Rex have any leads as to who was smuggling diamonds through the Butterfly House?"

"Not that we know of," Blake said. "With Dan's murder that lead has grown cold."

"Do you think somehow the two murders are related?" Wanda asked.

"Most likely," I said and stood. "Thank you, ladies, for your time."

"Oh, Allie," Blake said. "Do be careful. I understand Sean Grady is out on bail."

"I'll keep an eye open," I said.

Jenn and I walked away from the house in silence.

"Do you think Sean Grady kidnapped Victoria?" Jenn asked.

"My guess would be that Rex would have checked out Sean first." I stuck my hands in the pockets of my light jacket. "If Barbara had dirt on almost everyone on the island, that means our suspect pool is huge."

"Not really," Jenn said thoughtfully. "Only the truly desperate would risk murdering Dan and taking Tori."

"You think the two are connected?"

"It's the only thing that makes sense. Whoever killed Barbara killed Dan, and Tori was close to figuring that out, so they took her as well."

My heart sunk. "That means that Tori could be dead."

"I didn't want to think so, but yes," Jenn said. "It most likely does."

We walked the rest of the way to the McMurphy in silence. What should have been a joyous day had just turned into a scary, somber one.

Chapter 21

"We need a murder board," Jenn suggested the next morning.

I had just finished the morning fudges and was getting ready to take Mal out for her walk. "I don't know. The last time we did that it made things worse."

"Our mistake was keeping it in the lobby," Jenn said. "This time we'll keep it in the apartment."

"Fine," I said with a sigh. "I gave Frances the morning off. She wasn't feeling well. I think she's taking Tori's disappearance and her wedding postponement hard."

"Mr. Devaney's taking it hard as well. He's usually grumpy but I've never seen him this grumpy."

"Do you blame them?" I asked. Mal had her leash on and was tugging me toward the back door. "We'll talk when I get back."

"I'll handle the front desk."

"Thanks," I said and let Mal pull me down the hall and out the back door. "See you in a bit."

We stepped out into the early sunlight. Mr. Beecher was walking toward us. He was a regular in the alleyway behind the McMurphy. Mal rushed to her small patch of green grass on the opposite side of the alley to do her business.

"Hello, Mr. Beecher. How are you today?"

"I'm doing well," he said and smiled. Mr. Beecher was retired but always dressed well in a sport coat, dress shirt, and slacks. Sometimes he even wore a vest and he always wore a bow tie. He was old and swore the morning walks were the only things that kept him going. "I heard about your cousin. I'm terribly sorry."

"I'm not counting her out yet," I said. "She's a lot like me. We are strong."

He nodded. "I agree."

"You didn't happen to have seen her recently, did you?" I asked as Mal finished her business and came over to sit in front of Mr. Beecher and raise a paw in greeting.

Mr. Beecher smiled and shook her paw then slipped her a small treat. Since I got Mal earlier this season, he had begun to carry little dog treats in the pocket of his suit coat. "The last I saw of her she was talking to Sean Grady. It was on the other side of the police station out of view of most, but I like to cut through there on my way. There are a lot less tourists in the back ways."

"She was talking to Sean? Was this before or after he was arrested?"

"After," Mr. Beecher said. "I believe it was right after Sean got out of jail on bail."

"What kind of conversation were they having?" I asked. "Did they look like they were fighting?"

"No," he said. "If anything, it looked as if Sean was asking Victoria for help. He had his hat in hand, so to speak."

"What could Victoria do to help?" I asked out loud.

"That's a good question," Mr. Beecher said. "I'm sorry, I don't know the answer."

"Well, thanks for the information," I said. "Come on, Mal, we have more walking to do. Have a great day, Mr. Beecher."

"Thanks, dear," he said. "Try to stay safe."

"I will." But I had made the decision to go see Sean Grady. He may have been the last person to see Victoria. If so, I needed to know what they were talking about.

I sent a text to Jenn a moment before I knocked on Sean Grady's apartment door. The man lived above the carriage house next to his grandmother's home. The stairs up to the door creaked and moaned as Mal and I climbed them. I knocked on the door.

Sean opened it a crack. "What do you want?"

"I wanted to talk to you about my cousin, Victoria," I said. Mal wiggled her nose between the space of the open door and sniffed. "She's missing and Mr. Beecher told me you might have been the last person to see her."

"I don't know anything," he said. "Go away."

He tried to shut the door, but I got my foot under Mal and kept it open. "Look, I'm not here to accuse you of doing anything to Victoria. I just need to know what you talked about."

He scowled at me. "Why should I tell you? You're the one who got me arrested in the first place."

"I didn't make you steal anything."

"Go away!"

"Sean, this is important. Tori is missing. I don't want to have to go to Rex and tell him that you were the last one to see her. He will haul you back in and this time you won't get bailed out."

"Darn it," he grumbled and opened the door.

Mal sat and I refused to go in. "I know she was investigating Barbara's murder. What did she ask you?"

"She figured out I stole the keys to the Butterfly House for someone else."

"And you decided to lift Mrs. Gilmore's house keys while you were at it?"

He shrugged. "It was too easy. Doc says I got a compulsion."

"Who hired you to steal the keys to the Butterfly House?"

"That Dan did," he said. "The one that went and got himself killed."

"Aren't you afraid that whoever killed Dan would kill you?"

"Naw," Sean said. "I don't know who Dan was working with. Besides, the cops got eyes on me." He nodded to the right and I turned to see Rex come storming up the sidewalk. "You best go."

"Yeah, thanks for the info."

Sean closed his door and Mal and I stepped off the porch just as Rex got to us. "What do you think you're doing?"

"I'm walking Mal," I said.

"That's not what I mean and we both know it." He looked like he wanted to shake me and kiss me at the same time.

"I'm fine," I said. "He didn't threaten me. He also didn't take Victoria."

"Of course he didn't," Rex said. "He was in my custody when Tori was taken."

"But he was seen talking to her."

"Who saw them?"

"Mr. Beecher," I said and raised my chin. "So I came by to see what they talked about."

"Tori was investigating Barbara's murder," we both said at the same time.

Rex made a face and walked me down the sidewalk. Mal jumped up on him, but when he didn't pet her, she decided to lead the way. "Tori is missing," Rex said. "She could be dead like Dan."

"She's not dead," I said. "She can't be dead."

"She could be dead because she was investigating. I need you to promise me that you will stop investigating right now."

"I can't."

He stopped and put his hands on my forearms and squeezed to emphasize his words. "I can't have you dying on me."

"Why not?" I whispered.

There was a thick tension in the air. I searched his face. He opened his mouth to tell me something, and then I saw the moment he changed his mind. "I've seen enough murder on the island. I don't want to see any more."

I swallowed as he let go of me. Mal jumped up on him again. He reached down and gave her an absent pat on the head as if he was collecting himself.

"Tori isn't dead," I said. "I know she isn't. We need to find her."

"Let me and my guys do that," he said through gritted teeth. "We're trained for it. Promise me, Allie."

"I promise."

"There's a lot going on. I'll walk you back to the McMurphy."

"Thanks," I said. We walked in silence for a moment. The streets were full of tourists. "Frances and Douglas were supposed to be married now."

"I know." He ran a hand over his shaved head. "Trust me, the last thing I wanted was to keep those two apart."

"They are a match made in heaven, aren't they?"

"Yeah," he said.

"Sean said he told Tori it was Dan who hired him to steal the keys to the Butterfly House. How come Dan didn't make a copy of his own?"

"That's a good question. I figured Dan and his accomplice have been smuggling diamonds in for a while now. Dan wasn't the brightest."

"He didn't expect to be fired."

"So he didn't think to make a copy."

"Exactly, and I think he got killed over it."

"You think they killed Dan first?"

"The coroner concluded that he was killed at least a day before Barbara was murdered."

"So whoever killed Dan then tossed the Butterfly House looking for the diamonds. Most likely Barbara interrupted them and they murdered her as well."

"And now you found the diamonds," Rex said. "Whoever killed Dan and Barbara has to be sweating out the loss of over a million dollars in diamonds. People don't export them just to hang on to them. Most likely they were to make a payment for a debt."

"Some debt," I said as we turned down the alley toward the McMurphy. "Sounds like something out of a movie."

"Whoever needed those diamonds is not happy right now," Rex said. "They know you found them. Like I said, I don't want you to go out alone for a while."

We walked up to find Trent leaning against the banister of my staircase.

"Hello, Manning," Trent said and didn't look too happy. Mal was happy to see Trent and jumped up.

"Jessop," Rex said with a nod. "I'll leave you here," he said to me. "I meant what I said about not going out alone."

"I understand."

"Good-bye." He put on his hat and walked off.

"What did he mean by that?" Trent asked.

"Tori is missing."

"I heard. I came as fast as I could but you weren't here."

"I took Mal for her walk," I said and climbed my stairs. Trent followed behind us.

"How did you end up with Rex?"

I turned and looked over my shoulder. "Are you jealous?"

"Should I be?"

"No." I unlocked my door and let Mal in, unhooking her leash so she could run inside and get water. "It's not like you and Tori."

"I told you she was thanking me."

"Well, changing the locks didn't help keep her safe." I chewed on the inside of my cheek, suddenly aware of how upset I was. I held the door with my hands and didn't ask Trent inside.

"Allie—"

"I'm not ready, Trent. I need to see that Tori is safe. I think you should go."

"I'm not going far," he said. "I heard Rex tell you not to go out alone."

"Good-bye, Trent."

"Good-bye, Allie."

I closed the door and leaned against it. Jenn stood on the other side of the bar. "What was that all about?"

I sighed and put on a kettle for tea. "I went to see Sean Grady."

"That's what your text said. Are you nuts?"

"No," I said. "Mal and I ran into Mr. Beecher in the alley. He told me he saw Tori talking to Sean. So I wanted to know if Sean could tell me anything that would help with her disappearance."

"That was brave."

I shrugged and got down mugs and pulled out tea. "I don't think Sean hurt anyone. He was too cautious in his robberies. I don't think he was the one who tossed the Butterfly House and hurt Barbara. So I didn't think he'd do more than close the door in my face. Which he tried to do, but Mal helped."

"How?" Jenn asked, watching me pour hot water into the mugs and then pushing her favorite tea toward her.

"She got between his door and the jam enough I could get my foot in there so he couldn't close the door."

"Please tell me you didn't go inside his home."

"I didn't go inside," I said.

Jenn out a long breath. "What did you find out?"

"That Dan was the one who hired Sean to make a copy of the key."

"That's it?"

"Rex found me and walked me home after that. He is worried that the killer might be enraged about my finding the diamonds and come after me next. So he wants me not to be alone."

"Sounds reasonable to me," Jenn said. "Especially with Tori missing."

"I can't just sit here and make fudge while my cousin is missing."

"I know," Jenn said. "We can go out together tomorrow morning. I have a plan."

"What's the plan?"

"To go to the senior center," Jenn said. "If anyone knows anything. It's the seniors."

"True." I smiled and saluted her with my mug. "Here's to a good plan."

"Here, here," Jenn said and clinked mugs. We both sipped. "Now," she said as she put down her mug, "tell me what is going on with you and Trent and Rex . . ."

I sighed. "It's complicated."

Brown Sugar Cinnamon Pecan Fudge

Ingredients

14 oz. can sweetened condensed milk
1 cup of butter
2 cups of brown sugar
2 cups of toasted pecans
1 tsp cinnamon

Directions

Pour sweetened condensed milk, butter, and brown sugar in microwave-proof bowl. Microwave on high for 10 minutes, stopping every 2 minutes to stir. Remove and let mixture cool slightly. Mix with electric beaters for 5 minutes. Stir in pecans and cinnamon until well blended. Pour into buttered 8-inch square pan. Let cool 3 hours. Cut into 1 inch squares and enjoy!

Chapter 22

"Allie, are you okay?" Victoria's mother, June, said with a slight California accent. She smothered me in a hug and a cloud of Chanel No. 5.

"Yes, I'm fine," I said. "I'm sorry we have to see each other under these circumstances."

"Allie," Tori's father, Alex, gave me a quick hug. "What do you know about my little girl?"

It was the next day and we were at the police station. My uncle and aunt had insisted that they come to the station before they went anywhere. We were in Rex's office. They left their suitcases outside the door.

My uncle was a serious and imposing man. He stood six foot two and was well muscled. A former athlete, he was now retired from real estate. Today he wore a dress shirt and slacks that were wrinkled from travel.

My aunt, on the other hand, was soft, and rounded from age with champagne colored hair that was curled and hair sprayed to last through a hurricane. She came dressed in white capris and a blue silk blouse.

It seemed weird that she was Papa Liam's sister—but my aunt was fifteen years younger than my papa and she and Uncle Alex had had Victoria late in life.

"Rex Manning," Rex said and offered his hand to my uncle. "We spoke on the phone."

"Yes. Rex, didn't you go to school with Tori?"

"I did," Rex said. "Please have a seat."

"I'd rather stand," my uncle said. "We've been sitting a while now."

"Have you heard anything from Victoria?" June asked. She wrung her hands and tears welled up in her eyes.

I reached into my pocket and pulled out a small packet of tissues and handed it to her. She sent me a watery smile. "Thanks," she said. "My baby is out there somewhere and there's nothing I can do."

"We're doing all that we can," Rex said. "I've got my officers scouring the island. No one saw her getting on a ferry."

"But they could have taken her by plane," Alex said.

"I've interviewed the people at the airport. That seems like a dead end as well," Rex said calmly. He stood. "Can I get you some water or coffee?"

"Water would be great," Aunt June said.

Rex left the office, allowing my aunt and uncle time to collect themselves. Uncle Alex put his arm around Aunt June. She turned to him with a sob and he held her tight.

"I'm so sorry," I said. "I didn't realize anything was wrong. Tori and I . . . well, we've not been exactly speaking."

My aunt turned toward me and dabbed at her tears. "Yes, Victoria told me that you were the one who found her as she tried to resuscitate that poor dead woman."

"I did," I said. "Please know that no matter what Tori thinks, I never once thought she would harm Barbara."

"She doesn't think you do," Uncle Alex says. "She told us that you let her stay with you when the power went out at the cabin."

"Unfortunately she only stayed one night," I said. "There was a break-in at the McMurphy. Tori was very brave and helped me catch the thief."

"I'm the one who arrested her for the incident," Rex said. He handed my aunt June a glass of water. "It was a misunderstanding. I saw her standing over a man with a knife to his throat. I did what every good cop does. I neutralized the situation and asked questions after."

"Tori blamed me," I said. "And I blame me as well. You see, I thought the man was a thief and gave him the opportunity to copy my key."

"You what?" Rex said.

"I thought he would take the key to the hardware store and make a copy like he did with the other keys," I said. "I had Mr. Devaney at the hardware store ready to catch him. But he didn't go to the hardware store."

"And you thought you were wrong," Rex said.

"I thought he suspected what I was up to," I

said. "Victoria told me it was a bad idea and she was right."

"I don't understand," Aunt June said.

"He copied the key with a 3D printer and broke in," I said. "Someone could have been badly hurt but Tori saved us and then Rex arrested her for it. She was hopping mad and blamed me." I swallowed hard. "She took her things and stormed out."

"Victoria is a bit of a hothead," June admitted. "She gets it from her father."

Uncle Alex crossed his arms. "She gets her strength from me as well. I'm certain whoever has her is wishing they didn't."

"Someone has my baby," Aunt June wailed.

I took the water glass from her and she buried her head into Uncle Alex's shoulder.

I patted her back.

"I've backtracked her actions as best I can," Rex said. He leaned against his desk. "She must have gone back to the cabin. An investigation of the cabin showed us that someone cut the power. There was some sort of break-in and struggle. It's why we are sure she is missing."

"Why would anyone do that?" Uncle Alex said. "Everyone knew we kept a spare key outside."

"I told you we should have never done that!" Aunt June said and smacked him with the back of her hand.

"I think Tori had the locks changed," I said. "The last time I saw her she was talking to Trent Jessop and they kissed." I crossed my arms, still feeling vulnerable about it. "Trent told me that

Victoria came to him because she wasn't feeling safe. She had a death threat so Trent sent a guy over to change the locks at the cabin. Supposedly Tori was thanking him."

"Supposedly?" Uncle Alex repeated.

"I'm dating Trent. He told me the kiss was Tori thanking him."

Uncle Alex looked at me for a moment as if to contemplate whether I would have harmed Victoria.

Rex cleared his throat. "We believe she was investigating Barbara's murder when she got too close to the killer."

I raised my hands. "I haven't seen her since. I didn't know she was missing until Rex notified me."

"How long ago was that?"

"Sunday afternoon," Rex said. "Trust me, we haven't stopped searching. We know every hour counts."

"Oh please, please don't tell me they killed her. I couldn't take it."

"I don't think they would," I said. "Everyone on the island loves Victoria. They wouldn't risk the wrath of the islanders."

"But they killed Barbara."

"We think it was unplanned. Barbara caught them in the act of vandalizing the Butterfly House and they must have fought. Whoever did it picked up a garden trowel and stabbed Barbara and then ran out."

"So what are they doing with Tori?"

"Do you think Victoria might be hiding some-where?" I had to ask.

Everyone looked at me as if I lost my mind. I shrugged. "She might be hiding from the killer."

"Why wouldn't she just come to me?" Rex asked.

"You arrested her twice," I pointed out.

"No," Aunt June said. "She would have called us. She wouldn't put us through this."

"What can we do?" Uncle Alex asked.

"I need a list of people and places Victoria might go. Anyone she may have told you she was talking to in the last week."

"I can do that," Aunt June said and took the pad of paper and pen from Rex's hand.

"I hope you'll both stay at the McMurphy," I said. "I've got a room on the second floor waiting for you and can have your things brought over."

"We have the cabin," Uncle Alex said.

"It's still under investigation," Rex said. "I think it would be best if you stayed with Allie."

"Fine," Uncle Alex said.

"Thank you," Aunt June said.

"We're going to find her," I said and patted my aunt's hand. "Rex and his team are awesome."

"I have to believe that," Aunt June said. "She's my only baby."

"I'll see she gets home," Rex said. There was a promise in his tone, but I noted he didn't make a promise with his words.

* * *

Tori had been missing for more than forty-eight hours. They say in a murder investigation the first forty-eight hours are crucial. In missing persons, every hour counts. I called Sandy in to make fudge as I couldn't focus on fudge making. I had slept only a few hours last night and then badly.

Mal barked to be let out. I pulled on jeans, a T-shirt and jacket and took her out into the alley. The sun was breaking over the horizon. There was a note taped to my back door.

Mal did her business and I took the note down and read it.

> *"Return the diamonds if you want to see your cousin alive."*

A chill went down my spine. I hurried back inside and locked the door. Whoever did this could have been out there while I was out with Mal. Stupid of me to go alone. It was habit really.

I called Rex.

"Yeah, Manning" He sounded as if I woke him up. I looked at the kitchen clock; it was five AM.

"Rex, it's Allie."

"Are you okay?"

"Yes and no," I said. "Someone left a ransom note taped to my back door."

"I'll be right there," he said.

"I'll put on the coffee," I agreed.

Jenn wandered into the kitchen in her pajamas, her hair sticking up and her eyes bleary. "What's going on?"

"Someone left a ransom note on the back door,"

I said and pointed to the note lying flat on the counter. "Don't touch it."

"Don't worry," Jenn said and treated the note as if it would bite her. "So Tori was officially kidnapped. Why did they wait so long to send a ransom note?"

"I don't know. Maybe the original intent had nothing to do with ransom. Either way, they want the diamonds back now," I said. "But I don't have them. Rex does."

"Whoever left the note has to know that."

"I know. It was in the paper that I turned the diamonds in."

Jenn pulled a mug out of the cabinet and poured herself coffee, interrupting the flow. "That means they know that you and Rex are friends. They're counting on you to get the diamonds back."

I got a phone call. Frowning, I saw that the caller was Trent. "Hello?"

"Allie," Trent said. "I got a ransom note for Tori."

"Wait, what?"

"Someone left a ransom note taped to my door this morning," Trent said. "They want two million dollars to see Tori again."

"That's not right. I got a ransom note as well asking for the diamonds."

"What diamonds?"

"The ones I found smuggled into the packaging at the Butterfly House. I thought you knew about them."

"Right. I remember now."

"So each of us got a ransom note. Why? Are

there two different people taking credit for Tori's disappearance? Or one person who thinks we aren't talking to each other?"

"I think we need to talk to Manning."

I frowned. "Yes, he's on his way here. I bet he'll want to see both notes and compare them. Does yours tell you where to send the money?"

"No."

"Mine doesn't tell me anything about where to send the diamonds, either. They must plan on more notes or a phone call."

"I'll be right over and bring my note," he said. "Don't answer the phone until they can set up a trace."

"Won't the kidnappers know we'd do that?"

"Sure, but maybe they think they can play divide and conquer. I'm going to head out now. Don't answer the phone unless it's me or Manning."

Trent hung up.

"What was that all about?" Jenn asked.

"Trent got a ransom note, too. He's coming over here to give it to Rex. Should we call Shane?"

There was a knock at the door and I peered out to see Rex standing on the deck with his hat in his hand. I opened the door. "Hey, come in."

"Good morning," he said. "Hello, Jenn."

"Hi, Rex."

"Tell me what happened."

"I took Mal out this morning and I noticed this note on my back door." I pointed at the note on the counter. "I pulled it off the door and put it here, then called you."

"So Tori has been kidnapped."

"Maybe," I said. "Weirdly, Trent just called. He got a ransom note, too."

"For Tori?" Rex narrowed his eyes and shook his head in disbelief.

"Yes, he's bringing it now. Maybe we can compare the handwriting."

There was a knock at the door and I opened it up to see Trent standing there. He looked gorgeous in a pale blue polo shirt and jeans. "Hey, Allie," he said and bent to give me a kiss. But I took a step back. He frowned.

"Rex is here to compare the notes," I said and opened the door wider. Trent came in. Jenn sent me a look like *Why did you brush off a kiss from your boyfriend?* I narrowed my eyes at her. She was supposed to be on my side about this thing. I was still mad at Trent for kissing Victoria. That didn't change just because she was missing.

I was aware of a weird tension in the room between the two men. It was subtle but odd. "You got a note?" Rex asked Trent.

"Yeah. This was left on my door." Trent pulled out his note. He had placed it in a plastic bag. Unlike my note, which was handwritten, his note was printed on a printer.

Rex frowned. "These don't look authentic," he said. "It looks as if someone is trying to scam you both."

"What if the people who killed Dan are the ones who took Tori?" Jenn asked. "It's not so far-fetched since they want the diamonds."

There was a knock at my front door. I went over

and peered out. My aunt and uncle stood in the hallway. I let them in.

"We heard you got a ransom note," Uncle Alex said.

"Wow, word spreads fast," I said. "Come on in. It seems I'm not the only one who got a ransom note. So it's a bit confusing."

"Who else would have gotten a note?" Aunt June asked. She blinked at Trent. "Hello, Trent. What brings you here so early?"

I glanced at my watch. It was eight AM already, which might be early to some, but for me it was midday. "Trent also got a ransom note."

"Why would Jessop get a note?" Uncle Alex asked.

"Good question," Rex said.

Trent cleared his throat. "I was helping Victoria with her investigation. Whoever left the note must have thought we were involved."

I hated how my gut twisted at Trent's admission. "Well you knew I wasn't the only one to see you two kissing."

Rex and Jenn sent Trent dirty looks.

"Nothing was going on between us," he said and put his hands up as if we were about to shoot him between the eyes. As much as I would like to, Rex was watching.

"Why didn't I know you were helping Tori with more than finding a locksmith?" I asked.

"Because Tori asked me not to tell you," Trent said. "I agreed because I didn't want you getting involved in yet another murder."

"I am already involved," I said and put my hands

on my hips. "You lied to me about why you were on the island and didn't tell me."

"No, I didn't lie," he said. "I did have a horse buyer who wanted to fly in to see my horses."

"You just skipped the part about helping Tori."

Trent didn't say anything.

"When was the last time you saw Tori?" Rex asked. He had his arms crossed over his chest and his legs spread wide as if to intimidate.

"The day after we kissed," he said. "She told me that Mrs. Gilmore's mahjong group knew something about Barbara that might have gotten her killed. She planned on confronting the ladies."

"She was gone the next morning," Rex said.

"We talked to the mahjong group," I said at the same time as Jenn. "Jinks," we both said again.

"What did they tell you?" Trent asked

"Nothing specific," I said.

"Just that Barbara blackmailed a lot of people," Jenn said.

"That she was a master manipulator and they weren't surprised that someone killed her," I said. "Maybe we should go back and find out if they talked to Tori."

"No one is talking to those ladies except me," Rex said. "Is that understood?"

"What about the ransoms?" June asked. "We don't have the diamonds or two million dollars."

"We need proof of life," Uncle Alex said.

"What you all need to do is sit tight and wait for further contact," Rex said. "I'll have the state police send out their negotiating team and wiretap your phones. In the meantime, my team and I will talk to the mahjong group. I recommend you all stay in the McMurphy. Trent, you have your phone on you in case they call?"

"Yes," Trent said.

"Anyone in this room who gets a call, let it go to voice mail until we can get the experts out here with the proper equipment. Do you understand?"

"I do," I said. Jenn, Trent, my aunt and uncle agreed.

"Good," Rex said and picked up the two ransom notes. "I will messenger these over to Shane's office in St. Ignace. He should be able to find any links between the two. If we have a copycat, I need to know sooner rather than later." Rex put on his hat.

"Wait," Uncle Alex said. "Shouldn't we be trying to raise the money? I mean even with proof of life, there's no guarantee they won't hurt our daughter if we don't give them what they want."

"I agree," Rex said, surprising me. "Let people know you are trying to raise the money. That way the killer will think you will meet their demands."

"And when we don't?"

"We'll cross that bridge when we come to it."

"I don't like it," my uncle said. "You are playing Russian roulette with my daughter's life."

"Tori already did that when she started to investigate. Now, stick to the plan. Do not deviate unless I tell you to. Is that understood?"

"Yes," we all said.

Rex left through the back door. Jenn looked from me to Trent to my aunt and uncle. "Who wants omelets?"

I wasn't hungry. Too many things could go terribly wrong. All I could do was hope and pray that, when we get proof of life, we got a picture of Tori holding a newspaper, not a picture of some cut-off body part.

Maybe I did watch too many crime shows on television . . .

Chapter 23

My phone didn't ring. It took four hours for the equipment to arrive and for the police to set it up. With all the coming and going, I figured whoever taped the note on my door had to know what we were doing.

I paced in my apartment. My Aunt June sat in a chair and twisted a tissue that she would use to dab at the tears that kept falling. Uncle Alex was in the office with Jenn contacting people about borrowing the two million dollars.

Trent went back to his place where similar equipment was being set up on both his cell phone and the house phone. Officer Brown was with me, Brent Pulaski was with Trent, and Rex continued to supervise the investigation into Tori's whereabouts.

Frances and Sandy ran the McMurphy and the fudge shop as if nothing unusual was happening. I felt as useless as a newborn baby. Whenever I was upset or worried, I made fudge. So I spent the time experimenting with new flavor combinations.

Bubblegum Fudge seemed happy. Jawbreaker flavored fudge was colorful even if it took forever to crush the jawbreakers into tiny pieces. I used a hammer to get my frustrations out.

Finally, finally the phone rang. The door to the apartment was left open and at the sound of the ringer, everyone came rushing in. I grabbed the phone and waited until the policeman pointed at me and picked up the land line.

"Hello, this is Allie. How can I help you?"

"If you want to see your cousin alive, you will give me my diamonds back." The voice was warped as if the person spoke through a machine.

"Who is this?"

"I want my diamonds or your cousin dies."

My aunt gasped. Officer Brown held up his hand to silence her.

"How do I know she's not already dead?" I asked as I followed the script. "Put her on the phone. I want to talk to her."

"No."

"Put her on the phone," I said again. "I can't do anything unless I know she's still alive."

"I've sent you a text."

My cell phone vibrated and I opened the text. There was a picture of Tori holding the Wednesday morning newspaper. It creeped me out that he had my cell phone number. "This is the morning news. How do I know she's still alive?"

"I want the diamonds," he said.

"I don't have them. I gave them to the police as evidence."

"You have two hours to get the diamonds. I'll call back with instructions on where to drop them."

"But the police—"

He hung up.

"Did you get that?" I asked.

"No," the man with the equipment said. "They hung up too soon."

"What about where they sent the text from?" I said. "Can you ping the cell tower and find out their location?"

"Not without a warrant, and even then there's only one cell tower on the island. All it would tell us is if they are on the island or off."

"This is so frustrating," I said.

"Let me see that picture," Uncle Alex said. I handed him my cell phone. Tori was sitting in a chair with her hands and feet bound, holding the paper with today's date circled.

"My poor baby!" Aunt June said and sobbed.

"If I get my hands on these guys . . ." Uncle Alex growled.

The call came over the police communicator that Trent received a call the same time I did. They sent him the same text picture and told him they would call him back in two hours to get the $2 million.

Fifteen minutes later we were huddled around my table. My aunt and uncle and my entire team looked to Rex on what to do next. "They are definitely acting in coordination," Rex said.

"Why two different demands to two different people?" I asked.

"I don't know," Rex said with a frown. "It's clear they have one agenda."

"Take the diamonds and the money and run," I said. "Clearly they know I would have access to the diamonds."

"And they know the Jessops have money," Uncle Alex said. "But why not contact June and me?"

"That is a very good question," Rex said. "Perhaps they are unaware that you are on the island."

"They most likely know we don't have the kind of money they are asking for," Aunt June said.

"What is going on?" I asked. "I thought you owned your own business in California."

"The economy is not what it was," Alex said. "I had to sell off a lot of our assets. All we have left is our home and our retirement and that doesn't add up to two million dollars. Not even close."

"So whoever the kidnappers are, they are aware of your financial situation," Rex said. "Who have you spoken to lately?"

"No one," Uncle Alex said.

Aunt June sniffed and dabbed at her eyes. "I spoke to Irene. We were talking about Barbara's tragic death and Irene told me that she had lost a lot of money investing in something that Barbara had told her was a sure thing. I told her I understood losing everything."

"Irene Hammerstein?" Rex asked and stood.

"Yes," Aunt June said.

"Sounds like she has a motive for murder," Rex said and moved to the door.

"But why kidnap my baby?"

"Victoria was meeting with Irene," I said. "She must have figured out that Irene had a motive to kill Barbara."

"If it is Irene then she has no reason to release Victoria safely," Jenn pointed out.

"Jenn!" Frances and I said at the same time.

Aunt June sobbed and turned into Uncle Alex's arms.

Jenn cringed. "I'm sorry," she said.

"We're going to do all we can to get her back safe," Rex said. "I'm headed over to Irene's house with a few men. You stay here and wait for the next call." Rex left us with Officer Charles Brown.

"I hate waiting," I said and paced. A thought occurred to me. "Aunt June, why don't you go into my bedroom and lie down? We have over an hour before they call back."

"They'll know you aren't going to the police station to get the diamonds," Uncle Alex pointed out.

"Jenn and I will head that way," I said. "Frances will stay here to answer the phone."

"What if they call on your cell phone?" Charles said.

"I won't pick up," I said. "Not until we're back here and I'm attached to the machines."

"But what if they hurt my baby because Allie doesn't pick up?" Aunt June said. She looked terrible, as if she would shatter into a million pieces at any time.

"Please go lie down," I said. "You aren't any good to her this way." I gave Uncle Alex a hard look and he took her by the arm.

"Come on," he said. "I'll stay with you."

They both went into my bedroom. I hooked Mal up to her leash, then looked at Officer Brown. "Can you let Rex know that I'm off to the police station to retrieve the diamonds?"

"You can't."

"The kidnappers don't have to know that."

"You think they are listening in to our radio conversations?"

"It wouldn't hurt to be cautious," I said. "I'll text Rex and let him know what is going on." My fingers flew over the keypad on my phone and I sent off the text. A moment later he sent the thumbs-up emoji in reply. "We're good to go."

"I'm going with you," Jenn said.

"We might as well go out the back," I said. "If they are watching they would know it is the quickest route."

We went out the door, down the stairs, and waited while Mal did her business in her favorite patch of grass. "I was thinking," I said low. "Maybe we can figure out where Tori is by what's around her in the picture."

"Even if we figure it out, how are we going to get there?" Jenn asked low. "We're supposed to be going to the police station."

"We go into the front door," I said, "and sneak out the back."

"Okay," Jenn said. "Let me see the picture."

We both looked at the photo. The room behind Victoria was dark, but it looked like it was paneled.

She sat in an old wooden chair and the floor was covered in a rag rug.

"That could be anywhere," Jenn said with exasperation.

"Looks like a remodeled basement," I said as Mal finished, kicked up the dirt, and came toward us. I used a poo bag to clean up after her and stuck it in the Dumpster before we headed toward the police station.

"Most of the cottages on the island have a basement," Jenn pointed out.

"Yes, but most are not finished. We need to figure out who has a finished basement."

"Do you think they'll hurt Tori?" Jenn asked. "I mean for real?"

"I don't know," I said. "If these are the same people who killed Dan and Barbara, then my guess is that they wouldn't think twice about another murder."

"Victoria must be terrified."

"I think she's probably angry," I said. "I know I would be. We have to find her."

"What we need is someone who has lived on the island long enough to know who might have a paneled basement."

"What about Liz?"

"Oh, she might know," Jenn said.

I texted Liz to meet us back behind the police station. She texted that she was on her way. Jenn and I made a show of entering the station and asking the policeman at the counter to release the diamonds to us.

"I can't do that and you know it," he said. His name tag said WILLIAMS.

"Just loan them to me," I said. "I'll bring them back once Rex figures out who the kidnappers are."

"I can't do it. They are locked up in the evidence vault. I don't have a key."

I leaned over the counter. "So let's pretend you do have a key," I said low. "In case the kidnappers are watching. Have me follow you to the back."

"Right," Officer Williams said. "Why don't you and Ms. Christensen follow me to the back? I'll see if I can't help in some way."

We followed him as he opened the door for us and led us through the offices to the evidence locker.

"Thanks," I said. "I know you can't give me the diamonds, but it needs to look like you did. The kidnappers may be watching us."

"I understand," Officer Williams said. He was about five foot ten inches and solid muscle. "I wish I were out helping look for her."

"Oh," I said. "Did you grow up here?"

"Sure," he said. "Fifth generation of full-time islanders. Why?"

"Look at this picture," I said. "Do you know anyone who might have a room or basement paneled like this?" I showed him the photo.

"Gee, it could be anyone," he said and ran a hand through his blond hair. "Paneling basements was big in the seventies."

"What about the chair?" Jenn said.

He shrugged and peered at the picture. "It looks like any other chair. Sorry I'm no help."

"Thanks anyway," I said. "We're going to go out the back door. Okay?"

He frowned. "Don't you want them to see you leave?"

"No," I said. "I have some things to check out first."

"Rex briefed us all to keep an eye on you," Officer Williams said. "We don't need three of you in trouble."

"We're meeting Liz McElroy," I said. "We'll go straight back to the McMurphy after."

"Fine," he said. "But you'd better or I might lose my job." He led us to the back door and opened it for us.

"Don't worry," Jenn said and patted his cheek. "We'll be as safe as always."

"That's what worries me the most."

Chapter 24

"What's up?" Liz asked as she came around the corner of the white building to meet us at the picnic table in the back.

"Are you covering Tori's kidnapping?" I asked.

"Yes," she said. "Do you have anything new for me?"

"Do you recognize this room?" I asked and showed her the picture of Tori.

Liz winced. "Wow, poor thing. That scares the bejeezus out of me."

"Don't look at Tori," I said. "Look at her surroundings."

"Okay, paneling, rag rug, old kitchen chair. It looks like a basement apartment of some sort."

"Anyone you know have a place like this?" I asked.

"Hey, they didn't have the courtesy of using our paper," she pointed out. "It's the *Cheboygan Daily Tribune* paper."

"Oh man," I said and looked at Jenn. "Tori could be off the island."

"That's not good," Liz said.

"Do we get the Cheboygan paper here at Doud's Market?"

"Sure, but it's usually late."

"Rex would know that, wouldn't he?" I asked.

"Sure," Liz said. "Why?"

"Because he said he was going to Irene Hammerstein's house to look for Tori."

"Well, I can tell you for a fact that she's not at Irene's house," Liz said.

"Why's that?" Jenn asked.

"Because Irene doesn't have a basement," Liz said. "She lives in a bungalow on the cliff face. The rock is too close to the surface to dig a cellar out. Plus, she likes floral prints. There's no way she would keep paneling in her home."

"Does she have family in Cheboygan?" Liz asked. "They could have flown Victoria off the island."

"Rex already checked with the airport. Let's talk to Sophie. She would know if anyone scheduled a flight path to Cheboygan." Sophie was the private pilot for The Grand Hotel and knew everything that went on at the small Mackinac Island Airport.

"Hey, Allie"—Officer Williams stuck his head out the back door—"Officer Manning called. He said you and your friend need to get back to the McMurphy. You have thirty minutes to the next call and he has new instructions."

"Fine," I said. "Thanks for the info, Liz."

"Remember, I want an exclusive," she shouted at our backs.

"You'll get it."

We went back through the police offices and out the front door. I held my hands in my pockets as if I were carrying the diamonds. We arrived back at the apartment with no further delay.

"Hi all, anything new?" I asked.

"Nothing," Frances said.

"We pretended to pick up the diamonds," I said. "Frances, do you know anyone who would donate a handful of crystals? We need to fake the diamonds for the possible drop-off."

"I'll call my friend Marlene who owns a craft shop," Frances said. "I'll see if I can't get her to porter over a bag full of fake diamonds."

"Good idea," Officer Brown said.

"We have less than an hour," I said. "Any word from Trent?"

"Nothing further," Officer Brown said.

"What about Rex?" I asked.

"Irene allowed them to search her house, but they didn't find anything," Officer Brown said. "Rex is taking Irene down to the station for questioning now."

"We were looking at the picture, and the paper she is holding is the Cheboygan paper with today's date. So the timeline seems off. Today's paper doesn't get on the island until about now." I checked my watch. It was three PM.

"Do you think she is being held off the island?"

"Yes," I said.

"But no one saw her leave by ferry," Frances said.

"I'm going to call Sophie. If anyone took Tori

by plane, Sophie would know." I dialed my friend and private pilot for the Grand Hotel. Mackinac Island had an airport, but it was very small. If anything out of the ordinary was going on, Sophie would know.

"Hello?"

"Sophie, it's Allie," I said.

"Hey, Allie, what's up?"

"You might have heard that my cousin Victoria is missing."

"I did hear that and I'm sorry."

"We received a ransom note for her today and they sent us a picture as proof of life."

"Oh no, how scary. Poor Tori!"

"Listen, she's holding a Cheboygan paper and we're worried they took her off the island. No one saw her leave by ferry. Is there any chance someone could have flown her off?"

"Well, I'm not here all the time," she said. "I do travel to Chicago and Detroit and Green Bay so I am hours off the island."

"I see," I said.

"That said, we log in and out of the airport," Sophie continued. "As soon as I heard Tori was missing, I checked the logs. No one unusual flew out in the last thirty-six hours. Just me and Robert Langtree. He flies in supplies and mail and such. What about the paper makes you think she's not on the island?"

"She's holding today's paper before it arrived at Doud's."

"I see," Sophie said. "I can understand how that would worry you."

"Is there any other way on or off the island?"

"By private boat," Sophie said. "Your kidnappers might own a yacht."

"Shoot," I said. "That means it could be half the island."

"It also gives them a way on and off the island without detection," Sophie pointed out.

"Thanks," I said and hung up.

"She didn't fly out?" Jenn asked.

"No, that leaves only private boats," I said.

"There are a ton of those."

I pulled the picture again. "Do you think the paneling isn't a basement but perhaps the inside of a boat?"

"It could be," Frances said as she looked over my shoulder. "It would make the most sense. They could hold her and keep moving. It would be simple for them to pop up on the island for the ransom and then pop off."

"Tori's eyes aren't covered," I noticed. "If she can identify them, then it doesn't matter if we pay or not; she will be killed."

"Please don't say that," my Uncle Alex said as he came out of the bedroom. "I don't think your aunt June could take that kind of talk."

"Rex is on the case," I said. "If anyone can find her in time it will be him."

"We think she's on a boat," Jenn said. "Do you know anyone with this kind of paneling on their yacht?"

I showed him the picture and he groaned. "Don't look at Victoria," I said. "Look at her surroundings. Do you recognize anything?"

"No, nothing," he said and ran his hands over his face. It was clear he hadn't slept at all. "But I haven't lived on the island for over ten years."

"Okay." I patted his arm. "It's okay."

There was a knock at the door. It was Rex. I let him in. "How'd it go with Irene?"

"She doesn't know anything," Rex said. "Her alibi checks out for the morning Barbara was killed."

"We think Tori is on a boat," Jenn said.

"Why?" Rex furrowed his brow at the thought.

"Well," I said, "look at the photo." I lifted my phone up. "She's holding the Cheboygan paper before it arrives at Doud's, and it's today's paper. So at first we thought she might be off the island. We contacted Sophie and she said no one unusual came or left the airport. Then we looked at the paneling behind Tori . . ."

"I already checked with airport personnel," Rex said. "You should not have involved Sophie. That said, it does look like the inside of a yacht. It makes sense."

"A call is incoming to Trent Jessop," the machine operator said.

Then my cell phone rang as well. I waited for the signal and picked up. "This is Allie."

"Do you have the diamonds?" the machine voice asked.

"I do," I said. "Let me talk to Victoria."

"Take them to Turtle Park. Drop them in the trash can at the park entrance."

"Not until I can talk to Victoria."

"You have ten minutes to comply." The phone went dead.

"Well, heck," I muttered and looked at Rex. He was on his cell phone. They had gone radio silent after figuring out that the kidnappers were listening in.

"Trent says the kidnappers want him to leave the money in a duffel bag at the mouth of Arch Rock. They also gave him ten minutes to comply."

"How can they be at two places at once?" I asked.

"There is more than one," Rex replied. "Neither caller said anything about releasing Victoria."

"That's not good, is it?" Aunt June said as she came out of the bedroom. Her eyes were ringed with dark circles and bloodshot. Her hair stood up on one side.

"We can't put any meaning into it," Rex said.

"But we don't have the diamonds or the two million. If they check before they let her go then they will kill her."

"Trent has the money," Rex said. "The bills are marked so there is no way they can spend it without getting caught."

"I have fake diamonds," I said and held up the small bag of bling the porter had brought over. "But it will take too much time to check if they are real or not."

"What shall we do?" Jenn asked.

"I'll contact the coast guard. They can keep an eye on any vessels that move around the island. Allie, go leave the fake gems where they instructed. I'll have plainclothes policemen in the area. Do not stay at the park. Come immediately back here. Do you understand?"

I swallowed hard. "I understand." I grabbed the diamonds, put Mal on her leash, and went out the back door. The walk to Turtle Park took up a great deal of the time allotted. I wish I had ridden my bike, but I wanted Mal with me. I checked my watch as I dropped the bag in the trash at the entrance to the park. I was two minutes late. Two minutes that may be detrimental to Tori's health.

I noted four men near the park cautiously looking around. They could all be policemen or one could be a kidnapper. There was no way to tell.

"Come on, Mal," I said. "Let's go home."

We walked back. My heart raced and my hands trembled. I got into my apartment to find most of the policemen had packed up and gone.

"Well?" My aunt grabbed me the minute I walked in.

"I was two minutes late," I blurted out. "So I don't know."

"Did you see Victoria?"

"No," I said. "I only saw four guys. I don't know what happened after I left. I walked straight back here as Rex instructed in case I was being watched."

"My baby, my baby." Aunt June sat down hard on the bar stool and sobbed into her hands.

I looked at Jenn; she looked as stricken as I felt.

Officer Brown stood silently near the doorway. I looked at him. "Did Trent make his drop on time?"

"I'm waiting for word from Office Manning," he said.

I bent down and let Mal off her leash. She went over to her water bowl and took a long drink. Mella was in Jenn's lap. Jenn stroked her for comfort. Frances came in through the doorway.

"Any word?" she asked.

"Nothing," I said and sat down hard. "I was two minutes late."

Frances put her hand on my shoulder. "You did everything you could. I'm sure between Rex and his men and the coast guard, they will find her."

The waiting was the worst part. Minutes dragged by like hours. Finally, a call came through Officer Brown's cell phone.

"Brown . . . yes . . . okay. I'll let them know." His face was stoic and we all held our breath. "They found Victoria."

"Yes!" We all jumped up.

"Wait, is she okay?" my aunt asked, breaking into our celebration.

"The kidnappers threw her into the lake with her hands tied."

"Oh my goodness." June sat down hard and put her shaking hands to her mouth. "Is she alive?"

"Yes," he said. "Barely. She managed to tread water until the coast guard found her."

"Where is she now?"

"She's been life-flighted to Cheboygan. Rex asked me to take you there now."

I grabbed my purse.

"No," Officer Brown said. "Just Victoria's parents. She is in critical condition and they don't want to tire her. We need her to tell us everything she knows."

"But I can't just stay here and wait."

"You have to," Officer Brown said. "It's for the best if you act as if nothing is out of the ordinary."

"Why?"

"We haven't caught the kidnappers yet."

"So they got away with the money?"

"And left the fake diamonds," Officer Brown said. "It's as if they knew what was real and what was not."

"But we didn't tell anyone the diamonds weren't real."

"Except the porter and the shopkeeper and everyone working the case. . . ."

"You mean the kidnappers have a mole."

"We certainly hope not, but Rex isn't going to take any chances. Only Tori's parents will be allowed to leave. Everyone else will be debriefed."

My aunt and uncle headed out the door with Officer Brown. "I'll porter your suitcases over to Cheboygan," I said. "Please tell Victoria that I love her."

They closed the door and Jenn and Frances and I sat in silence for a moment. I was lost in my thoughts. Whoever had done this was still out there and could strike again.

Chapter 25

"Tori's in a coma," my aunt told me when I called for an update. "She had a lot of water in her lungs and they drained them. The doctors put her in a coma until they know if she has pneumonia."

"I'm so, so sorry," I said.

"What is the update on the kidnappers?"

"Rex tells me that they got the money, but not the fake diamonds. Either they knew the diamonds were fake or they weren't able to pick up both ransoms or perhaps they saw the cops. The diamonds might have even been a decoy."

"A decoy?"

"Yes, they have to know that the police department has limited staff, so they could have used the diamonds as a way to split up the staff."

"Ah, as a distraction."

"Yes," I said and sighed. "I'm just glad we got Victoria back. What are the doctors saying?"

"They are keeping an eye on her and she may

be in a coma for a few days. There is no real way to tell, but they think she will recover."

"I can't imagine what she went through," I said. "I can't wait to find the people who did this and see that Tori gets justice."

"We feel the same way," Aunt June said. "I've got to go now. Take care, Allie."

I hung up the phone. It was early evening and Jenn and I sat with Frances and Douglas in my apartment. I had made a cold pasta salad for dinner and we all had a glass of wine.

"What's the prognosis?" Frances asked.

"Tori's in a coma," I said. "They had to drain fluid from her lungs. The biggest worry is pneumonia."

"I can't believe they tossed her in the water with her hands tied," Jenn said. "It makes me want to strangle them."

"Tori's strong and a good swimmer to be able to tread water with her hands tied," I said and sipped my wine. "Rex recovered the fake diamonds. But they got the money."

"Two million is a lot of money," Douglas said.

"Trent and his family came through with the marked cash."

"I certainly hope they are able to recover the money," Frances said.

"Oh I'm sure the kidnappers will see that the bills are marked. There is no way to spend it. I'm still convinced this has to be connected to Barbara's murder," I said. "Rex said he ruled out Irene. That means it is far more likely that Barbara caught the smuggler in the act of tossing the Butterfly House."

"You aren't seriously thinking about investigating," Frances said. "Not after what they did to Victoria."

"I think I should investigate *because* of what they did to Victoria," I said. "Someone has to pay."

"I think you should let Rex take care of that," Frances said.

"Let's change the subject," Jenn said. "When are we going to have a wedding?"

"Jenn," I admonished. "Tori is in the hospital."

"And safe."

"There's a killer and kidnapper on the loose."

"And Rex will take care of them," she said and turned to Frances and Douglas. "How about three days from now? That will give us time to reschedule everything and for the baker to make a new cake and the caterer to create new hors d'oeuvres."

"Oh, I'd quite forgotten about the food in all the fuss," Frances said.

"That's what you have me for," Jenn said. "I donated the cake and hors d'oeuvres to the St. Ignace homeless shelter. I've also talked the vendors into charging only for cost on the second round."

"Thank you," Douglas said. "My pocketbook thanks you."

"That sounds fine to me," Frances said and patted Mr. Devaney's knee. "Is that all right with you?"

"I'd say tomorrow, but then you wouldn't get

the cake and such that you want," he said. "I guess three days will have to do."

"Perfect," Jenn said and clapped her hands. "I've reserved the park again so there is nothing further for you to worry about."

I smiled at my friends, but didn't feel happy inside. With a killer on the loose, there was still a chance that something could go terribly wrong at the wedding. It made me want to find them even more. Could I catch a killer in the next two days?

Early the next morning while I was making the day's fudge, I put together a suspect list in my head. Sean Grady was still a suspect as far as I was concerned. He didn't work alone. Although his partner Dan was dead, I believe there was someone else higher up on the food chain. Someone who needed to smuggle diamonds to keep up their lavish lifestyle.

Someone with an accomplice who was able to kidnap Victoria and distract the police long enough to get away with $2 million.

That was a lot of people on a small island. Someone had to know something. As I said before that someone was probably at the senior center. I made an extra batch of salted pecan dark chocolate fudge. Then once the senior center opened, Mal and I went for a walk with a basket of bribes in hand.

"Hello, Allie," Mrs. O'Malley greeted me at the

door. "I see you brought a friend to visit us." She bent down and gave Mal a pat on the head.

"Oh, what a cute puppy," Mrs. Green said. Mal jumped up and did a twirl, then sat down and lifted her paw to shake. Mrs. Green clapped her hands in delight and shook Mal's paw. "You are a smart one, aren't you?"

"I'm sorry to hear about Victoria," Mrs. O'Malley said. "How is she doing?"

"She is in intensive care," I said. "They are watching her for pneumonia."

"Oh, poor thing," Mrs. Green said. "Who would do such a thing?"

"I was wondering if you all might know," I said. "I know you hear the local gossip first."

"Well"—Mrs. O'Malley took me by the arm and dragged me over to the craft table where five ladies worked on crochet squares—"we were talking about that this morning."

"We heard that they kept Victoria on a yacht."

"Yes," I said and pulled out my phone. "Here's a picture they sent us as proof of life."

"Oh no!"

"Poor dear."

"I had no idea!" They all responded with tsks and worried looks.

"Don't look at Victoria. Look behind her," I encouraged. "Do any of you recognize the inside of the boat?"

"It could be any paneled yacht," Mrs. Green said.

"I've seen that rug before," Mrs. O'Malley said.

"Really?" I felt my excitement grow. "Was it at someone's home or in a boat?"

"Well, now I can't remember." Mrs. O'Malley frowned.

"Oh." Disappointment filled me and dropped my posture. "What do you remember about the rug?"

"Where did I see it?" Mrs. O'Malley looked at her friends as if they could help her.

"Let me see that," Mrs. Finch said as she came to the table. I showed her the picture. "That's the Sikeses' boat."

"Wait, Wanda and Fred Sikeses' boat?" I said. "Are you certain?"

"I'm sure," Mrs. Finch said. "Agatha Sikes was my best friend. Back in the day we used to take the boat out all the time. She bought that rug at a flea market in 1975. The chair was part of the original dining set in the yacht."

"Oh yes, that's where I saw it," Mrs. O'Malley concurred. "I remember now. They used to have parties on the yacht. Before Agatha died. None of us have been invited since. The younger generation. They have no regard for their elders."

"Why would the Sikeses kidnap Victoria?" Mrs. Green asked. "It doesn't make any sense."

"No, it doesn't," I said. "Perhaps someone borrowed their boat."

"It could be one of their employees," Mrs. Finch suggested. "We have marina workers who take care of our boats. Perhaps they were having work done and one of those workers kidnapped your cousin.

If I were you, I'd go over there and ask Wanda. She might be horrified that such a thing happened in her boat."

"I agree," I said. "Thank you all so much for your help."

"Don't forget to leave us the fudge," Mrs. Finch said when I turned to walk away.

"Oh right."

"What kind did you bring us this time?" Mrs. O'Malley dove into the box and pulled out a one-inch-sized piece.

"It's ultra-dark chocolate and salted pecan," I said.

"Yum," Mrs. Finch said.

"We talked about nuts," Mrs. Albert said.

"You don't have to have any," Mrs. Finch said.

I smiled. "Enjoy, ladies."

"When are you going to bring us gents some fudge?" Mr. Oxford shouted from the card table in the corner.

"Next time," I said. "For now, ask the ladies to share."

"No way," Mrs. O'Malley said. "Those old coots didn't do anything to deserve the fudge."

"Come on, Mal," I said to my pup and pulled her away from Mrs. Hamilton's lap. She was enjoying the old woman rubbing her behind the ears.

We left the senior center and headed straight for Wanda Sikes's house. I knew I didn't like Fred Sikes. I wondered if he was the one behind it all. He certainly had the shipping company that could have smuggled the diamonds. Perhaps Victoria got too close. Or maybe it was as simple as Mrs. Finch suggested. Maybe someone who worked for the Sikeses was behind the kidnapping and possibly the murders.

I knew I couldn't go to Rex without proof. It occurred to me that it would be better to find the Sikeses' boat and get inside to take a picture of the interior. If it matched, then Rex would have to investigate.

Chapter 26

Luckily the marina was on the way back to the McMurphy. I was proud of myself for not going straight to the Sikeses' home. This was better. Safer.

The marina was filled with yachts coming and going. I flagged down a young man in a white polo and khaki shorts with a logo on the shirt. The logo said SKIP'S BOAT REPAIR.

"Excuse me," I said as we approached. Mal jumped up on the boy and he reached down to pat her head.

"Who do we have here?" he asked.

"This is Mal," I said. "She's a bit friendly."

"Oh, right, you are Allie McMurphy, aren't you?"

"Yes," I said and drew my eyebrows together. "How did you—?"

"Know? Easy. You and this pup have quite the reputation. Didn't you drag some girl out of the marina last month?"

I felt the heat of a blush rush up my cheeks. "Yes, that was us."

"You are such a smart pup, aren't you?" He rubbed Mal behind her ears. "I'm Matt Alvin."

"Hi, Matt," I said "Nice to meet you. The logo on your shirt—do you work for a boat repair company?"

"Yes."

"What's that like?"

"Good work, but tough sometimes."

"What kinds of things do you do?"

"We work on engines, clean the boats, fill up the gas tanks, work on rigging, anything that is part of the maintenance of the boats."

"Are you the only company that works on the boats?"

"No, there's us and then Owens. But the really cool people choose us," he said with a wink. "Are you thinking about getting a boat?"

"No, I was wondering about the Sikeses' boat. Do you work on that? I believe it's kind of old."

"Sure, yeah, it's a classic seventies yacht. We specialize in the older boats. The Sikeses are basically hands off on the maintenance of the *Scoundrel.* That's the name of the boat."

"Do they take the boat out very often?"

"Once or twice a season," he said. "I understand that before the old lady died, the family used to take the boat out at least once a week. But Mr. Sikes is too busy, and his wife, Wanda, isn't interested in water sports. It's a shame really. Old beauty like that needs to go out in the water at least once a week to keep it up and going."

"Do they ever have anyone else take the boat out?"

"Sure, a boat like that needs to run out on the open water. We usually take it out for a spin around the island just to keep things oiled up. It's good for the engine."

"Is that the *Scoundrel* over there?" I walked Mal down the docks toward the older boat on the end of docks.

Matt followed me. "Yeah."

"Can I see the inside?"

"Why?" he asked. "Are you working on a case?"

"A what?"

"You know, one of your investigations? Did something happen on the *Scoundrel*?"

"I don't know," I said. "No, I was just at the senior center and they were telling me about the parties they used to have on the boat. They told me they thought it hadn't been remodeled since the seventies."

"Well, that's true," Matt said. "It's kind of like a mini museum to the era. I'm sure they won't mind if I showed you inside."

I picked Mal up and Matt helped us up on the deck. The boat had a beautiful teak deck and was two levels plus the inner cabin. "I'll give you the basic tour," he said. "The main deck was built for parties. You see the deck and the inner cabin are the same size. That way they could move in and outside as the weather permitted with the same number of people." He walked me through the covered middle deck that had a bar in the corner and a couple of bar tables with chairs. They were bolted down and looked like they were straight out of a time capsule.

"Up here is where you steer," he said.

I put Mal down and climbed the metal stair up to a small room with two captain's chairs. There was room for four people up here and it had windows on all four sides. "Wow, I've never been in this part of a yacht," I said and ran my hand along the well-polished, wood wainscot beneath the windows. "You can see a lot from here."

"It's really helpful when you take it out. I like to sit up here to get the best views of the islands and the mainland when we take it out."

"There's a lot of room here," I said. "Do they have a galley?"

"Oh yeah," he said. "That's the best part. It's so seventies. Even the dishes are straight out of the era." He went down the small flight of metal stairs and I followed him. Mal followed from the deck as he opened a door under the stairs and went into the belly of the boat. It was dark inside, so he turned on a light.

Mal came down with us, happy to sniff. She was especially interested in the rag rug that sat on top of the teak floorboards. She barked and wagged her stub tail as if to say, "I found it!"

I swallowed hard as I recognized the paneling and the rug. The chair was moved back to a small side table that was bolted down. "This is amazing," I said. "Can I take some pictures?"

"Sure," Matt said with a shrug. "I don't think the Sikeses would care."

I snapped a few pictures with my cell phone.

"This is really cool," I said and fussed over the carved cabinets and the avocado green dishes. "Oh, would you take my picture?"

"Sure," Matt said.

"I'll drag this chair over here by the wall so you can get Mal and me," I said as casually as possible. I handed Matt my phone and pulled over the pine chair to the spot I estimated was where Tori's picture was taken. Then I sat down with Mal in my lap.

"Smile," Matt said and took the picture.

Mal barked and leapt out of my hands.

"What is going on here?" Fred Sikes said as he came down the stairs.

My heart went into my throat. He didn't look happy at all. "Um, Matt was showing me around." I took my phone from Matt.

"Sorry, Mr. Sikes," he said and stood up straight as if at attention. "She asked to see the inside of the boat."

"Why the heck would you want to do that?"

I swallowed hard and secretly sent the picture of me and Mal to Jenn's phone. "The seniors at the center were telling me about the parties your mom used to throw."

"Why would they do that?" he asked, his eyes narrowing as he advanced toward me.

"I was looking for a rag rug," I quickly made up the lie. "They said that there was one on the boat that was authentic to the seventies."

"And that made you think you could barge onto my property without my permission?"

"Oh no. You see, I ran into Matt and asked about

the *Scoundrel.* He told me how great the boat was,"
I said. "He said it was in mint vintage condition."

"So now you're interested in old boats," he said
and took me by the elbow. "I think you need to
leave. Now." He practically dragged me to the
stairs. Mal barked and grabbed a hold of his pant
leg and shook it, growling viciously. I'd never
seen her act like that. "What the heck? Get this
dog off me."

"I'm sorry," I said and gathered Mal in my arms.
She continued to growl at him. "I've never seen
her like this. We'll be leaving now."

I hurried up the stairs and out into the sunlight. Mr. Sikes strode purposely behind me. "Get
off the boat and don't come back. Have I made
myself clear?"

"Yes, sir," I said and scrambled down the gangplank to the dock.

"If that dog so much as looks at me again, I'll
call animal control. We have leash laws you know."
He brushed his suit coat. "Matthew Alvin, you are
fired."

"Oh no, don't fire him. It was my fault. I asked
him to—"

"This is none of your business, Miss Busybody."

"But."

"It's okay, Ms. McMurphy," Matt said and climbed
down the gangplank. "I should have known better."

"No, it's not all right," I said. "Really, Mr. Sikes,
I didn't take anything. Matthew was simply showing me the boat."

"Good day, Ms. McMurphy," he said and stormed
toward the cabin.

"I'm so sorry," I said to Matt.

Matt shook his head. "It's okay. He's right. I shouldn't have showed the boat without his permission. It's just that he never comes down here. I didn't expect him to be anywhere near the *Scoundrel.*"

"I don't know what to say."

"It's okay. I can't work on his boat, but there are plenty of others who don't mind being friendly."

Mal and I walked off the docks. My phone dinged and I looked down at the text from Jenn. It said, **Holy Moses, are you okay?**

I texted back. **Yes, I'm fine. Going to see Rex.**

Okay.

"What were you thinking?" Rex practically shouted at me when I showed him the picture. "If anyone saw you on the boat, you could have been hurt."

Mal squirmed in my arms and whined at Rex's tone of voice. "We didn't get hurt. It seemed harmless enough. I ran into Matt Alvin and he showed me the boat." I didn't tell him the part where Mr. Sikes showed up. It seemed incidental. . . .

"Are you kidding me? You were trespassing. It's as bad as breaking and entering. The Sikeses could have you arrested and you come here to show me proof that you did this?"

"No, no," I said. "I didn't break into the boat. Matt gave me a tour is all."

He ran his hands over his face and sat down. "What made you want a tour of the *Scoundrel?*"

"I showed the seniors at the center Tori's proof of life picture," I said. "I wanted to know if they recognized the rug or the chair and they did. Mrs. Finch told me it was the interior of the *Scoundrel.*"

"Allie—"

"Don't get mad," I said. "If I had brought you this information, you would have said that you couldn't do anything."

"So you went to the marina and broke into the boat to see if it was the crime scene."

"Yes—no, I went to the marina and Matt said he could give me a tour," I said. "He told me that the Sikeses only take the boat out once or twice a season. Instead he or a member of his care crew take the boat out once a week to keep the engine in proper working condition. It's a classic."

"You took a terrible risk," Rex said. "You need to stop this. You saw what happened to Victoria. I don't want that to happen to you."

"It won't," I said. "I'll be careful."

"Careful isn't good enough," I said. "The perpetrators have already killed two and tried to kill your cousin. They would think nothing of killing you or anyone else who got in their way."

"Yes, well, I've dealt with killers before."

"And you have been extremely lucky," he said and sat back. "Allie, one of these days your luck is going to run out."

"That day isn't today." I raised my chin in defiance. "Are you going to get a warrant for the *Scoundrel?* I think I've given you enough cause."

"Yes, I'll look into it. Now, please, Allie, let me and my team do our job. The last thing I want to do is have to drag you out of the water half-dead."

"That won't happen," I said with more bravado than I actually felt.

"How is Victoria?" he asked.

"I talked to my aunt on the way over here. She told me that they are taking Tori out of the medically induced coma today. She should be up and talking by this afternoon."

"Good," he said.

"Rex."

"Yes?"

"We make a good team. Don't you think?"

He looked up at me, his gorgeous blue gaze sincere. "I do think so."

I swallowed hard. There was a sudden tension in the room that I hadn't felt in a while. "I mean as crime solvers."

"Yes, that, too," he said.

"Yeah, okay, well, let me know what your people find out about the boat."

He tilted his head. "I'm sure you'll have Jenn ask Shane to give you all the particulars."

A blush rushed up my cheeks. "It doesn't mean I don't like to hear your take on things."

"Good-bye, Allie."

"Keep me posted, Rex."

"Sending me that photo was not funny," Jenn scolded me when I arrived back at the McMurphy. "You scared me half to death."

"I didn't mean to scare you. I sent the photo because Mr. Sikes caught us taking pictures on his boat, and if he was the killer I wanted someone to have proof of where I was before I disappeared."

"You are crazy," Jenn said. "Seriously. What if he had been the killer?"

"Then you would have taken the picture to Rex and he would have found me."

"You take too many chances," Frances scolded me.

"I only went to see if the *Scoundrel* was the boat that held Victoria hostage. When I saw that it was, I took pictures. Rex says I need proof to back up my accusations. So I got proof."

"You don't think Mr. Sikes did it?" Jenn asked.

"I don't know," I said. "According to Matt, the Sikeses only use the boat once or twice a year."

"And yet the minute you are on there taking pictures, he's right there to throw you off the boat."

I chewed on the inside of my mouth. "It does sound suspicious, but all he did was kick me off."

"He saw you taking pictures?"

"Yes, well, Matt was taking pictures with my phone, and Mr. Sikes didn't take my phone away," I pointed out. "It hardly sounds like the actions of a guilty man."

"Did you ask him about Victoria?" Jenn said. "Did you show him the pictures?"

"No," I said with a shake of my head. "I'm letting Rex do that."

"Well, at least you are getting smarter," Frances

said. "Now, the couple in 201 want to stay an extra night. Where do you think I should put the new arrivals who have booked that room?"

After the afternoon fudge demonstration and some bill paying, I called my Aunt June to check on Victoria.

"She's awake and talking to the police," Aunt June said. There was relief in her voice. "Officer Manning just left."

"Did Tori say who took her?"

"She said they wore masks."

"Oh," I said. "Well, good, then they didn't mean to kill her. Listen, I discovered the boat they held her in belongs to the Sikeses. I took pictures of the interior and they match."

"The Sikeses? Why would they hurt my baby?"

"I'm not sure they did," I said. "I was talking to a kid from the marina and he told me that they only use the yacht once or twice a year. Anyone with access to the keys could have taken Victoria."

"Tori says it was two males and they were pretty strong and she thought they were young."

"Why did she think that?"

"She says their voices weren't as low as grown men."

"So perhaps guys in their late teens, early twenties?"

"Yes."

"That confirms the theory that it wasn't the Sikeses," I said. "Did she tell you why or how she was taken? Did she get close to finding out Barbara's killer?"

"She said that she was walking behind the Butterfly House retracing her steps from the morning when she found Barbara. She remembered seeing someone running toward St. Anne's church. At the time she didn't think anything about it. They were in jogging clothes and it was early morning."

"Did she remember who it was?"

"A woman," my aunt said. "But before she could remember anything more, they grabbed her from behind, put a bag over her head, and hauled her away."

"Wait, the cottage door was open. I thought she was taken from the house?"

"Tori said they wanted us to think so," my aunt said.

"Wow, that was pretty brave to grab her in the daylight," I said.

"Whoever it was knew the back routes away from the tourists and even the workers."

"Do you think she'll be able to ID their voices? I'm certain Rex will get them for kidnapping and attempted murder."

"She thinks she can," Aunt June said. "Tori says she'll never forget their voices."

"Is she safe? Does Rex think they will come back once they find out she's alive?"

"Rex has a policeman stationed at her door."

"It's for her protection, right? Surely not because she's still a person of interest in Barbara's murder."

"Rex said Tori was free to leave Mackinac. After the kidnapping he is certain she didn't do it."

"Oh good. Did Rex give you any idea who his new suspects are?"

"No," Aunt June said. "But he did say that he thinks that Barbara's death was not planned. He thinks she was killed by the diamond smugglers who killed Dan."

"What about the woman Tori saw running?"

"It could be anyone up early for a jog," Aunt June said.

I thought about my early walks with Mal and shuddered. "Is there anything else Victoria remembers?"

"Frankly the coma scrambled her thoughts a bit. They have her sedated still," Aunt June said. "The doctors told us they are going to keep her one more day to ensure she doesn't get pneumonia and then release her."

"Oh good," I said. "Please let her know that I'm wishing her well. I sent flowers."

"She got them," Aunt June said. "I tell you what—when they release her I'm taking her back to California with me and not letting her anywhere near the island again for a long time."

"Aunt June," I said.

"Yes, dear?"

"Are you and Uncle Alex angry because Papa left the McMurphy to me? Tori was pretty upset with me for getting all the rights to the place."

"Oh no. In fact, Alex asked Papa to leave that headache of an old monstrosity to you."

I felt relief inside. "But Tori said she wanted her fair share. In fact, she was so angry she wasn't talking to me when she first got on the island."

"I love my daughter, Allie, but after this I'm not going to let her anywhere near Mackinac Island or the McMurphy."

"I'm pretty sure the island is safe, but the McMurphy does seem to take a lot of upkeep."

"See, quite frankly we're glad you took over that money pit."

"I wish Victoria felt the same way. She said she was going to sue me for a portion. I told her I would give it to her."

"Don't you dare. It's your inheritance. I'll have a talk with her."

"Thanks, Aunt June."

"Stay safe, Allie," she said. "I don't want to find you in the hospital as well."

"Yes, ma'am." I hung up my phone and stared off. So Victoria wasn't taken because she found a clue to the murders. At least it didn't seem like it. So they took her for the money? Why take Tori? Why not me or Jenn? She had to have seen something. She had to have remembered something.

I chewed on my lip. Was the jogger a clue? If so, what did she look like? Maybe Tori's memory would return eventually. Maybe she did have a clue who was behind everything.

I blew out a long breath. Aunt June was right. The McMurphy could be a money pit, but it was my money pit and I'm glad she understood that. All I had to do now was hope that Victoria would agree with her parents.

* * *

Later that night I walked Mal outside on her last nightly trip. We walked out the back door and down the alley. Mal used her favorite patch of grass to do her business. I heard a noise and turned quickly to see a man come out of the shadows. My heartbeat raced. Mal started to growl again.

"How is your cousin Victoria doing?" Mr. Sikes asked.

I swallowed my fear and pulled Mal over toward me. "She's out of the medically induced coma," I said.

"I see," he said and put his hands in the pockets of his dress slacks. He wore a dress shirt with the sleeves rolled up. "And she's talking, I presume."

A nudge of fear crept up my spine and I took two steps back as he advanced. "My Aunt June says that her memory is scrambled from the lack of oxygen." I lied. "Thanks for asking."

"But you know the truth, don't you, Allie?"

"Excuse me?"

"Those pictures were taken on the boat today. You gave them to the cops. They've been all over my boat looking for evidence. I have you to blame for that, don't I?"

"I don't know what you mean," I said and took two more steps away from him. Mal stayed beside me, growling. There was a Dumpster beside me. I could push it between me and him if I had to.

"I don't like liars," he said. "You have to know you've cost me dearly. Those diamonds are mine.

I want them back and I don't want any of those cheap knockoffs you tried to pass on as the real deal."

"Excuse me?"

"Come, come, Allie," he said. "Diamonds are etched with a serial number. The ones you tried to ransom your cousin with were fakes."

"You are the one who has been smuggling diamonds in with the butterfly chrysalises."

"Now you're catching on," he said. "I need my diamonds back."

"Don't be ridiculous," I said, my hands starting to tremble as I took another step back. "The cops will have them in evidence for at least thirty days. There's no way they would give them to me."

"That's not what I think."

Mal barked and I glanced behind me to find two men in ski masks approaching. I tried to duck behind the trash bin, but they grabbed my arms. I let go of Mal. "Run, Mal, get Rex!"

Mal raced past Mr. Sikes, but he caught hold of her leash. "Oh no, you don't, little dog." He pulled the leash tight until she was left dangling from her harness and whining.

"Put her down!" I said and struggled against the two men who held me.

"I want my diamonds, Allie," he said. "You are in no position to deny me."

"That's why you took Victoria, isn't it? For the diamonds. What about the two million dollars? What did you do with that?"

"That was a little deposit in case you didn't follow through." He stepped closer to me. "You see, young lady, you are a known troublemaker. I knew two million would hurt your family and the Jessops. They need that money back. I tell you what. You get me the diamonds and I'll let you have the cash back."

"You're lying," I said.

"I could be," he said. "But you won't know until you get me what I want."

"Let me go!"

"No. In fact I think taking you will more likely get me the diamonds than kidnapping your cousin." He tilted his head.

"They won't give you those diamonds," I said. I thought about screaming, but I learned a few months ago that no one could hear you when you were in the back alley at night. Screaming would do little good.

"This time the diamonds are not negotiable," he said. "I think we'll start with killing the dog."

"Wait! No!" I quit struggling when he lifted Mal up as if to wring her neck. "I'll call Rex right now."

"I see you love your dog more than your cousin," he said.

Tears welled up in my eyes. "I love my cousin. It isn't fair of you to compare the two."

He squeezed Mal until she cried out.

"I'm calling," I said. "So help me if you hurt her. . ."

"You'll what exactly?"

"See that you get your diamonds." I struggled against the two guys. "Let me go so that I can call."

Mr. Sikes nodded. "Let one arm go. I'm sure you can make a phone call with only one hand."

The man who had a hold of me lifted me up until I was on my tiptoes to relieve the pain. I hit the button to instant-dial Rex from my contact list.

"Manning," he answered grumpy.

"Rex," I said.

"Be very careful," Mr. Sikes said as he squeezed Mal again.

"Allie, what's going on?"

"Rex, please listen carefully. I need you to get the diamonds out of evidence lockup."

"Allie, I can't do that. You know that."

I swallowed hard. Mr. Sikes put his hands around Mal's neck. "Please listen. They are going to kill Mal. I need you to get the diamonds out of evidence." I looked up at Mr. Sikes. "And bring them where?"

"Leave them at the top of the trash can in front of the Butterfly House."

I repeated the instructions.

"Allie," Rex said. "Are you okay?"

"No," I replied and the second man grabbed the phone from me, ended the call, and threw the phone into the Dumpster. "Wait! You didn't give him a time frame."

"Too late," Mr. Sikes said. "You'd better hope Manning moves quickly." He made a motion as if to twist Mal's head, when my sweet puppy became a snarling mass of fur and claws. She clamped down hard on his hand. Surprised, he dropped her. "Darn it!"

"Run, Mal! Get Rex!" Mal took off down the alley, her leash trailing behind. I held my breath as Mr. Sikes attempted to grab her leash again, but missed. She was gone in the darkness.

"It doesn't matter," Mr. Sikes said as he took out a handkerchief to stop the blood flowing from the bite on his hand. "Manning knows we have you. He won't fake the diamond drop."

"How do you know that?" I said.

"Because the man is in love with you."

"No—"

"Take her to the boat," he ordered.

"No," I said as they dragged me off. "Rex knows about the *Scoundrel*. I told him."

"We aren't using the *Scoundrel*," Mr. Sikes said. "I'm no idiot. Shut her up."

There was a painful blow to my head and things went black.

Salted Caramel Fudge

Ingredients

14 oz. of sweetened condensed milk
2 cups of dark chocolate chips
1 tsp. of vanilla
¼ cup dulce de leche
Sea salt flakes

Directions

In a 2-quart microwave-safe bowl, microwave the sweetened condensed milk and chocolate chips on high for 1 minute. Let sit for 1 minute and stir.

(If chips are not all melted, microwave another 30 seconds.) Add vanilla and pour into a buttered 8-inch square pan. In a separate bowl, microwave the dulce de leche just until pourable—0-20 seconds. Pour over chocolate fudge. Use a cold butter knife to swirl the caramel. Sprinkle with sea salt. Cool completely. Cut into 1-inch squares and enjoy!

Chapter 27

I woke up in the dark tied to a pipe. My hands were bound with a plastic zip tie and I could feel the rocking of waves beneath the wood floor at my feet. "Help!" I shouted. "Someone, help!"

There was only silence in response. It seems they dumped me in the bowels of a boat. I had no idea how far out in the lake I was. Or even if there was a crew to hear me. I struggled against the zip tie. My hands were well and truly caught. They were raised above my head and the pipe. I felt the unforgiving metal. It was a good four inches around. There was no way I could break it. I had to try. Pulling just made my wrists hurt more.

My eyes adjusted a bit to the dark. I was with the engine of the boat. The smell of oil and gas filled my nostrils. I tried to stand but my feel slipped out from under me, making the zip tie dig further into my wrists. I imagined that I would have to break my bones to get out of the tie. I wondered if I could.

I was surprised they'd kept me alive, since I knew it was Mr. Sikes who smuggled the diamonds and kidnapped both Victoria and myself. Then I thought perhaps Rex would demand proof of life. Sikes would keep me alive as long as Rex stalled.

Still, it was a sure bet that I would be as dead as Dan and Barbara if Rex gave up the diamonds. I struggled against the plastic tie. I could feel the blood drip down my arm from the struggle. Was it possible to cut your wrist on a zip tie? I twisted and turned to no avail. "Help!" I shouted and kicked the side of the boat. "Help me."

Silence followed. Off in the distance I could hear a buoy bell. At least Mal was safe. When I closed my eyes I could still see Fred Sikes holding her as if twisting a dog's neck was something he did on a regular basis. It made me feel sorry for Wanda Sikes.

I opened my eyes and struggled again. I was getting tired. It felt like hours had passed, but I supposed it was only minutes. Sweat dripped down my back, blood down my arms, and I tried to break the bones in my hands to release them from the ties.

It was a lot harder than they made it seem on television. I had good bones. Dislocating my thumbs was also difficult, as all the pulling did was make my back and shoulders scream with pain.

I called out until my voice was hoarse, and my throat hurt every time I swallowed. There wasn't even the sound of footsteps above me. Did they have me on an empty vessel? Surely someone was at the helm. "Please," I said. "I won't tell if you let

me go. Please." It came out as a croak. My lips
were dry. My head pounded. I wondered if I had
a bump on it. My hands were too far above my
head for me to feel anything.

I looked at the pipe in the semidarkness. It ran
along the length of the boat and into what looked
like the shape of a water heater. I was on a boat
with hot water. It was yards away, but if I could
work my way over there I might be able to follow
the curve of the pipe and bring my arms down
below my head.

After what seemed like days, I had inched my
way long the pipe to the bend in the elbow. But
the circumference of the pipe was larger at the
elbow and there was no way I could get the zip tie
over it. Frustrated, I kicked at the water heater.
Tears welled up and poured down my face, adding
to the salty brine of sweat.

The kicking dislodged the pipe from the unit. I
swung precariously by a pipe hanger that wasn't
meant to hold my weight before the pipe jerked
violently and came down on my head. It hit me
so hard I saw stars.

"You're okay," I said to myself as the stars
cleared. I listened for any reaction to the loud
noises I was making. But no one came. It was clear
they had left me alone on the boat. I couldn't be
that far from shore. They would have had to take
a dinghy back to the island. I wondered if Rex had
given up the diamonds. Or if Mal appearing at the
police station would have been enough for him to
wait for a ransom note.

I didn't want to think about the fact that Mr. Sikes

was a killer. Instead I concentrated on the zip tie, which was now at eye level. I stood up on my tiptoes and it brought the tie to my mouth level and I chewed on the plastic. If I could chew the square head off, the zip tie should pull right apart.

I chewed and chewed, then stopped to rest my aching legs. The square part was just high enough to make it difficult. My entire body ached. Finally, I felt it pop in my mouth and I spit out the bit that held the tie in place.

Unfortunately, I also heard a motor approaching the boat and the banging sound of a dinghy hitting the side. I pulled as hard as I could to dislodge the zip tie from its mooring. Stupid zip ties were designed to stay in place with the tiny hooks. I got my legs up against the side of the boat when I heard voices and footfalls above. I pushed off with my legs and the zip tie broke free, tossing me across the bottom of the boat.

I held my breath. They had to have heard me tumble. Whoever had come aboard was also holding their breath, and neither of us made a sound. The plastic tie dangled from one wrist as I inched my way across the floor and into the space behind the engine to hide.

Footfalls stormed down the stairs along with male voices. "What the heck was that?"

"Who's down here?"

I kept quiet and hugged my legs to my chest. The heat of the engine warmed me. The upper door burst open and a hand with a gun came down first. "Whoever you are, show yourself!"

The man inched down the steep steps. He flipped a switch cautiously and my eyes closed against the glare of a single lightbulb.

"Darn it. The pipe broke," I heard him call to whoever was still above him.

"What pipe?" came the second male voice.

"The waste water pipe to the storage tank," he said and walked over to where I had broken the pipe. "What the heck? There's blood everywhere." He raised the gun again and pointed it in my direction. "Who's in here?"

I swallowed and kept quiet. Was this a ruse? Were these bad guys or good guys? Did they own the boat? Would they tie me back up and toss me overboard once they realized I'd seen their faces?

"I said, who's there?"

There was a bumping noise and more footsteps above. "Coast guard, freeze!" came the shout above.

"What the—" The man took off toward the stairs.

I listened as the sound of boots and shouting filled the air. A man wearing a coast guard uniform appeared through the entrance. "Allie McMurphy? If you're down here, show yourself."

I squeezed out of the small space with my hands up. He pointed his gun at me for a long moment and my heart raced.

"Allie McMurphy?" he asked.

"Yes," I said.

He put his gun away and walked toward me. "Cameron Piece," he said. "Are you okay?"

"Yes," I said. "What happened?" I started to shake.

He took me by the arm and I cried out as pain shot through me. "Hold on," he said. "Let's get you up into the light where we can see you."

I scrambled up the steps to the cabin below decks. Two men I'd never seen before were sitting at the table with their hands cuffed behind them. Rex rushed to me. "Allie!"

He hugged me and I cried again. This time through the pain for joy. "How did you find me?"

"We got Sikes to confess," he said.

"How?"

"We'll talk about that later. You're shaking and you need medical help."

I ignored the men in the cabin and went up into the morning light. "What time is it?"

"It's around eleven AM," he said. "You've been missing for twelve hours."

"Felt like a lot longer," I admitted. He helped me into a dinghy to take me back to shore. "Who were the two men in the boat? It sounded like they didn't know I was there. But they had a gun so I wasn't sure if they were good or bad."

"They claim they didn't know," Rex said. "But I'm checking into it. The boat was part of a movie set. They claim they were there to set up explosives. They did have a permit to blow up the boat. It's why it was moored offshore."

"And why no one heard my shouts for help," I said. My voice was reduced to a harsh whisper.

"Shh," Rex said. "You need to rest your voice."

We went the rest of the way in silence. It was a

shockingly short trip to the shore where Frances, Jenn, and Mal waited for me on the dock. I was surrounded by hugs and questions and tears.

"You're contaminating the evidence," Shane said from behind.

I shook my head. "I thought you had a confession," I croaked.

"Still need to collect evidence in case he rescinds his confession," Shane said and carefully took me by the arm. "Come on. George is waiting by the ambulance. I hate to say it, Allie, but you look like hell."

"Shane!" Jenn said.

"Well, she does," Shane said. "That's a good thing. We will take photographic evidence and put this guy away for years."

The ambulance was backed up to the end of the dock and the doors were open. George and Shane helped me to sit on the edge of the vehicle. Shane took pictures while George worked on cleaning my wounds. He gave me a bottle of water that tasted like heaven. I hadn't realized how thirsty I was.

George wanted to take me to the clinic, but I said I preferred to just go home. So Frances, Jenn, and Mal got into the back of the ambulance with me. George and Shane drove me carefully through Main Street and around the alley to the back of the McMurphy, where I had less exposure to the crowds of tourists.

"Sandy is taking care of the fudge shop," Frances said. "Megan has the reception desk."

Mal sat on my lap and licked my cheeks. I couldn't

help the overwhelming smile. "I didn't think I would ever see you all again."

"We were so worried." Jenn helped open the doors and jumped out. "Let's take you upstairs."

"How did you find me?" I asked again. My voice was less hoarse with the water in me.

"We got a tip about Sikes," Rex said as he came around the ambulance. Rex had walked the short distance from shore.

"I'd really rather you came to the clinic for an IV or two," George said. "You're severely dehydrated."

"I just want to be home," I said as I climbed out of the ambulance.

"Then I'll bring the IV up to your apartment," George said.

"I need to debrief you as well," Rex said.

"I need to document the physical evidence," Shane said.

"Well, then, let's get everyone upstairs," Frances said and took me by the arm and helped me up the stairs to the back of the apartment. I felt like I had a parade of people.

"Really, everyone," I said. "We're drawing a crowd."

Even coming around the back of the McMurphy, there were so much commotion that people had gathered in the alley. Liz pushed through the crowd. "Hey," she shouted from the bottom of the stairs. "Allie, are you okay?"

"She's fine," Rex said to Liz and addressed the crowd from the deck at the top of my back steps. "Let's give her some space, people."

Relief filled me and caused tears to form in my eyes as I walked through the kitchen and into the living room. I was home.

After two hours, a thorough documentation of my injuries, my time on the boat, an IV, and a good hot shower, I was in clean pajamas and sitting in the living room with Frances, Jenn, and Liz. Rex hadn't left my side. Trent was on his way back from Chicago.

"Now," I said and leaned back against the pillows, Mella in my lap and Mal by my side both demanding attention. I absently petted both of my fur babies. "How did you find me?"

"We got a tip it was Sikes," Rex said.

"Who? How?"

"It was Tori," Frances said.

"Tori?"

"Yes, she started remembering things. When you went missing, she remembered why his voice was so familiar to her. It was the same voice of the man who kidnapped her. She called Rex and he went to find Mr. Sikes."

"We were able to get a search warrant," Rex said. "We found evidence that he was writing another ransom demand note."

"Rex hauled him into the police station and grilled him until he confessed."

"So Mr. Sikes was behind the smuggling and break-ins? Did he kill Dan?"

"No," Rex said. "He lawyered up. We made a deal to get to you. He'll go down on kidnapping but not murder."

"Not murder?"

"He swears he had nothing to do with Barbara's death or Dan's."

"Then who?"

"We may never know," Rex said and patted my knee. "It's time I go and let you get some rest."

After he left, I made a phone call to Victoria.

"Hello? Allie? Are you okay?" Tori asked.

"Hi, Tori. Yes, I'm a bit bruised but okay," I said, and tried not to rub the bandages around my wrists. "I understand your tip led to my rescue. I wanted to call you and thank you."

"Oh, you're welcome," Tori said. "I'd come to the island and hug you, but my mom won't let me."

I smiled as I pictured Aunt June as I last saw her. She had sworn not to let Tori onto the island for a long time to come. "It's okay," I said. "Did you hear that Mr. Sikes swears he wasn't involved in the murders?"

"Yes, I heard."

"Do you believe him?"

"Sort of," Tori said. "I've been thinking about it. I mean, would a man use a garden trowel as a weapon?"

"So you think it was a woman who killed Barbara?"

"Yes," Tori said. "I was close to figuring out who when I was kidnapped," Tori said. Her voice sounded frustrated. "I wish I could remember who I was thinking did it. But I can't."

"At least you remembered Mr. Sikes's voice," I said. "It saved me. Thanks again."

"You're welcome, cuz," she said.

"If your mom ever lets you back on the island, promise me you'll stay at the McMurphy."

"I promise," Tori said. "Take care of yourself, Allie."

"You do the same," I said.

We hung up. "I'm glad you and Tori buried the hatchet," Frances said.

"I think we've been through enough," I said.

"Me, too," Frances said. "Will you be up to walking in my wedding tomorrow?"

"I wouldn't miss it for the world," I said.

"Good," Frances said. "I'll let you get some rest." She kissed my forehead. "Call your mom. She's worried about you."

"I will."

I closed my eyes and tried not to dream of being trapped on a boat.

Chapter 28

Trent came by later that night. Jenn opened the door and let him in. "Hey, Trent, come on in. I've got to take Mal for a walk." She hooked up Mal's leash. "You two be good now."

"Hi, Allie," Trent said and came in and sat down on the couch next to me.

"Hi, Trent, how's Chicago?"

"Fine, good. I didn't come here to talk about work. I need to know how you are." He took my hand and looked at my bandaged wrists. "I understand they had you tied to a pipe in a boat set for demolition."

"Yes," I said. "I'd rather not think about it." I rubbed my wrists.

"I'm sorry about things," he said. His gaze was filled with sincerity. "Tori and I have been friends for years."

"I know," I said. "I keep running up against that here. Everyone has been here longer than me."

"It's not personal," he said.

"Kissing my cousin is personal," I said. "Pushing me away when things get tough—that's also personal."

He took my hand in his. "I love you, Allie. I want to be in your life. I want you to be in mine."

"You have a funny way of showing it," I said and blew out a long breath.

"Can we start over?"

"How?"

"Let me take you out."

"It has to be after tomorrow. Frances and Douglas have rescheduled their wedding."

"I heard." He paused. "I thought I could be your plus one."

I chewed on the inside of my lip. "I wanted you to be my plus one, but now . . ."

"Now you know that I'm sorry and I love you." He ran his hand over his face. "When I think about you being abducted, that you could have died, it eats me up inside."

"It's not always about you, Trent," I said.

"I know that," he said with frustration.

"Maybe we should take a break," I suggested.

"What? No, I don't want to take a break," he said. He ran his fingers through mine. "Please, Allie, listen. Let's start over."

I put my hand over his. "Trent," I said, "you're always off on some business trip or other. Your family doesn't like me because I don't have your country club experiences."

"I don't give a darn what my family thinks."

"That's not true," I said. "When push came to shove, you shut me out."

"I didn't want you to get hurt."

"I get hurt no matter what," I said. "I'm not certain we work. There're just too many differences. You were raised on the island. The people here still consider me a fudgie. You have multiple businesses, I have only the McMurphy. My life is my work. Your life is your work. We aren't seeing each other."

"All small things," Trent argued. "I'm in love with you, Allie."

I closed my eyes. "I'm trying to tell you that I'm not certain how I feel—except alone and exposed and raw from watching you kiss Tori."

"Allie—"

"No, I think we need a break," I said.

"Fine," he said and stood. "I respect your wishes, Allie, because I love you. I'll give you some space if that's what you need."

My heart broke. "It is what I need. At least for now. Go back to Chicago, Trent."

"I want you to know that I'm not letting you go that easy," he said. "I will be around, Allie. When you're ready, know that I love you and nothing is going to change that."

"Okay," I said. "Okay, can you go now?"

"Sure."

He left and I stared at the flowers he'd left resting on the table. I should get up and put them in water, but at the moment I wasn't motivated enough to do anything but close my eyes and let

Mella patty-cake my side. Her nails were prickly,
but there was something comforting in knowing
she wasn't going anywhere.

The next morning, I went downstairs to be with
Sandy while she made fudge. There was a knock
on the door just before eight AM. I opened the
door to find the ladies from the senior center.
"Allie, are you okay?" they asked as they tumbled
into the McMurphy.

"I'm okay," I said and tugged my sleeves over
the bandages on my wrists. I was sore from large
bruises I'd gotten from my efforts to get free. At
least I hadn't needed to break my hand to get out.
It meant I could go back to fudge making soon.
"Come on in. I have coffee."

"We brought you cookies and doughnuts,"
Mrs. Finch said and lifted a big pink box from the
Island Bakery.

"Sounds yummy," I said. "Come in and have a
seat." I waved toward the sofas and the wingback
chairs in front of the elevator in the lobby. They
were closest to the coffee bar that was ready with
coffee twenty-four hours a day for our guests.

"How are you after your ordeal?" Mrs. O'Malley
asked. "Was it horrible? What did you do? Did the
twelve hours seem forever?"

"Was Mr. Sikes evil with his threats? How did he
capture you?" Mrs. Finch asked.

I smiled. "You all sound like Liz McElroy."

"Inquiring minds," Mrs. Green said with a soft smile.

They each got their coffee and sat down, snitching doughnuts or cookies depending on their mood. I had a cup of coffee in my hand. Sandy was making the last batch of fudge until the eleven AM demonstration. I settled into the couch and answered all their questions.

"So Mr. Sikes claims he didn't murder anyone?" Mrs. O'Malley said.

"That's right," I said.

"That means there is a killer still out there," Mrs. Finch said.

"It could be," I said.

"Barbara did have a lot of enemies," Mrs. O'Malley said. "You think a woman killed her?"

"That's the thought," I said. "Although it takes a lot of strength to murder someone with a gardening trowel, a man would most likely use a different object. Not one quite so blunt."

"Well, Barbara did have a lot of women angry because of how she manipulated their husbands."

"She did sleep around a lot and it didn't matter to her if the man was married or not," Mrs. Green stated.

"But if an angry woman killed Barbara, who killed Dan?"

"It is a quandary," Mrs. Finch said. "If the two murders aren't connected then we have two murderers."

"I think we only have one," I said. "If Dan helped Mr. Sikes smuggle things into the Butterfly House, then he might have done something else illegal on the side. Whoever he worked for found out he was going to be caught and got rid of him."

"So the obvious creature is the wife of whoever had an affair with Barbara last," Mrs. O'Malley said, a look of satisfaction on her face.

"We need to discover who was sleeping with Barbara last and work it out from there," Mrs. Finch said.

"I thought we knew that already."

"Well, we were clearly wrong," Mrs. O'Malley said. "We need to dig deeper."

"How are we going to do that?" I asked.

"Oh, honey, the grapevine knows all," Mrs. O'Malley said with a grin. "We simply need to put out the word."

"Let me know when you know," I said. "I'll tell Rex."

"Oh, honey, don't get Rex involved just yet. We have to get the guilty party admitting to the crime."

"Like they do on the crime shows," Mrs. Finch said. "Maybe we can finagle it so that they confess on tape."

"That would be marvelous," Mrs. Finch said with a clap of her hands.

"Where is Frances?" Mrs. Green asked as she looked at her watch.

"I gave Frances the day off," I said. "She and Mr. Devaney have rescheduled their wedding for later this afternoon."

"Oh, well, nice of her to tell us," Mrs. O'Malley said in a pique.

"It's my fault," I said. "I was supposed to send

out new e-mail invitations, but I got—how shall we say it?—tied up with something."

"Ha!" Mrs. Finch said and slapped her knee. "Good one."

"Okay, dear, all is forgiven," Mrs. O'Malley said.

"We need to get going," Mrs. Finch said, looking at her watch. "We have a water aerobics class in fifteen minutes. Enjoy your doughnuts, dear, and we'll see you at Frances's wedding. It's still at sunset, right?"

"Yes," I said. "Still at sunset and at Turtle Park."

"Great. Bye, dear."

They all gave me careful hugs and kisses on the cheek.

I frowned at their backs. There was still a killer out there. It was kind of them to offer to find out who had the most to gain from Barbara's death, but it worried me that they were putting themselves at risk by asking.

If anyone was aware of the dangers of asking the wrong people the right questions, it was me.

Chapter 29

The day was uneventful. I could only supervise Sandy with the fudge demonstrations. My injuries made things difficult to make fudge on my own. Jenn had Frances back at the salon getting her hair done. I just left the salon with my own hair done in a top bun and hair sprayed to within an inch of its life. I swear it was shellacked in place. But I had to pick Mal up from the groomer. She was also being bathed and brushed and having bows put on her ears. We were going to look marvelous for the wedding.

I picked up Mal. My adorable pup looked extra adorable with pale blue bows. I carried her so that she didn't get dirty on the streets busy with foot traffic and horse traffic. Finally, I was able to put her down and travel the back alley. She was happy to do her business at her favorite place of business.

"Allie McMurphy."

I turned to see Wanda Sikes step out of the

growing shadows behind my stairs. "Oh, Wanda, you startled me."

"You are a meddling sort, aren't you?"

"I'm sorry?"

"Because of you my husband is in jail right now."

"No, I think he's in jail because he kidnapped me."

"If you hadn't taken the diamonds out of the Butterfly House he wouldn't have needed to take such a drastic step."

I noted that Wanda wore a track suit. She had on athletic shoes, her hair was in a tight ponytail. There was a glint from something metal in her hand. I took a step back as she advanced.

"Wanda, I'm not responsible for your husband's incarceration," I said and raised my bandaged wrists. "I have the wounds to prove it."

"You took the diamonds," she went on. "Now you have the seniors asking questions they shouldn't ask. It's no one's business who Barbara was sleeping with. She's dead. Her affair is over."

She raised her hand and I saw she held a knife. My heartbeat picked up and I reached down, grabbed Mal, and held her to me. "Barbara was sleeping with your husband, wasn't she?"

"You know, I knew others would always betray me, but not Barbara. She was the one person I could always count on," Wanda mused.

"Until you found out her latest conquest was your husband."

"I didn't think it was true. Barbara wouldn't do that to me. I was her best friend for life—through thick and thin."

I swallowed at the crazy glint in Wanda's eye. "You met with her that morning at the Butterfly House."

"No," Wanda said. "No, you don't know anything."

"I know you have a knife."

She glanced at her hand as if it didn't belong to her and then looked back at me. "I followed Barbara that morning."

"You saw your husband leaving her home, didn't you?"

"Fred was always a weak man, but he was my weak man," she said.

"You followed Barbara to the Butterfly House and confronted her."

"She could do anything she wanted but she crossed a line when she went after my Fred."

"You argued," I said and took another step backward, pulled my phone out. I hit the button on my phone twice and it dialed the last person I'd talked to—Rex. I hoped that even if he didn't answer, his voice mail would record Wanda.

"She had the audacity to laugh at me. Me! Her best friend."

"It made you angry." Mal wiggled in my arms when Rex's voice said hello on the other end of the phone. "Wanda, put down the knife." I prayed Rex could hear me over Mal's happy barking.

Wanda's eyes were lost in memory. "She said that I, of anyone in the world, should know what she was capable of. I didn't believe it. I couldn't believe that she would betray me like that."

"You picked up the garden trowel."

"She wasn't even the least bit afraid," Wanda said. "She said I didn't have the strength to do anything with it. She laughed harder and said I was a weak pathetic woman who couldn't keep her husband happy. She said I deserved to lose him to her. She said more terrible, horrible things."

"So you stabbed her."

"I saw red," she said. "I didn't think. I just struck. I didn't mean to hurt her, just to make her stop laughing. Stop betraying me with her words. The things she told me. I had to make her stop."

"What did you do?"

"I ran," Wanda said. "When I realized that Victoria was coming in the back door, I ran out the front.

"She saw you jog by the greenhouse."

"I had my hood up," Wanda said. "There's no way she could have identified me."

"Did you know about your husband's smuggling?"

"No," she said and shook her head. "Barbara told me. She told me that she knew more about Fred than I ever would. She called me a fool, but I fooled her, didn't I?"

"Who killed Dan?"

"Dan?" She shrugged, her gaze focusing on me and Mal. "He had to die. He was ready to go to the police with what he knew once he realized you were tracking him down. Tori had gone to visit him. He said he could keep one of you from knowing the truth but not both. He was going to go to the police."

"So you killed him."

"It's easier the second time," she said. "It gets easier every time you do it."

"Do what, Wanda?" I asked as loud as I could so that Rex could hear.

"Kill someone," she replied and advanced on me. She raised her arm with the knife. "I'm sorry, Allie, but you crossed the line when you put my husband in jail."

"He did that to himself," I said and stepped back far enough to press myself against the fence that separated me from the hotel behind the McMurphy. "Put the knife down. The alley behind the McMurphy is no place to kill someone."

She rushed me. I flashed my phone light into her eyes and she shouted, pausing a fraction of a second. It was long enough for me and Mal to run. My goal was to get inside. I hit the stairs running. She was right behind me. I fumbled with the keys to my apartment as she grabbed at my leg. I kicked her back and she fell two steps; I stuck my key in the lock. I could feel Wanda closing in.

"Police! Freeze!" Rex's strong voice cut through my panic. I froze for a second and so did Wanda, but then she swiped the knife toward me, barely missing me.

I pushed her back. Mal barked in my arms. Rex let off a shot and I froze as everything seemed to go into slow motion. The sound of the shot rang in my ears. Wanda crumpled at my feet, the knife rattled to the deck floor. I pushed the door open behind me and stepped into the cool darkness of my apartment. Rex raced up the stairs and called 9-1-1. "Yes, Charlene," he said into his radio.

"Shots fired. I need backup and an ambulance at the back of the McMurphy."

I heard her say something. Rex pushed the knife away from Wanda's reach. "Are you okay?"

"I'm okay," I said. Mal wiggled in my arms, begging to be let down. Mella wound her way around my trembling legs.

"Don't let the animals out," he warned.

I closed the screen door and put Mal down. Then I leaned against the door frame as officers arrived. "Is she dead?"

"No," Rex said and pressed on Wanda's shoulder wound. Wanda moaned. Rex looked up at me. "You were smart to call me."

"How much did you hear?" I asked as sirens filled the air. Officer Brown came running up the stairs.

"Enough," Rex said.

"Is everyone all right?" Officer Brown asked, his gun drawn.

"I've got a suspect down," Rex said. "Everyone else is okay."

My legs gave out and I collapsed on my kitchen floor. Mal barked at all the men gathering on the porch. George came up and assessed Wanda's wounds. I held my pup to keep her from pushing the screen door open. I watched as they hauled Wanda off on a stretcher.

"What will happen to her?"

"She'll be airlifted to Cheboygan," Rex said. "George said they will have to do some surgery to take care of the gunshot wound." He hunkered down in the kitchen beside me. "Are you okay?"

"I'm fine," I said. "How's my hair? Jenn will kill me if I mess it up before the wedding."

Rex laughed. It was a nice round sound that warmed my heart. "It looks perfect," he said with a shake of his head. Mal jumped up and licked his cheek. Mella rubbed against him. "I guess you found another killer."

"I wasn't even really trying this time," I said. "The seniors came to see me. We speculated that the killer might have been the wife of whomever Barbara was sleeping with. So they put out some feelers out on the gossip circuit to figure out who was Barbara's last lover."

"Let me guess. Fred Sikes."

"Yes," I said. "The seniors hadn't even gotten back to me when Wanda jumped me in the alley."

"You have a busy alleyway," he said and helped me to my feet.

"Yes, I do," I admitted. "But there's no way to fix that. It's Mal's backyard."

"Speaking of Mal," he said and patted the pup on the head. "She looks good, too."

"I'm surprised she kept the bows in," I said. "Maybe they hair sprayed them in like my hair."

The front door to the apartment burst open. "We saw the ambulance leaving," Jenn said. "Are you all right?"

"I'm fine." I said as Jenn hugged me. Her hair was as stiff as mine. We had matching beehive dos with buns in the back.

"You scared the bejeezus out of us," Jenn said.

I glanced over to see Frances with tears in her eyes. "It was Wanda Sikes," I said.

"Allie phoned me and I got here before anything could happen," Rex said.

"But the ambulance . . . is Wanda dead?"

"No," Rex reassured her. "She's only wounded."

"So wait. Why did Wanda . . ."

"She jumped me in the alley," I said. "I guess she heard that the seniors were looking into who Barbara's last romance was. She knew it wouldn't take long before everyone knew it was her husband."

"That must have been devastating," Frances said. "To find out your best friend was sleeping with your husband."

"Apparently Wanda and Barbara fought and Wanda killed her."

"Oh my," Frances said and sat down. "Did Wanda also kill Dan?"

"That's what she said," I slipped onto a bar stool. "She blamed me for all her troubles."

"So she came after you?" Jenn asked.

"With a knife," I said.

"That had to be scary."

"I'm thankful it wasn't a gun or I would be dead." Frances looked at Rex. "How did you know?"

"Allie called me. I heard most of the confession."

"Smart to call him," Jenn said.

"How did you do that?" Frances asked.

"I hit redial," I said. "I was hoping at the very

least it would be recorded on Rex's answering machine."

"It's a good thing Rex was the last person you talked to on your phone."

"Allie, are you all right?" Trent came in through the open front door.

"Yes," I said. He came over and kissed and held me.

"I heard that the ambulance was headed to your apartment and I got worried."

"It seems you aren't the only one," I said. I hadn't put my arms around Trent. I wasn't ready yet. It was a bit awkward.

"She had Mal in her arms," Rex said. "I think she's getting multitalented with the speed dial."

I laughed. It broke the tension as Trent stepped back. "With everything that goes on here, it's handy to be good with a phone."

"I bet," Rex said.

Trent's expression faded and he stuck his hands in his pockets. "What happened?"

I retold the story yet again.

"So Wanda killed Dan?" Trent asked.

"I think so," I said. "I know she confessed to killing Barbara and she tried to kill me."

"Thankfully she didn't."

"Should we put the wedding off another day?" Frances asked, a worried expression on her face.

"No!" Jenn and I said at the same time.

I went over and patted Frances's hand. "No," I assured her. "I'm fine. Mal is fine. What we really need is a celebration of love right now. If you're okay with getting married, then we're okay with you getting married."

"Oh, honey," Frances said and gave me a big hug. "I've been ready for days now."

"Good!" said Jenn and she jumped up. "Let's get things over to your house and get you ready. Rex, call Mr. Devaney and make sure he gets to the park on time. I'll take care of everything else."

"I hope it's okay if I invited the senior center ladies," I said.

Frances laughed. "The more the merrier at this point. I just want to get married."

"Then let's do this," Jenn said.

We got everyone out of my apartment, grabbed our bridesmaids dresses, and went to Frances's condo. It was time for a celebration.

The evening air was cool with a gentle lake breeze. The sunset made the sky a lovely rainbow of pinks, blues, and reds. The park seats were packed. It seems word had gotten out that there was to be a wedding in the park. All the island regulars were there.

Jenn had done a bang-up job. There were rows of white folding seats, each row with a ribbon on the end. Luminaria bags lit the aisles with the gentle glow of candles. The bags had star cutouts and cast star shadows on the white paper runner.

The arched arbor was covered in white twinkle lights and white flowers. The Pastor Neaveau stood in a black jacket under the archway. A harp began to play music as Rex, Shane, Ted and Mr. Devaney stood beside the preacher. All the men wore black tuxes and bow ties except Mr. Devaney who wore gray. They looked like elegant James Bond types. Jenn started down the aisle, then me, then finally Maggs. I smiled at the townspeople, feeling like I had finally made townie status. When Maggs arrived across from Rex and Mr. Devaney, the harp picked up the sound and chords. Everyone stood as Frances came down the aisle in her elegant gown. Her face beamed with joy and happiness.

The flowers in her hands trembled slightly. She was a gorgeous bride. She arrived at the front and I arranged her dress in the back then took her bouquet as she took Douglas's hands in hers.

"Ladies and gentlemen," Pastor Neaveau began. "We are here tonight to join this man and this woman in the bonds of holy matrimony. A wedding is a celebration of love, where two pledge to become one. To care for each other, to cherish and love one another for the rest of their days. Douglas Devaney, please recite your vows."

Mr. Devaney cleared his throat. "Frances, since the first moment I met you I knew you were special. I wanted to get to know you and all the mysteries of you. Every day my love grows stronger and I promise to spend every moment of the rest of my life cherishing you, loving you, and being the partner you need in love and in life."

"Frances?" the pastor said.

"Douglas, since the moment I met you, I knew you were a very special man. In fact, the very man I wanted to know better. I love and cherish you and

I promise to spend the rest of my life loving and cherishing you and being your partner in love and in life."

"You may now exchange the rings."

Douglas took Frances's hand. "With this ring, I thee wed," he said and put the ring on her finger.

Frances took his hand. "With this ring, I thee wed." She put the ring on his finger.

"By the power invested in me by God and the State of Michigan, I now pronounce you husband and wife. You may kiss the bride."

They kissed and we all clapped and cheered. When they turned to face the crowd, I handed her back her bouquet. The harpist played a happy march and they went down the aisle together. People pelleted them with birdseed and blew bubbles.

Rex held out his arm and I put my hand on it and we went down the aisle. Shane and Jenn came behind us.

Frances and Douglas got into a horse-drawn carriage for a trip around the island. Meanwhile, everyone else went back to the McMurphy for a buffet of finger foods, an open bar, and a small swing band.

Sandy had made a chocolate sculpture for the cake topper and everyone wished the new couple well when they entered the McMurphy. It was a happy party. Mal loved dancing with people. Mella hung out on the top of the stairs and watched all the goings-on from a distance. People were not her big thing.

As the night wore down, the band played a slow

song. Rex came over and asked me to dance. I took his hand and slipped easily into his arms.

"They make a great couple, don't they?" I asked as we watched Douglas and Frances dance slowly around the floor. It was late and people had started to go home, leaving only the die-hards.

"They do," Rex said. "They make me think about doing it again."

"After two marriages?"

He chuckled and it was a warm rumble of his chest. "I'm a die-hard romantic."

We danced silently for a moment. It was a comfortable silence between friends. "I wanted to thank you for rescuing me today," I said and looked up into his gorgeous blue eyes.

"I was afraid I wasn't going to make it," he said, his expression fierce. "I sprinted over to you."

"I think I need a constant patrol in the alleyway," I teased.

"Maybe you do," he said and paused for a heartbeat. "Or maybe you need more of a police presence in your life."

I smiled at him. "I think I already drive the police crazy."

"In more ways than one," he said and leaned down and kissed me. My arms were around his neck. His hands on my waist. His mouth was soft and warm on mine and a thrill went through me. I might have leaned into the kiss. He might have deepened it.

Someone cleared their throat. I pulled back to see Shane and Jenn dancing beside us. Shane nodded his head toward the door. I looked over to see Trent in a tux. He turned on his heel, and left the McMurphy.

"Oh no," I said and disengaged myself from Rex. I went after Trent, but when I got out onto Main Street he was gone. I hurried to one end of the block, then the other, but never found him.

Rex came out with a jacket and put it on my shoulders. Our breath mingled in the cool night air. "I'm sorry. I didn't mean to cause trouble. It's just that it seemed the right thing to do."

"We're on a break," I said halfheartedly.

"I know. I heard that you saw him kissing Victoria."

"I asked him not to come."

Rex reached down and picked up a bouquet of roses that were on the ground just outside the door. "It looks like he came anyway." He handed me the flowers.

My heart squeezed. "I'm sorry," I said.

"I know. I'll go." He lifted my hand and kissed my fingers. "Good night, Allie. Please pass on my congratulations to Frances and Douglas."

"I will," I said and watched him leave. I walked back into the McMurphy alone with Trent's flowers in hand. Jenn and Shane met me at the door.

"Are you all right?" Jenn asked.

"Yes," I said, even though I didn't feel all right.

"Frances and Douglas are saying their good-byes," Jenn said.

Shane put his jacket across Jenn's shoulders. "We're going to the Grand for a nightcap. Did you want to come?"

I looked at them and realized they needed to be

alone. "Thanks," I said. "But I'm going to stay here and clean up."

"You don't have to," Jenn said. "I've hired a crew to come in."

"A crew?"

"Okay, two teenagers and a parent. They cleaned up the park and I paid them for an extra hour to clean up the McMurphy," Jenn said. "I didn't think it was right to leave it all to you."

I sent her a smile and gave her a hug. "Just like you to think of everything. You two go on and have a nice night." I watched them leave and went over to find Frances and Douglas.

"Congratulations," I said and gave them both a big hug. "It was a beautiful wedding."

"I couldn't have asked for better," Frances said. "Thank you to you and Jenn."

"You're most welcome. Now I don't expect you two back to work until Monday at the earliest. What are your honeymoon plans?"

"If we told you, there wouldn't be a honeymoon," Mr. Devaney said and winked at me.

"Just call if you need more time off," I said. "Life is short. Enjoy it while you can."

"We'll be back on Monday," Frances said and patted my hand. "Now that we're married every day will be a honeymoon."

I waved them off with rice and best wishes. I said good-bye to the last of the party-goers and let the cleanup crew in. I let them do their job. But I wanted to save the top layer of cake for Frances as tradition said. So I grabbed a box and slid the top layer inside and wrapped it up. Then

I placed the chocolate sculpture of the bride and groom walking into the sunset in another box. The rest of the cake was put in boxes to be distributed at the senior center the next day for lunch.

I helped the cleaning crew finish up and then went upstairs to my apartment. It was quiet there. I tried not to think too much about the kiss. Tried not to wonder what it meant. I put Trent's flowers into water, wondering why I kept them. I touched my mouth. We were on a break. I let Rex kiss me.

I wondered if my romance with Trent was truly over. I thought back to my first month on the island. That first kiss. A lot of things had changed since then. I hoped Papa Liam would be proud of most of them. The papers had come from the lawyer ceding a quarter of ownership of the McMurphy to Victoria. I hadn't read them over yet. I wasn't ready. I wasn't even sure if she still wanted legal rights or if family rights were enough.

I dialed her number. It was late, but she was back in California so it wasn't quite so late there. "Hello?"

"Hi, Tori," I said. "It's Allie. How are you doing?"

"I'm fine," she said. "How are you?"

I looked at the ligature wounds on my wrists. "I'm alive," I said with a small laugh. "Thank you for saving my life."

"I was just returning the favor. So do you know who the killer was?"

"Wanda was the killer," I said. "She had some serious issues."

"Wanda, I would have never thought of her."

"She wasn't my first pick either," I admitted. "Changing the subject, Frances and Douglas got married this evening."

"Good for them," she said and I could hear her delight. "I'll send a card. They are a great couple."

"I kissed Rex," I blurted out. "Trent saw me."

"Ouch," Tori said, and I heard her settle into her seat. "What are you going to do now?"

"I don't know," I said. "But I think I have a better understanding of you kissing Trent. I wanted to say I'm sorry for everything."

"Me, too," she said. "And don't worry about legal rights to the McMurphy. I had a long talk with my parents. I don't think I'll be back to visit the island for a long time to come."

"What about the fund-raiser?"

"Irene is going to hand that back over to the committee. While I was in the hospital I wrote down the plan and all the contacts and other important information. They have it now."

"You will be missed."

"You're always welcome in California," she said. "Come see me sometime."

"I will," I promised, said my good-byes, and hung up. I made a cup of tea and curled up on the couch with Mal and Mella and wondered what the future would hold. "Tomorrow is another day, babies," I said and petted both of them. "As long as I have you by my side, everything will be okay."

And I knew it would be.

Acknowledgments

Special thanks go out to the crew at the Original Mackinac Island Butterfly House and Insect World. They very kindly answered my questions. Any errors made in the book are completely mine as I do blend bits of truth in my fictional world. I want to acknowledge my editor, Michaela Hamilton, for her encouragement, cheer, and wonderful eye for editing. Also the rest of the crew at Kensington, for all the hard work they do to make a book become a reality. Thanks to my agent, Paige Wheeler, for putting up with all my crazy ideas and helping my stories reach readers. Most importantly, thanks to my readers for continuing to buy the books and allowing me to live in this wonderful fictional world on Mackinac Island.

Don't miss the next delicious
Candy-Coated Mystery
by Nancy Coco

Forever Fudge

Coming soon from Kensington Publishing Corp.

Keep reading to enjoy a sample excerpt . . .

Chapter 1

"Allie, have you heard the news?" Jenn, my best friend and this season's assistant manager of the McMurphy Hotel and Fudge Shop, came bouncing into the office.

"There's a town hall meeting tonight," I said and didn't look up from my work on the finances. Labor Day weekend was the official end of the season on Mackinac Island. I was working up the numbers to see how successful the season had been and if I could stay in business.

"Yes." Jenn sat on the edge of my desk. "But do you know why?"

I set down my pencil. "Tell me."

"They are announcing that a television pilot for a mystery series set on the island will be shot starting next week."

"A mystery series set on Mackinac?" I sat back. "That's cool."

"It is so cool. Marsha Goodwin told me that a Hollywood producer visited us on vacation a year or so back and wanted to do a series set here. They finally got up the funds to shoot the pilot. They will be doing outside shots here and then inside shots back in their L.A. studios." She wiggled into place on my desk. "Now here's the fun part. For a mere two thousand dollars, they will include shots of the exterior of the McMurphy. We could be part of the opening credits for the run of the show!"

"I'm familiar with reality TV," I said, thinking back to this summer's cooking show I got roped into. "While a pilot is cool, that doesn't mean a show will get made."

"But it's a shot you can't pass up," she said and crossed her arms. "What if the series takes off? You could be on the opening for years and on reruns forever."

"Two grand is—"

"Not that much money for that kind of exposure. Think about how business has picked up since that cooking show."

I looked at my computer screen. Our online fudge sales had doubled. We only had a limited amount of rooms to rent so we were turning people away. "It has been good for business," I mused.

"And you want to keep up the exposure," she advised.

"But we are already running to capacity. Any more orders and I'll have to stop making batches by hand and start farming it off to a factory."

"Why would that be bad?" Jenn frowned at me, confused.

"Because we are known for our handmade fudge,"

I said. "Anyone can make fudge in a factory. We make fudge in the kitchen by hand."

"So hire in another candy maker and start another shift," she said. Then she hopped down and planted her hands on my desk. "The Old Tyme Photo Shop and all the others on this side of Main are pitching in for the exterior shots. You don't want to lose to the other side."

"What other side?"

"The other side of Main." Jenn waved her hand and straightened. "People will be counting on your support tonight."

"No pressure," I muttered sarcastically and rubbed my hands over my face. "If I do this, I'll have to take the money out of the roof remodel fund. That means we would not have the patio roof for events next year."

"They are both long-term investments," Jenn pointed out. "But I think this television show has a chance to really take off."

"Why?"

"It's starring Dirk Benjamin," she said with an exaggerated sigh.

"Dirk Benjamin?"

She jumped up and pulled out her phone. "Yes, you know, he did that made-for-TV movie about broken hearts where the older guy has Alzheimer's and the older woman falls for the younger handyman. . . ."

"I don't watch much TV," I said.

"Oh, you know him," she said. "I'll pull up his

IMDb page." She flipped through some screens on her phone and then turned it toward me. "See?"

On the screen was a headshot of a very handsome man. I swore there was a twinkle spot of light coming off his teeth. "He is nice looking."

"He's more than nice looking," she said and turned the phone back toward her. "He is the latest 'it' guy for the small screen. He's been slotted to play the local police detective. There is no way this pilot won't take off."

"So wait, that guy is playing Rex Manning?" I chuckled at the idea that a young Hollywood actor with so much hair and a toothy smile would be playing Rex. Rex Manning was rougher around the edges, with a bald head and with more of an action movie guy looks than romantic hero looks.

"Well, not exactly," Jenn said. "The series is about a Mackinac Island writer. You know, an updated version of Jessica Fletcher. She finds clues to murders and he steps in to arrest people."

"Oh boy, I bet Rex loves that idea," I said. Rex wasn't very happy with my meddling with his investigations. I highly doubted he would be happy about a television show depicting the Mackinac Island police as needing an old woman's help to solve crimes.

Jenn smirked. "Rex hates it. I heard that Dirk is shadowing Rex for the next two weeks to get a feel for how he does his job."

That thought made me laugh. "Okay, now I have to call Rex and see how he's taking it." I picked up my phone.

"Before you call"—Jenn interrupted—"are you in for the two thousand?"

"I don't think so," I said with a shake of my head. "The pilot could get made and not picked up or even shown to anyone for years. I think I'll keep my roof improvements."

Jenn stuck out her bottom lip in a pout. "Sad. I think your neighbors aren't going to be too happy."

"We just can't do everything," I said with a shrug. "They are business owners. They'll understand."

Later that afternoon I took Mal out for her afternoon walk. We went out the back of the McMurphy and across the alley to Mal's favorite patch of grass.

"Allie." Mr. Beecher called my name. Mr. Beecher was an elderly gentleman who wore three-piece suits and walked twice daily around the island. He reminded me of the snowman narrator from the Rudolph stop-action television show. Or more specifically, he reminded me of Burl Ives.

"Hello, Mr. Beecher. How are you today?"

"I'm well, thanks," he said. "I hear that you aren't going to put in for the pool to get the television show to shoot your side of the street."

I sent him a weak smile. "Word travels fast around here."

"You've got some folks up in arms over it," he said, reached into his pocket, and took out a small treat. Mal raced over and did her tricks for him. "I told them that you were entitled to spend your money as you saw fit."

"Thank you," I said. "I'm saving up to remodel the rooftop. It will make a great space for weddings and bridal showers and other kinds of parties."

His eyes twinkled. "Like I said, you are entitled to spend your money as you see fit. I think your grandfather would be proud of what you've done with the place."

"Thanks," I said. "I wish Papa were here for my first season, too."

"What's our little friend up to?" he asked and pointed out that Mal was sniffing around the side of the Dumpster two buildings down.

"Mal," I called. "What are you doing? Get over here." I clapped my hands. Mal refused to come. "I'm sorry," I said. "Sometimes she can get really stubborn."

"Do take care. They like to put poison out by the Dumpsters to keep the rats away."

"Oh no." My heart rate sped up. I don't know what I would do if Mal got poisoned. I hurried down the alley to the Dumpster, calling her name. "Mal. Mal, come here, girl." It wasn't rat poison she was sniffing around, but a pair of men's tennis shoes . . . with the person still wearing them. "I'm sorry," I said and pulled her off the man. "She has never met a stranger."

The guy was half sitting, half lying down against the side of the building. His head rested against the Dumpster, a hat covering his face as if he needed a nap and wanted to keep the sun out. He didn't make a sound. I froze.

"Is he sleeping?" Mr. Beecher asked as he rounded the Dumpster.

"Oh boy," I said, noting the dirty jeans and torn sweatshirt he wore. "Hello? Sir?" I reached down and jiggled his shoulder. The hat popped up and revealed brown eyes wide open, but opaque, staring at nothing. "Sir?" I put my hand on his neck to feel for a pulse, but one touch let me know he was dead. The body was cold.

I straightened; my nerves were on edge. Mal wiggled in my arms. Mr. Beecher stuck his hands in his pockets and whistled.

"So you've found another dead man," he stated.

"I think so," I said and fumbled for my phone. "Do you recognize him?"

"He sort of looks like Jack Sharpe," Mr. Beacher mused, tilting his round head to get a better look at the body. "Of course, Jack is a better dresser."

"Nine-one-one. What is your emergency?" Charlene's voice was clear on the other end of the phone.

"Hi, Charlene, it's Allie."

"Oh, dear me, who's dead now?" She sounded pained.

"I don't know," I said. "I'm in the alley behind Main Street . . ." I stepped back to look at the store names stenciled on their back doors. "Behind Doud's Market and Mackinac Gifts."

"I'll send Rex out," she said. "But he isn't going to be happy."

"I'm not responsible for making Rex happy," I replied.

"That's not what I hear." Charlene chuckled.

"I've sent a text out to Shane as well to get CSI over there. There is a dead body, right?"

"Yes," I said solemnly. "But just because I call you doesn't automatically mean someone died."

"Honey, the only time you ask for help is if someone dies," she pointed out. "Are you alone?"

"No, Mr. Beecher is here, too."

"Well, good. Who found the body?"

"Mal did," I answered.

"That pup has a nose for the dead," Charlene said.

In the distance I heard the sound of sirens. The alley wasn't very far from the administration building where the ambulance and police were housed. The ambulance was one of the only motor vehicles allowed on the island.

"I hear them coming," I said into the phone. "Thanks, Charlene."

"Take care, Allie."

"Well, this certainly is an interesting turn of events." Mr. Beecher kept his hands in his pockets and bent over to peer at the body. "I wonder what killed him?"

"Let's hope it wasn't foul play," I said and held Mal securely in my arms. Movement caught the corner of my eye and I turned to see Rex come striding down the alleyway with a tall, impossibly handsome man behind him.

"Allie, Mal, Mr. Beecher." Rex acknowledged us all but didn't introduce the man with him. He turned to the body. "You reported him dead?"

"Yes," I said. "Mal pointed him out and we

thought he was sleeping. So I knelt down and shook him to wake him up, but he was stiff and cold."

"Wow, a real dead guy. Just like that . . . in the alley," the handsome man said and ran his hand through his mass of blond hair that was thick and glossy.

"Hello," Mr. Beecher said and stuck out his hand. "I don't think we've met."

"Right. Dirk Benjamin," the man said and shook Mr. Beecher's hand. "You're Beecher?"

"Mr. Beecher," he replied.

"The man is definitely dead," Rex said, interrupting. He knelt beside the body and used his pen to pull the hat off the dead man's head. There was blood and gunk on the inside of the hat.

Dirk Benjamin turned very pale. "Is that like brains?"

"Yes." Rex answered, his mouth a grim line. Dirk turned and got sick on the other side of the Dumpster. "Amateurs . . ."

I looked from the hat to the dead man's head and saw that he had a bullet hole right above the eyes.

"I'm thinking it was foul play," Mr. Beecher said out loud.

"Do you think?" Rex muttered sarcastically.

The ambulance cut its sirens as it crept along the alley toward us. George Marron got out of the vehicle. "Mr. Beecher, Allie," he said. "What happened?"

"That's what we're trying to figure out," Mr. Beecher said.

"Did either of you hear gunshots last night?" Rex asked as he stood.

"No," I replied. "Mal would have barked."

"It might be a body dump," George said as he squatted down to take a look. "There's not a lot of blood here." He squinted up at us, his dark black gaze serious. "Probably killed somewhere else and moved here."

"Why here?" I asked.

"People know you walk this alley," Rex said. "And with your reputation."

"What reputation?" I put one hand on my hip and held Mal with the other.

"Of finding dead men," George said.

"Mal finds them," I pointed out. "What does that have to do with anything?"

"They probably killed him then brought him back here, posed him to look like he was sleeping, and left him here for you to find."

"Are you sure he didn't kill himself?" Mr. Beecher asked.

"No gun around," Rex said, taking in the scene.

"It could be under the Dumpster," I pointed out.

"Jack Sharpe was right-handed," George said. "The Dumpster is on his left."

"So it is Jack Sharpe," Mr. Beecher said. "I thought so."

"I'm going to have to rope off the crime scene until Shane can get here," Rex said. "George, take a look at Mr. Benjamin. He lost his breakfast and might be in shock. Allie, keep Mal away from the body. You and Mr. Beecher should go sit on the steps to your apartment until I can square away the scene."

"Yes, sir," I muttered.

"Come on, Allie." Mr. Beecher took my elbow in his hand. "This is the best adventure of my life."

"Well, Mal and I wish it wasn't a normal occasion in ours," I said as we scooted past the ambulance. Dirk Benjamin sat on the back of the ambulance. George had draped him in a blanket and was checking his pulse. I remembered seeing my first dead body. It didn't make me sick, but it did put me into shock.

Mr. Beecher gave Mal another treat as we settled onto the steps to my apartment. "I don't know why Rex leapt to the conclusion that the body was left for me to find."

"It was my first thought, too," Mr. Beecher said.

"Why?" I asked. "You walk down this alley twice a day. The body could have been there for you to find."

"Then they were successful as I did find it, too," he said. "But most likely it was left for you."

I rolled my eyes. "You can't rule out Doud's Market or Mackinac Gifts, their owners, and patrons," I said. "It's a stretch to say that it was left for me."

"Not much of a stretch," Rex said as he approached, his gloved hand holding the corner of a piece of paper. "They left you a note."

Connect with Us

Visit us online at
KensingtonBooks.com
to read more from your favorite authors, see books
by series, view reading group guides, and more.

 Join us on social media

for sneak peeks, chances to win books and prize packs,
and to share your thoughts with other readers.

facebook.com/kensingtonpublishing
twitter.com/kensingtonbooks

Tell us what you think!

To share your thoughts, submit a review,
or sign up for our eNewsletters, please visit:
KensingtonBooks.com/TellUs.

Grab These Cozy Mysteries
from
Kensington Books